For my wee gran, May.

KILL ORDER

A Maggie Black Thriller

JACK MCSPORRAN

inked entertainment

Series Guide

The main Maggie Black Series consists of full-length novels featuring secret agent Maggie Black.

The Maggie Black Case Files is a prequel series of self-contained missions which Maggie completed prior to the events of the main Maggie Black Series.

Both series can be read before, after, or in conjunction with the other.

Maggie Black Case Files
Book 1: Vendetta
Book 2: The Witness
Book 3: The Defector

Maggie Black Series
Book 1: Kill Order
Book 2: Hit List (Coming Spring 2018)

Want a FREE Maggie Black book?

Full information on how to get your FREE copy of
VENDETTA sent straight to your email inbox can be
found at the back of the book. Happy reading!

Chapter 1

Maggie Black scanned the top deck of the luxury yacht and searched for her target.

A sea of people crowded the open space. Everyone from A-list actors and rock stars to wannabes and groupies were all there for the annual Cannes Film Festival. Even the patient onboard staff seemed impressed as they waited on Hollywood royalty.

The security guards were less impressed. Maggie made sure to keep an extra eye on them. They wandered among the guests in suits that strained against muscled arms, their postures rigid and wires barely hidden in their ears. Blending in wasn't on their list of priorities – unlike Maggie's.

"What did you say your name was again?" asked an irritating brunette to Maggie's left. The stench of cigarette smoke and vodka assaulted her with the woman's every breath.

"Eva," Maggie replied, swirling her glass of water on the rocks. She leaned against the rails of the balcony and looked over the woman's shoulder, feigning interest in whatever it was she was saying.

Music blared from a deejay booth in the center of the partial deck as people well past drunk danced under the glow of the moon, its light glittering off the water as the yacht bobbed a half mile out from the port.

"And what do you do?" the brunette asked, who'd introduced herself as Brooke. Or Becky. Or something like that.

"I'm a model." Maggie didn't bother looking at her conversation partner. She was far more interested in the guard nearest her, and the flash of his pistol as he adjusted his jacket. A black Smith and Wesson from the looks of it. Her hand itched for her own 9mm Glock 19, but it was back in her hotel room.

The crew had searched everyone before coming onboard, and her tight-fitting red dress could hardly conceal a weapon like that. Tonight, Maggie was armed with her wit and her fists.

"Funny, I don't recognize you," Brooke said, the hint of a sneer edging at the corner of her ruby lips.

"Most of my work is international. I did a shoot in Japan last week."

The shoot – two bullets in a Japanese businessman. One in his chest and one in the head to make sure. The British government didn't take too kindly to those caught selling malware to their enemies. In this case, a militia group planning a cyber-attack against the National Health Service.

Maggie flipped her waves of long blond hair to the side and turned to gaze over the deck below.

Plush sofas sat in clusters around glass tables, each of them covered with champagne bottles and bowls of suspicious-looking white powder piled high in the center.

She moved from face to face, evaluating then discarding them one by one. None of them matched the image of the reporter she'd memorized.

Then she saw him. Adam Richmond. Investigative reporter, trust fund playboy, and seller of classified information.

Brooke yapped in Maggie's ear about some movie producer she was seeing, but Maggie paid her no mind. She focused all her attention on the tall, dark, handsome man chatting up a beautiful woman near the bar.

The woman touched his arm and laughed at whatever Adam said. Her clear interest seemed to bore Adam, and his gaze moved from the woman to the rest of the party.

Condensation dripped down Maggie's glass as she took a sip. The day's heat lingered into the night, making Maggie's pale skin glow amid the humid air. The sky had bled out and bruised to a dark purple, promising another ideal day for the film festival. Though not everyone onboard would see the sun rise.

Adam's eyes traveled towards the top deck and landed on Maggie. He grinned at her, the woman beside him forgotten. Maggie watched him with open interest and tucked a strand of hair behind her ear.

He gestured to the bar, where a barman placed two glasses of bubbling champagne on the counter. *Smooth.*

Maggie abandoned her spot at the railing, leaving a flustered Brooke behind without a goodbye, and made her way to him. She took her time travelling down the stairs, allowing her leg to peek out from the slit of her dress, feeling his eyes take her in from head to toe.

As she reached the bottom step, Adam dug into his jacket pocket and brought a cellphone to his ear. His face grew serious as he spoke, his attention stolen from her. Maggie frowned. She made for the bar, but a group of partiers interrupted her path and blocked her view of the target.

When they dispersed, Adam was gone.

Maggie picked up her pace and reached the bar. "The man who was just standing here, where did he go?"

The barman shrugged, busy shaking cocktails and hounded with calls for service from the other guests.

Maggie scanned the bar, but Adam was nowhere to be found. *Shit.*

She scoured the whole deck in search for him, heat rising to her cheeks. A drunk man stumbled into her and stood on the bottom of her dress, pinning her to the spot. Maggie yanked the dress back and shoved the guy away from her. If only she could have worn trousers instead of an insufferable dress.

Holding the train away from her feet, she weaved through the party and headed inside, closing the heavy watertight door behind her.

The bass from the speakers outside hummed through the wooden floors, adding to the rocking of the water as Maggie hurried down the corridor. Her sea legs had suffered much worse than the tame waves of the Mediterranean, allowing her to move with ease, even in killer heels.

Passing a lounge area with a grand piano nestled in the corner, she smiled at those standing around it, singing songs and taking shots of amber liquid. *At least someone gets to enjoy the cruise,* she thought as she continued deeper into the heart of the yacht.

Maggie rounded a corner and took a flight of stairs leading down to the sleeping quarters on the deck below. Voices made her freeze.

"No," said a muffled voice. "I don't want to."

"Yes, you do." The second voice was deep. Slurred. "You've been hanging over me all night."

"Please."

"Shh," the male voice cooed. "You know you want it."

Maggie leaned down to get a look.

A man in his fifties had a young girl pinned against the wall, a meaty hand covering her mouth to stop her from calling out or screaming.

Maggie's nails dug into her palm. She continued down the stairs and marched up behind the man. "Hey," she called, grabbing the man's shoulder.

"We're busy here." His scowl was soon replaced with a sloppy smile. He whistled, looking Maggie up and down. "Want to join in?"

Maggie grimaced at the man, whose shirt was soaked through with sweat. "Get your hands off her."

The man laughed and returned his focus to the frightened girl. "If you're not interested, piss off before I lose my patience."

Maggie took a deep breath. She couldn't afford to cause a scene or waste time. She needed to find Adam.

The man laughed at her and shook his head. "Stupid bitch."

Maggie grabbed him again and spun him around to face her. She smashed her fist into his bulbous nose, the bone cracking with a delicious snapping sound.

Blood flooded from his nostrils and ran down his chin.

"You broke my fucking nose!" The man lunged at her, but Maggie was ready for him. She caught him with a mean right hook, sending him crashing to the floor with a thump.

The girl leaned against the wall and blinked at Maggie. Her eyes were dilated, and black hair stuck to the sides of her face.

"You okay?" Maggie asked.

The girl stared at her knocked-out attacker and gave a little nod.

"Good. Get out of here and don't tell anyone what happened."

"What about him?" she asked.

"I'll deal with it. Now go, and make sure you drink plenty of water until the yacht gets back to the port." Cocaine and alcohol was one cocktail the girl could do without.

"I will. Thanks." The girl backed away then ran upstairs and out of sight.

Maggie rested her hands on her hips and sighed. She kicked the big lump with the tip of her shoe, then hoisted him up by the arms and dragged him into a nearby supply closet. Maggie shut the door and allowed herself a brief moment to catch her breath before moving on. The dead weight of the man, combined with the heat, sent trickles of sweat down her back.

The lower deck was deserted, the hum of the party echoing from above. Maggie walked towards the aft until the music died enough to hear waves sloshing against the sides of the yacht. She reached a wide hallway with numbered rooms running along either side. Someone had left a door ajar, which revealed a large suite with a king-sized bed and a private balcony.

Her reports said Adam Richmond was staying onboard the yacht during his stay in Cannes. One of his many high roller friends owned the vessel, an investment banker on Wall Street. Adam must have a private room. Somewhere.

Maggie strained her ears and listened for any signs of life. She tried the first door, but it was locked. As was the next.

This is taking too long. Maggie felt around for the light switch. She flicked off the lights and allowed her eyes to settle. There. At the end of the row to the left.

Light emanated in a thin strip from under the bedroom door. She grinned. *Bingo.*

Maggie turned the lights back on and crept toward the door. She pressed her ear against the wood, careful to stay out of view from the peephole. Footsteps. She was sure of it.

Maggie gripped the door handle, hoping it wasn't locked, and turned it. The door swung open and she stumbled inside, pretending to lose her balance.

Adam jumped in his chair, closing his laptop before turning to face her.

"Oh," Maggie said, wobbling on her feet, "this isn't Brooke's room."

"No, it's not." Adam got up from his chair and ushered her towards the door. He stopped when he got up close to her, his face brightening. "You're the woman from the top deck."

"And you're the man from the bar." Maggie let out a laugh. "I'm sorry. I was looking for my friend, and I got the room numbers mixed up."

"A happy coincidence." Adam crossed the room and opened a minibar, taking out a bottle of cognac. "How about that drink?"

Maggie looked back out into the hall. "I should really be getting back."

"Oh, come on. Just one drink. I insist." Adam shot her a wide smile, his schoolboy charm laid on as thick as his upper-class drawl.

Maggie pretended to consider his offer and shrugged. "Well, if you *do* insist." She closed the door behind her with a soft *click*.

She eyed the closed laptop as Adam poured the drinks into curved crystal glasses. Maggie didn't know what secrets lay inside the hard drive or who the reporter planned on selling them to, but she knew one thing. The transaction would never take place. Not on her watch.

Adam returned and handed her a filled glass. He held his own to hers and they clinked their glasses.

"I'm Adam, by the way."

"Eva," Maggie said, biting her lip. She tossed back her glass in one gulp, and the cognac burned down her throat in a comforting warmth.

Adam's eyebrows rose and then he followed suit,

smacking his lips.

"The party couldn't hold your attention?" Maggie asked, brushing her hand against his.

"Let's just say things have certainly picked up, thanks to you."

Maggie gave him a playful push. "Charmer."

He grinned at that, and Maggie suppressed the urge to roll her eyes. A light breeze swept in from the balcony, the curtain sweeping up like a phantom warning of things to come.

"I don't mean to be forward," he said, stepping closer so his chest pressed against hers, "but what would happen if I tried to kiss you right now?"

Maggie raised her head and whispered into his ear. "Why don't you try and find out?"

Adam closed his eyes and moved his head towards her with parted lips.

Maggie placed her hands at either side of his face and leaned towards him. Before Adam Richmond's lips could touch her own, she tightened her grip and jerked her hands with a savage twist.

His neck snapped. A clean, precise break.

They always were.

Maggie let go, and Adam collapsed to the floor, his head lolling to the side.

She stepped over him and sat down at the desk, the seat still warm from the reporter's body, which now grew cold on the floor.

She opened the laptop, took out a portable USB stick from her bra, and plugged it into the port at the side.

Taking a quick glance at the folders stored in the hard drive, Maggie transferred the files onto the USB.

Five percent complete. The green bar grew longer as each file downloaded. *Ten percent.*

A loud knock rapped on the door. "Mr. Richmond, are you okay? We heard a crash."

Maggie's heart leapt in her ribcage. The man's phrasing was not lost on her.

We.

Maggie tapped the side of the laptop. "Come on, come on."

Twenty percent complete.

Sliding out of her heels, Maggie slipped off her dress and stripped down to the thermal bathing suit concealed beneath. She leaned down and collected one of her heels.

Fifty percent complete.

Maggie stared at the body. The man behind the door called again. "Mr. Richmond? I'm coming in."

Bollocks.

The door swung open as Maggie charged across the room. She surprised the first guard, swinging her shoe to meet his head. The heel hit his temple, and blood spurted out like oil from a well.

The next guard was ready for her.

She sent a punch to Maggie's gut, forcing the air out her lungs. The woman reached for her gun, but Maggie charged into her side and rammed her against the door. Their impact slammed the door shut and they tripped over the fallen guard, who squirmed around like a fish out of water, holding his head to keep his brain inside.

Maggie scrambled to her feet, but the woman grabbed her hair and sent her reeling back.

She went with the momentum, hissing as hair ripped out from her scalp. Maggie rolled into the fall and kicked up, her bare heel connecting with the woman's jaw.

The guard collapsed beside her now unconscious partner.

Maggie returned to the laptop, picking up the woman's gun as she went.

Eighty percent complete.

Footsteps sounded outside, coming closer. She counted four different gaits before she sent six rounds through the door.

Ninety-five percent complete.

There was a commotion outside the door, and it barged open, hitting the fallen guards.

Ninety-eight percent complete.

Someone grunted on the other side of the door as they shoved, sliding the fallen guards forward across the floor.

One-hundred percent complete.

Maggie pulled out the USB and scooped up the laptop. Behind her, the guards shoved the door open enough to fit through.

She reached the balcony and launched the laptop

overboard. It landed in the water with a satisfying splash and sank to the murky depths below.

A call came from behind her as the first guard slipped through the gap. Maggie aimed and shot the guard through the thigh. He fell to the ground as three more entered the room and more guards shouted in the corridor.

Maggie dropped the gun and turned back to the balcony. She ran forward and leapt in the air. Her body passed over the railings, and she positioned herself into a dive and met the water as gunshots carried out through the night.

Chapter 2

LONDON, GREAT BRITAIN
19 MAY

Maggie turned the keys in the lock and entered her apartment. A pile of letters lay on the floor waiting for her. She bent down with a groan, her muscles aching from the events of the night before, and nudged the door shut with her foot.

Bills, junk mail, bank statements, take out menus. Nothing important. She tossed them onto the kitchen counter with her keys, kicked off her boots, and wheeled her suitcase into her bedroom. She'd unpack later.

The air in the apartment was stale from disuse. Maggie lit a lemon scented candle, sitting it on the table beside the large living room windows. She peered out at the city skyline, the River Thames flowing past The O2 arena, illuminated like the towers behind it, which belonged to Canary Wharf's most influential banks.

Her reflection stared back at her. She looked tired, her hair pulled back from her face and bags resting under her ice blue eyes.

Maggie turned away, taking off her coat and draping it over her leather corner couch. A red flickering light caught her attention, the answering machine blinking to alert her of a new message.

Just one. She hadn't been home for over two weeks.

Maggie played the message and plodded over to the fridge to appease her grumbling stomach. Empty, aside from a jar of pickles and a container of something that had long since passed its sell by date. Maggie dumped the container in the bin and ran a hand over her head.

The message played and a woman's voice filled the open plan living space.

"Hi, this is Laura from First Class Travel. I'm calling to fill you in on some of our latest deals as you bought a holiday from us eighteen months ago. I guess you're at work right now, so phone me back when you can. Remember, life isn't all work and no play. You deserve some down time, and we have the perfect hot spots for you to choose from. Bye for now."

Maggie deleted the message and stared at the now empty answering machine. It felt like all she did was travel, though never for pleasure. Even the trip Laura the travel agent mentioned went unused; Maggie was stuck undercover in Morocco at the time.

A familiar shadow crossed the floor of her balcony and pressed up to the sliding door.

Maggie let the black cat in, her only visitor to the riverside apartment since she bought the place last year.

"Hello, Willow." Maggie scratched the cat behind the ears.

Willow rubbed herself against Maggie and circled around her legs, purring up at her. For a stray, Willow was a rather affectionate feline.

Maggie rummaged through the cupboards in the kitchen in search of a can of tuna to feed her furry friend, but like the fridge, they were a barren wasteland.

Willow meowed.

"Chinese food it is then."

Maggie called the restaurant around the corner and placed her usual order. Thirty minutes later, her chicken chow mein and spring rolls arrived, along with steamed fish for Willow.

She switched on the TV, but nothing held her attention for long. There was a spy film showing on one of the movie channels, and Maggie laughed at the ridiculous gadgets featured. Give her an old-fashioned gun or knife any day.

Turning off the TV, Maggie finished her meal in peaceful silence. She fell back on her couch, still smelling as new as the day it arrived, and pulled her bare feet up, closing her eyes as Willow snuggled into her.

A few minutes later, Maggie was back on her feet, pacing around her unused home. It was always like that after a mission, especially one that involved wet work. Unlike her television, Maggie couldn't simply press an off switch. She'd lost count of how many lives she'd taken over the years, her first at the ripe young age of fifteen. Perhaps she didn't want to know the number.

She could ring Ashton, but he would be busy. The man had never seen a Friday night he didn't like; not that he needed the weekend as an excuse to get up to no good. Besides, she hadn't spoken to him for almost a month. Hopping from one job to the next was a sure-fire way to annihilate any resemblance of a social life.

Her thoughts travelled to Leon, but Maggie was fast to shove them aside.

Fed and watered with a belly full of fish, Willow gave herself a shake, leapt off the couch, and left the way she came in, back out into the night and leaving Maggie alone.

It took all of five minutes before Maggie collected her computer from the coffee table and fired it up. She inserted the USB stick from her mission and downloaded the files she copied off Adam Richmond's computer.

Hours passed as Maggie combed over the contents, reading articles the reporter had penned himself, scrolling through emails from his work and personal accounts, and clicking from one image to the next in his photo folder.

It was almost midnight when she came across something that caught her eye, though it wasn't what she had expected to discover.

Maggie grabbed her mobile and rang one of the few numbers stored in her contacts. The person at the other end answered after three rings.

"We need to meet."

Chapter 3

Maggie arrived at Westminster Station by way of Canning Town, maneuvering through the crowds of eager tourists and early risers, and up the stone steps out onto Bridge Street.

Big Ben watched her as she buttoned her jacket and crossed Parliament Street, continuing down Great George Street. A mass of enraged gray clouds hung over her, threatening rain in typical British fashion for the approaching summer.

She stopped into a café for a much-needed coffee and then cut through St. James's Park. Maggie stopped by the bridge and sipped her drink while she watched some children feed the ducks. Boisterous pigeons swooped down and stole the pieces of bread from their little hands with the skill of London's best thieves.

Maggie arrived at her destination soon after, staring up at the five-story office building on King Street that served as the Unit's headquarters. Disguised as Inked International, a global stationery supplier, the boring nature of the business gave those not in-the-know no reason to walk through the doors.

The only time anyone ever tried to enter was when they stumbled home from The Golden Lion, an old-school pub next door where Maggie spent one too many nights drinking her way through their collection of whiskies in her early years as an agent.

Maggie swiped her security pass at the entrance. The locks clicked open, and Maggie walked to the elevators, her heels clacking on the marble floor. She entered the empty cab, pressed the button for the top floor, and waited.

"Hold on," came a voice before a foot wedged between the closing doors. The man pried them open and stood beside her in the confined space.

Maggie focused on keeping her face expressionless, her heart fluttering at the sight of him. She cleared her throat, the familiar woody scent of his favorite aftershave dancing in her nose.

"Hi, Leon."

"How you doing, Maggie?" he asked in his deep, gravelly voice.

"Just back from an assignment last night. You?"

"Can't complain." Leon hit the button for the fourth floor. "I thought you just came back from Japan the other week?"

"Are you keeping tabs on me?" Maggie craned her neck to meet his dark brown eyes for the first time. At six foot three, Leon Frost had over half a foot on her.

"I worry, that's all," he said, his white shirt crisp and bright against his black skin. "Every agent needs some downtime after being out there."

"I'm a big girl, I can look after myself."

Leon sighed and rubbed a strong hand over his close-trimmed beard. "I didn't mean it like that."

It was always like that these days. Both with so much to say to each other, yet saying nothing at all.

They stood in awkward silence until the elevator pinged and opened at Leon's floor. He stepped out, and the cab felt empty without him.

Leon stopped and turned back to her. "You look good, Maggie."

"You too," she said, gripping onto her jacket sleeve.

The doors closed between them, and Maggie took a deep, shaking breath. Seeing Leon was never easy, especially when she wasn't prepared for it.

Straightening her back, she swept her feelings to the side as the elevator stopped on her floor. By the time she stepped out, she was back to normal, her training kicking in.

Never let anyone see you sweat.

Brice Bishop was waiting for her in his office with a cup of tea in his hand.

"Maggie," he said, the remnants of a Manchester accent still in his inflection. "Nice to have you back."

Maggie sat down across from his desk. "Thanks."

Bishop's office was clean and Spartan, the result of a long career in the military before he joined the Unit. His phone buzzed and he read the message, tossing it back on the desk with a heavy sigh.

"Everything okay?"

"June," said Bishop, needing no further clarification. The divorce with his wife had been a long and messy one, their relationship barely civil and only so because of their kids.

"What now?"

"I finally get the girls next weekend, and she's trying to cancel."

"Why?"

"She and *Brian*," he said, the distain for his ex-wife's new fiancé clear from the way he growled the man's name, "decided to take a family holiday that week. If I cancel, I don't get to see them for at least another three weeks."

"And if you don't, you're the bad one for cancelling their holiday," Maggie finished. It had taken a while for Bishop to get back on good terms with his teenage daughters, both girls siding with their mother during the divorce.

Bishop leaned back in his chair. "June's design, of course. She should have been an agent."

"I'm sorry, Bishop."

Bishop tried to shrug like it was nothing, but he didn't quite pull it off.

For a man in his late fifties, he still clung to his brown hair which he kept cropped at the sides like he was still a soldier. Crow's feet perched at the corners of his eyes, his skin tough as leather, and nose bent out of shape from when Maggie had broken it during her first official mission.

To the untrained eye, Bishop appeared as just another businessman living in London who looked after himself and wore expensive suits. It was all deliberate, of course. Brice Bishop was so much more than that, and stories of his days as an agent still passed around the Unit like folktales. He was one of the best.

"Enough about that. I trust everything went well?"

Maggie nodded. "All according to plan."

"Excellent."

"There was one thing."

"Oh?"

"I couldn't find any of the stolen secrets on Richmond's laptop." Not one file. She searched for hidden folders and encrypted documents disguised as something else, but the laptop was empty.

"You read the computer files?"

"I figured I should check what the secrets were, in case

any of them were an imminent threat to national security." And out of sheer curiosity to find out what was so classified that Richmond had to die, but Maggie kept that to herself.

Bishop nodded. "Good thinking."

Maggie leaned forward in her chair. "But that's just it. I didn't find any."

"Nothing?" Bishop frowned.

"Not nothing, but not what we were looking for."

Maggie got up and turned on the computer. It was linked to a projector Bishop used when hosting meetings. Like she did at her apartment, she plugged in the USB stick and selected some of the files of note.

"I trolled through every file on here. Junk for the most part, but one folder in particular stood out." Maggie clicked the first file and it appeared on the projector screen on the wall. "Richmond was working on a story, investigating a private and commercial property developer named Brightside Property and Construction Limited."

Bishop clasped his hands. "What was his angle?"

"Corruption. Apparently, the company applied for planning permission on a plot of land in the East End, but it was declined." Richmond had acquired a copy of the application to prove it.

"Why?"

Maggie brought up an article that had made it onto the BBC News website. "The land is home to a row of government assisted houses owned by the local council. The residents are refusing to move."

"Where does the corruption come in?" Bishop asked, his tea growing cold on the desk.

"Brightside recently purchased the houses from the government, which now makes the homes private rentals. Brightside increased the rent payments to unaffordable levels to push the residents out."

Bishop shook his head. "Legally evicting them. Sly bastards."

"It's worked for the most part," Maggie continued, "but a few of the residents are causing a stink about it and going to the press. There have been reports of intimidation, too. Residents claim men knocked on their doors in the middle of the night and threatened them, warning them to move."

Richmond had gathered some written testimonies and a few names, but nothing concrete. It didn't take long for Maggie to find a way into the Metropolitan Police's records and hunt down police reports to corroborate the stories.

"I did some digging. Similar reports have been made against Brightside in other developments in London and surrounding areas over the years."

Maggie clicked on another file. A photo of a body appeared on the screen, an old man beaten to death, his face purple and swollen.

"Eric Solomon was found dead in his home, the victim of a supposed break-in."

Bishop examined the photos on the screen. "What makes you think he wasn't?"

"The week before his body was found, Mr. Solomon turned down a substantial financial offer from Brightside to move. He'd purchased the council house he was living in before Brightside took over and procured the surrounding land. His refusal to move would have stopped their plans to knock down the houses and build a shopping center on the land."

Maggie brought up the proposed plans for the construction. Richmond had really done his homework.

"With the old man dead, Brightside could carry on with their plans," Bishop said, tying up all the pieces with a neat bow.

"That's what I'm thinking." Maggie pulled the USB from the computer. "Though it seems strange for someone like Adam Richmond to investigate all this while preparing to sell classified documents to the highest bidder."

"Perhaps it was part of his cover," ventured Bishop. "He was an investigative reporter after all."

Bishop could be right. Maggie sat back down and slid the USB across the desk to him. "I don't know all the big players yet, but I will soon enough. I'm pretty sure Richmond was on to something here. Something big."

"Great work. Really." Bishop leaned back in his chair.

"I'll speak with the Director General and see if she can dig anything up from the guys at MI5. They might already be looking into the dealings of this company." He shook his head. "Richmond must have kept the stolen files somewhere else."

"I can contact Ms. Helmsley if you want," Maggie offered. The Director General was known as a pit bull in a power suit around the Unit, but Maggie liked her. She had a knack for seeing through bullshit and kept the men running around for her like they were little boys and she their headmistress.

"No, that's all right, I'll do it." Bishop slid a manila folder in front of her. "I have a favor to ask of you in the meantime."

"What?" Maggie eyed the folder but didn't pick it up.

"The Mayor of London is the keynote speaker at an international business conference in the financial district and has requested a chaperone."

Maggie sighed. "When?"

"Tonight," said Bishop. "Nina will be there, too, following the same orders for the Foreign Secretary."

"Why can't another agent do it?" The last thing Maggie wanted to do was go back out on a mission. She'd only just gotten home. "I saw Leon coming in."

"Leon is already assigned to another case. All my other agents are tied up."

Maggie remained quiet. If she wanted a career in babysitting, she would've been a nursery teacher.

"It's only for a couple of hours," added Bishop, giving her that pleading look she hated.

Maggie drooped her shoulders. "I can look after them both on my own. No need to send two agents for this type of job." If she wasn't getting the night off, at least Nina could.

"Nina is going, too. You really need to learn to work with others," Bishop said, not for the first time. "You can't do everything on your own."

Maggie folded her arms. It wasn't that she didn't like Nina. They had known each other since they joined the Unit at sixteen. She just worked better alone. "Fine, but I'm taking my annual leave after this."

"Of course." Bishop handed her the file containing what she would need to know for the evening's event. "Thanks, Maggie."

Maggie took the manila folder and left Bishop's office. Maybe she would call that travel agent back after all.

Chapter 4

The taxi took a left from Leadenhall Street and turned into St Mary Axe, where a swanky new hotel had opened on the corner of Bevis Marks, right next to The Gherkin.

Maggie paid the fare and stepped out into the cold. The sky's earlier promise of rain came through, and huge droplets plummeted down from the heavens.

She ducked under the covered entrance to the Baltic Hotel and shook her umbrella out.

"I'll take that for you, Madam," said a man by the door, ushering her inside.

"Thank you," she said. "I'm here for the conference."

The man pointed across the room to where a sign stood for the event. "Straight ahead."

Maggie walked through the foyer and arrived at a large and glamorous conference room, decked out with chandeliers hanging from the high ceilings that overlooked round tables. At the back of the conference room, Maggie noted the podium where the mayor would give his talk.

The tables were set with fine porcelain dishes, crystal glassware, and golden cutlery. The staff had even arranged the napkins into elegant swans. Ten seats a piece were tucked under the tables, upholstered in fine gold suede to match the intricate filigree design of the wallpaper.

Along the bar sat buckets of champagne resting on ice, ready for when the attendees arrived.

The organizers had spared no expense, appropriate given the high-profile guests could bring millions of pounds in foreign investments into London's private sector.

Nina stood waiting for her near the bar as staff milled around the room making final touches to the pristine layout.

"I've scoped out the place," announced Nina by way of hello. "Everything's in order."

She wore a sleek gown with a plunging neckline, the emerald fabric bringing out the green in her hazel eyes. It also did a good job of hiding the knives Maggie knew would be strapped to Nina's thighs. She had a fondness for getting up close and personal with her enemies.

"Good," replied Maggie, taking a quick look around. "Where are our charges?"

"Upstairs in one of the suites," Nina said as she headed out to the foyer and climbed the stairs.

Maggie followed, cursing the dress code. Why did she always find herself stuck in a dress? At least the black number she wore tonight wasn't hugging her hips. Her gun sat in its holster around her thigh, the familiar weight like a deadly comfort blanket.

"Here's your ear piece." Nina handed it over to Maggie along with a clipboard, both playing the role of event coordinators for their cover.

"It's already wired in to the right frequency." Nina spoke into the little microphone of her own device. "Testing."

"One, two, three," Maggie replied, securing hers around her ear, careful not to disturb her chignon hairdo. If she had to wear a dress, the least her hair could do was to stay out of her face.

"How was Cannes?" Nina asked, slowing down to walk by Maggie's side.

They were around the same height, but where Maggie was curved with vulpine features, Nina was lithe and all sharp angles, from her cutting cheekbones to her pointed nose.

"A pain in the neck," Maggie said. "The weather was nice though."

Nina shook her head. "Bishop really needs to stop sending me to places that require thermals."

"That's what you get for speaking Russian."

Nina huffed, a playful grin edging her lips. "You speak it, too, and you got to party on a yacht."

Maggie held up her hands. "Hey, I'm not complaining."

"Must be nice being the favorite," Nina teased, nudging her.

While preferring to work alone, if Maggie had to work with anyone, she was glad it was Nina. They were both teenagers when Bishop recruited them. Though they viewed each other as rivals at first, it didn't take long for them to become good friends. There weren't many women in the Unit, so they bonded quickly.

Like most old boys' clubs, the Unit had some work to do to bridge the gender imbalance. One too many meetings suffered from an overload of alpha-male testosterone. Not that Maggie or Nina had any trouble being heard. They just had to trample on a few toes first.

When they reached the third floor, Nina led Maggie to the corner suite, walking past two armed men who stood sentry before the entrance. Nina stopped in front of the door. "Fair warning, the Foreign Secretary is rather sloshed."

"Some boys just can't handle their drink," Maggie said with a sigh.

Nina ran a hand through her locks of straight chestnut hair and gave Maggie a wink.

The suite was as expected, given how the rest of the Baltic Hotel was decorated. The designers were fans of gold and rich creams, the primary colors of the sitting area that separated the bedrooms and bathroom. White lilies bloomed in several vases around the space and filled the air with their light floral scent.

A man got up from the couch on unstable legs. Nina was right, George Moulton was drunk, and from the triple measure in his hand, he had no intentions of stopping.

"Very nice indeed," he said, his voice loud and irritating. He studied them with glassy eyes, his fake tan a shade too orange to fool anyone into thinking it was real. "Why does Bishop only recruit sexy girls?"

Maggie responded with a raised eyebrow, biting her tongue to refrain from assassinating him with a response. At least she wasn't in charge of babysitting him for the night.

Nina stiffed at the mention of Bishop. "Is anyone else here?" she hissed.

"Relax, it's just us," said Moulton, shaking his head.

Nina glared at him.

Knowledge of the Unit was strictly classified due its propensity to cross the line of what was legal. Only those with a high enough clearance were made aware of its existence. Most of those working for the Secret Intelligence Service weren't even privy to their clandestine faction.

Ignoring the Foreign Secretary, Maggie walked over to the other man in the room. The Mayor of London was busy reading over notecards by the window. "Nice to meet you Mr. Worthington," she said and offered her hand. "I'm Maggie Black."

"A pleasure, and please, call me James," he said, his

shake nice and firm. "Thank you for doing this on such short notice. I'm afraid our little event resulted in some anonymous threats, and Brice felt some extra security was in order."

"He doesn't like to take any chances," replied Maggie, cursing Bishop. She could be curled up on her couch in her pajamas, reading a good book with a nice glass of wine right about now.

George Moulton cackled behind them, Nina giggling a polite yet strained laugh along with him. James scowled at the man's back and offered Maggie an apologetic shrug.

"Ready for your speech?" Maggie asked.

"As I'll ever be." James released a heavy exhale. "I'm not good with these things."

James Worthington was new in his role as mayor. His predecessor Edgar Johnston died at the beginning of the year.

The new mayor was a handsome man, in a stiff upper lip sort of way. Not a hair was out of place on his head, his face clean shaven. He wore a smart suit, yet nothing too flashy like the Armani suit Moulton had squeezed into.

Moulton continued spluttering behind them, cracking jokes and lighting a cigar. Maggie had heard better one liners from Christmas crackers. The tendrils of smoke from his cigar circled around the room, drowning out the fresh lilies.

Maggie lowered her voice. "I'm sure you'll do better than him."

That won her a smile. "Yes, well, there's that at least."

"I'm going to take Mr. Moulton down to his table," called Nina. Moulton wasn't due to talk until after the dinner. Hopefully by then he would have the ability to stand, never mind give a speech on UK business.

"See you down there." Maggie turned back to the mayor when the door closed behind Nina. "We've made a sweep of the hotel and surrounding areas and cleared the conference room itself. You're good to go."

"Excellent." James held out his arm. "Shall we?"

Maggie indulged him and linked her arm in his. "It's a nice hotel," she said as they walked downstairs, the armed men following close behind. Voices travelled up from the foyer as the guests arrived in time for the mayor's speech. And the free booze and food.

"Yes, named after the Baltic Exchange. Terrible business."

Maggie was too young to remember the bombing of the building, right on the very street they were in now, but Bishop had worked on the case. Three people had died that day, and another ninety-one injured.

"The drunken idiot is seated and behaving himself," came Nina's voice in Maggie's ear. "No signs of trouble."

The podium was to the back of the conference room and had its own entrance. The mayor stood behind the curtain, going over his notes one last time before going out.

The real event coordinator was behind the podium,

too, ordering helpers around, her cheeks flush and movements flustered.

Maggie watched everyone who came and went, taking in faces and checking all access points.

"All clear here," Maggie said into her microphone just as a man caught her eye.

He strode backstage, but not in an organized rush like the others around him. He moved with a purpose, and that purpose became clear as he approached and reached into his jacket.

Maggie was about to shout when the man lunged at the mayor.

The man pulled out his gun and aimed at his target. Maggie dived in front of the mayor, blocking the man's path. His finger inched toward the trigger, but Maggie got to him first, thrusting his arm into the air. The gun went off and shot into the ceiling, flecks of plaster falling around them like snow.

Screams erupted from the other side of the curtain as guests heard the shot echoing off the walls of the large room. Chairs scraped on the floor and footsteps stampeded as people spilled out of the conference room and into the foyer.

The man was fast, and before the mayor's two personal guards could move three paces, he shot bullets into each of their heads. They crumbled to the floor like lifeless dolls, blood already seeping out of the bullet holes.

Maggie jabbed at the assailant, but he blocked her punch, sending a ringing pain through her arm. He pointed his gun at the mayor once again, but Maggie timed a perfect roundhouse that sent the weapon flying from his grasp.

The gun landed out of sight and Maggie squared up to the assassin, making sure to stay between him and James. If he wanted to reach the mayor, he would need to go through her.

The assassin swung a fist at her, and Maggie ducked back avoiding impact. She reached for her own gun, concealed around her thigh, but the man was on her again, this time catching her in the jaw with a right hook.

Maggie's head snapped to the side, the metallic tang of blood filling her mouth.

With a yell, she bounded forward and kneed him in the stomach, doubling him over. When he straightened back up, he had a knife in his hand, the silver glinting under the light.

The mayor stepped toward her, but Maggie shoved him back out of the way.

The assassin took advantage of her distraction and sliced at her. Maggie noticed the knife at the last second and flinched back, the blade catching on the fabric of her dress. She grabbed his wrist and thrust her palm into the man's elbow, aiming for a break. The bone didn't snap, but the assassin yelped and dropped his weapon.

But the loss of his weapon didn't slow him down. The man spun and rammed into her with his shoulder, forcing Maggie back. He swept his foot across the floor and swiped his leg into hers, sending her careening to the floor in a graceless fall.

He made for the mayor, but Maggie scrambled to her feet and grabbed him by the back of his collar, using his momentum as he stumbled back to trip him up. He fell on the arm she damaged and hissed.

Maggie seized the moment and threw all her weight into a brutal kick to his abdomen. The man groaned a curse and rolled away, holding his stomach as he bounced back up on agile feet. Maggie made for him again, but he turned and ran, heading back the way he came.

"Stay here. Don't come out until I come back for you," she ordered the mayor. "Got it?"

James nodded, wide eyed and panting, leaning against the wall to keep him steady.

Certain he was okay and had heard her, Maggie abandoned her heels, leaped over the dead bodies of the guards, and sped off after the assassin.

The foyer was pandemonium, people pushing and shoving each other out of the way to race from the hotel, all pretense of civility gone. An old man lay on the floor covering his head as others trampled over him to get to safety.

Nina spoke in Maggie's ear. "Maggie what the hell is going on? I heard gun shots."

"Someone tried to take out the mayor," she replied. "I'm in pursuit."

"Where are you? Do you need my help?"

"No. Get the Foreign Secretary out of here. He could be a target, too."

"Copy that," Nina said, her voice cutting in and out. "Go catch the prick."

The alarm interfered with the wire's signal, and it screeched in Maggie's ear. She took it out and tossed it, continuing her chase.

Maggie fought her way through the crowd, eyes set on finding the one responsible for the chaos. Black hair, light brown skin, an unassuming face that blended in well. Spanish from the way he cursed, though she could be mistaken on that. Spanish wasn't on her list of fluent languages.

The alarms wailed through the hotel. New and louder screams followed, the sirens only panicking the people more.

Event Security tried to settle everyone down and restore order, but it wasn't working. The flight instinct in the guests was well and truly in effect. But not for Maggie. She was in full fight mode.

Maggie spotted Nina across the foyer in a splash of emerald among the crowd, heading out the front door with George Moulton. They met each other's eyes, and

Maggie nodded for her to go on. George could be in danger.

Maneuvering her way through the panicked people, Maggie scanned every inch of the room.

There.

The assassin had made it through the crowd and was running up the stairs Maggie had taken with the mayor. The man looked over his shoulder and spotted her moving his way.

Maggie ran, feet cold on the marble floor, and fought her way through the guests. She reached the stairs and took them three at a time, releasing her gun from its holster and gripping it with a firm hold.

She turned the safety off and made it to the second floor.

A door to her left was closing, but no one had come racing out to head downstairs. Maggie caught it before it clicked shut and ducked inside, weapon at the ready.

The tail of a black jacket flashed down the hall as someone turned the corner at a run.

Maggie sprinted after them, her heart pounding and hair slipping out from behind her head. She rounded the corner and laid eyes on her target. Aiming with both hands, Maggie kept running and shot at the assassin.

The bullets missed his head by inches, embedding into the wall. He made a right down another hall of the hotel floor, and Maggie heard a crash.

Sprinting after him, she spotted the busted door to one

of the rooms, the wood split off the frame. Gun at the ready, Maggie stepped inside. Something cold brushed against her bare foot, and she stole a glance down. A card. She bent to collect it, keeping her weapon pointed into the darkness of the room. It was a room key, but not for that one, or any other on the second floor. It was for the level above.

"I know you're in here," Maggie said, stepping inside.

Glass shattered further in, and she stormed through, ready to attack.

The assassin was at the window, the cold air blowing in through the broken pane. He took one last look at her before Maggie pulled the trigger.

The man jumped from the window and fell out of sight.

Maggie moved to the window and looked down. He wasn't there.

"Shit."

———

Things were still up in the air when she returned to the foyer, red faced and kicking herself at failing to apprehend the assassin.

She went to the back of the podium to return to the mayor and report what happened. So much for an easy couple of hours.

Maggie walked in to find the place deserted other than the two bodies lying in a heap on the ground.

She froze.

Not two bodies. Three.

James Worthington, Mayor of London and her charge, was dead.

Chapter 5

Maggie dropped to her knees and pressed her fingers against the mayor's neck. There was no pulse, but she knew there wouldn't be. The man before her was clearly dead.

An angry red gash sliced across his neck like a wide smile. Blood soaked the collar of his white shirt and pooled beneath him, smeared across the floor where he had struggled to hold onto life before it escaped him.

The mayor stared up to the ceiling, his gaze vacant and haunting, shock etched permanently over his features.

"I'm sorry," she said, closing his eyes.

Maggie stared at her hands, covered in his warm, sticky blood. She balled her fists, looking between James and his security men. She couldn't have been more than a few minutes late.

Something lay on the floor a few feet away, the shine

attracting Maggie's gaze. She reached over for it and held it in her hand. The assassin's knife.

The bastard must have slipped back inside to finish the job while she was still upstairs.

"Don't move."

Maggie put her hands in the air and dropped the knife. "This isn't what it looks like." She rose slowly to her feet and turned to face the voice.

"I said don't move!" Sweat beaded above the man's lip, his eyes darting between Maggie and the bodies lying at her feet. The gun in his hand shook, a Met police standard Glock 26. He wore a tactical vest and a grimace, brows burrowed down to reach the bridge of his nose.

"Stay calm," she soothed, conscious of his finger hovering over the trigger.

"Hands on your head." He raised the gun until it pointed at her chest.

Voices came from out in the foyer, shouting orders and directing people to exit the building. The rest of the young policeman's team had arrived.

Maggie stared the officer in the eyes, unblinking. She moved her gaze over his shoulder and sucked in a fake gasp.

The policeman turned to where she looked, and Maggie darted forward. She reached for the gun, twisted it from his grasp, and spun it back on him.

"Please, don't kill me," he said, flinching away from the barrel.

Maggie smashed the gun into his temple, sending him to the ground with a solid *thump*. His eyes rolled to the back of his head, but he was still breathing. Maggie discarded the gun, stepped back into her shoes, and darted down the other end of the podium, procuring a woman's coat which hung over a chair along the way.

Maggie made sure she wasn't followed and slipped out the back exit.

Police sirens and flashing blue lights filled London as she disappeared into the night.

Blood spiraled down the sink, stark red against white porcelain.

Maggie scrubbed at her hands, the soap suds mixing with the blood to form a pink froth. The water burned her skin, but she didn't care. Steam rose from the spurting tap and coated the mirror above, distorting her reflection.

Thoughts and theories raced through her mind, each of them fighting to be heard above the others. Why did the assassin want the mayor dead? Was it a hired hit or something more personal? James had mentioned threats against him at the event, but he was the Mayor of London. Threats were a daily occurrence for someone like him.

Maggie dried her hands and picked up the room key she'd found while chasing the assassin, twirling it between her fingers. The hit was planned, that much was clear. This wasn't a spur of the moment thing. A decision made in haste or out of anger. It was calculated and cold.

Professional.

Maggie wiped the mirror and looked at herself. Specks of blood scattered over her face like freckles. She thought of the men it belonged to, the mayor's guards. She hadn't even bothered to learn their names before they were shot protecting their charge.

Gathering a wad of tissues from the dispenser, Maggie soaked them under the water and dabbed at her face. Once clean, she used the pins from her updo to pull her hair back and secure it out of her face. The police would be looking for a blond.

Taking her gun from its holster, Maggie removed the magazine and checked inside. Eleven rounds left, plus the extra magazine in her holster. She shoved the magazine back in place and set her Glock on the side of the sink while she gave herself a once over. Blood stained her dress, but it wouldn't stand out against the black, especially outside in the darkness of the night.

Her phone buzzed against her chest, and she pulled it out of her bra, glancing at the caller I.D. "Bishop," she said, the phone to her ear.

"Maggie. What the hell just happened?"

"Someone killed the mayor." His dead face flashed in her mind.

"Yes, I'm aware of that," grumbled Bishop. "How?"

"Throat slashed. I think it was a professional hit." There was so much blood. The knife had torn through skin and muscle in one clean slice.

"This is a mess." Bishop's voice rose. "An officer reported seeing you kill Worthington."

Maggie imagined Bishop pacing his office, his plans for the evening—if he even had any—interrupted. It wasn't like he had his wife or kids to return home to anymore. Bishop was married to the job, just like most of them, and it had cost him a life outside of it.

"He put two and two together and made five," she said, returning her gun to its holster.

A fist slammed on something hard at Bishop's end, his maple desk or the nearest wall. "You're all over the news."

Maggie pried the bathroom door open and glanced out into the pub. A television hung on the wall behind the long bar, the usual programming interrupted by the words *BREAKING NEWS* splayed in bold letters across the screen.

Most of the patrons were more interested in the bottom of their glasses and chatting each other up than the news, but a few of the lone drinkers watched with interest.

A reporter stood outside the Baltic Hotel, the perimeter cordoned off with police tape and constables fresh on the job tasked with keeping civilians out. Text scrolled at the bottom of the screen, highlighting what happened. Maggie read it and pinched her nose.

Mayor of London killed by unknown woman.

"I didn't do it," she said, going back into the bathroom and locking the door.

"I tried to contain the story, but reporters were already on the scene covering the conference."

"Bishop, I did not do this," Maggie repeated, an unfamiliar worry curling in her gut. Bishop always trusted her. How could he think—

Bishop let out a deep breath, sounding tired. "It doesn't look good, Maggie."

"What do you mean? The policeman walked in on me checking James for a pulse." It didn't help that she was holding a knife at the time, but she certainly hadn't killed anyone. That night anyway.

"James?" Bishop asked, not missing the familiarity.

"Yes, James." Maggie held back a frustrated scream. "The fucking mayor. I didn't kill him."

Bishop was quiet for a moment, the silence deafening. "We've got access to the CCTV feeds."

"Good." Maggie leaned against the tiled wall. "Check them and you'll see who did this."

Another pause. "We did."

"And?"

"Put me on speaker, I'm sending you a file."

Maggie did as he said and waited for the ping of the email to come through.

Maggie touched the screen and downloaded the file. Pressing play, she watched the video as Bishop stayed quiet on the other end of the line.

It was pixelated, but Maggie could make out the mayor standing where she had left him before running off. Someone came into view from the door leading to the foyer.

Bile rose in Maggie's throat.

Someone in a black dress walked towards the mayor. He said something to her before she pulled out a knife and slashed it across James Worthington's throat.

Maggie watched as the mayor grabbed at the wound, blood spurting between his fingers. The blond woman watched him roll onto his back where he would bleed out before making her exit.

"That's..." Maggie started, her breathing labored. Her mouth grew dry, words sticking to her tongue. "That's not me."

She stared down at her dress, identical to the one the killer wore. The video replayed on a loop, and Maggie couldn't tear her eyes from it. The assassin's hair was styled in a chignon at the nape of her neck, clear despite the graininess captured by the CCTV camera.

The knife. Blood. James.

Her.

"I think you need to come in," said Bishop.

"Come in?" A tremor worked through Maggie's hand.

"Yes." Bishop was calm now, soothing. "We can get to the bottom of this."

"You know I didn't do this. Please, Bishop." Maggie

preferred her boss when he was harassed and shouting. The calm version of the man wasn't a good sign.

"It's over my head now. The Director General's been informed, and she's not happy."

Maggie huffed. "I can't say I'm thrilled either."

"Where are you, Maggie?"

Maggie closed her mouth. The higher ups were involved. Bishop couldn't do anything for her now. Something like this would need to be cleaned up, and fast.

"Maggie..." Bishop voice carried a clear warning.

"Director Helmsley can't let it leak that an agent assassinated the Mayor of London," she said, more to herself than to him. "You know that. They won't claim me as their own."

And if they wouldn't claim her, they couldn't risk her talking. They needed to contain what happened. Bury it. Remove her from the picture as fast and as clean as possible. A scandal like that could put the entire secret service and their activities into question. Frankly, Maggie was a liability they couldn't afford, innocent or not.

"Let me help you."

Maggie bit her lip. "No, you can't get involved. They'll investigate you, too."

"You know how it'll look if you don't hand yourself over."

Maggie knew the drill. "They'll already have me pegged for it. I can't explain that video. I mean look at it. That could be me."

Except it wasn't.

Maggie shook her head, nerves rattled. "Someone set me up."

"If you run—" Bishop began, but she cut him off.

"I'm not taking the fall for this." Maggie lashed out and struck the mirror. It smashed in the center, cracks splintering through the glass like a cobweb and slashing her reflection.

"Calm down, Black. Think this through."

Easy for him to say. He wasn't the one being framed for murder. "I have to hang up." How long had she been on the phone?

"Maggie, don't," he pleaded. "Talk to me."

They could be on their way for her now. "I'm sorry Bishop. Just know I didn't do this."

"I believe you," he said as Maggie hung up.

She had to move. Now.

The black mac jacket she procured was a little too big for her, but it would do. She shrugged it on and buttoned it up to the collar, tying the belt tight around her waist.

Maggie threw the hood up over her head and made sure her hair was hidden.

She exited the bar, keeping her head down and her back to the security camera in the corner. Rain poured from the sky, the road and pavement slick and glistening under the street lights. She walked off down the street in the opposite direction from the Baltic Hotel, resisting the urge to check over her shoulder every five seconds.

A bus stop was up ahead, and Maggie took out her phone. As she passed, she slipped it into the pocket of a young man and watched him hop on the bus as it pulled up.

They would be tracking her phone by now. Bishop and the like would know it was a pointless exercise, but her diversion would slow down the police and anyone else who might be after her. Smart phones were expensive tracking devices, and she had used that to her advantage more than a few times on missions.

The young man would receive an unwanted visit tonight, but whoever turned up at his door would not find who they were looking for.

Maggie disappeared like a shadow into the night, branded a traitor to the country she had served and risked her life for all these years.

Chapter 6

The streets were quieter around Mayfair than they were walking through SoHo, where the night was still young for those exiting West End shows and the people gathering outside of nightclubs to have a quick smoke before going in.

Maggie had walked the whole way, conscious that images of her face may already be making rounds at transport hubs and among the officers working the busy Saturday nightshift.

Turning left from North Audley Street, Maggie made her way down Green Street, keeping the brisk yet casual pace of a woman who knew her way around the city, but also knew not to wander too long alone at that time of night. Even in the well-to-do area she found herself in.

Another left and Maggie arrived at Park Lane.

Unable to return home, Maggie needed a place to rest and think over what the hell she was going to do next.

She milled down the road, eyeing the line of residential homes along the way. She watched for signs of life inside the high windows but didn't stop. A grand period building stood in the corner, drainpipes running up along the white walls, the windows on each floor curved and opening out into little balconies ideal for hot summer nights.

Maggie counted six flats in total, plus one night manager who sat at a desk and stared into space.

The lights were off in the top flat of the building, the only two-story dwelling on the street that came with a rooftop terrace overlooking Hyde Park. It was perfect.

Crossing the street, Maggie circled back and waited thirty minutes, staying out of sight as cars drove up and down the main road.

The night manager got up from his desk and entered a little room in the back—to go to the bathroom or to make a cup of tea. Maggie seized the moment. She ran at the building and leapt, grabbing hold of one of the drainpipes and scaling the wall.

Using the metal balconies as a boost, she hoisted herself up, her hands cold and slippery thanks to the incessant rain.

Reaching the roof, Maggie swung a leg over the top and rolled to safety, lying on her back while she caught her breath.

The terrace had an arrangement of outdoor furniture sitting among a garden of brightly filled hanging baskets, mini evergreen trees in large pots, and twisting vines that spread over the walls of the upper floor.

Maggie got up and crept over to the sliding door, peering inside with her hands around her eyes. No one was home.

The glass shattered easily enough with a little help from a garden gnome she found in one of the potted plants.

Slipping her hand in the gap, Maggie undid the lock and stepped inside.

Glass crunched under her shoes, her shadow reaching across the floor and clawing up the wall as she intruded into what should be someone's safe place.

Her knees bumped against a bed, unslept in and neatly made. God, she was tired. Her body ached, a mixture of adrenal fatigue and the aftereffects of the assassin's blows settling in.

Maggie crossed the room and felt around for a light switch. What she wouldn't give right then for a good meal and a scalding hot shower.

Her fingers grazed the switch, but she thought better of it. No lights. If the night manager noticed them on, it might raise suspicion. Especially if the resident told him they weren't going to be home.

Instead, Maggie left the room and walked down the hall, listening for any hint of life but hearing none. She was home alone. Downstairs, she walked through a large living area in search of the kitchen.

She was too late to react when she felt the tip of a gun press against the back of her head.

Maggie stiffened as the cold metal brushed the back of her hair. Had they found her already? Followed her there without her noticing?

The gun left her head.

"For Christ's sake, Maggie, I could've shot you."

The Glaswegian brogue was music to her ears, and she spun around to face him.

"Ashton." Maggie raised to her tiptoes and wrapped her arms around him.

He hugged her back, his bare torso and tattooed arms nice and warm. "Who else did you expect, the bloody Easter bunny?"

"You don't want to know," she said, letting him go.

He wore a pair of black lounging trousers, his feet bare. From the lack of styling product in his short brown hair, Maggie must have woken him out of bed.

Ashton pointed upstairs to the spare bedroom she entered from. "Did you have to break the door?"

Maggie smiled. "Send me the bill."

Ashton rolled his eyes and walked through to the kitchen. "What are you doing here anyway?"

Maggie stepped out of her shoes and removed the jacket before sitting at the breakfast bar, the kitchen modern with black marble worktops and chrome fittings. Ashton Price enjoyed only the best.

"I didn't think you'd be home," she said. "All the lights were off." The flat was one of Ashton's many properties, his main home an estate in Sussex. Scamming unsuspecting criminals paid much better than her government job. Even after her hazard pay bonus.

Ashton nodded back towards his room with a grin that exposed his dimples. "Aye, well, I'm entertaining."

"Oh," Maggie said, dragging the word out. "The actor?"

"Nope." Ashton wiggled his eyebrows. "Rugby player."

"Good for you," said Maggie. "Where did you both meet?"

"Maggie, what's wrong?" Ashton asked, cutting through her stalling.

"What do you mean?" She bat her lashes at him. "Can't a girl visit her best friend?"

Ashton gave a pointed look at her dress, blood stained and covered in scrapes and white dust from her climb. "She can, but it isn't every night she scurries up my building and breaks in. She usually rings around first. When she's not avoiding me, that is."

"I would have knocked had I known you were entertaining," Maggie teased. "And I haven't been avoiding you, I've just been–"

"Really busy with work," Ashton finished, opening the fridge. "Do you want a drink?"

"Tea, thanks."

Ashton returned with a glass of whisky. "You look like you could use something stronger."

Maggie tossed back the drink, wiping her mouth as the liquid warmed her cold bones. "I'm in trouble."

"I figured as much." Ashton leaned on the counter across from her.

She told him everything. From the moment she got the assignment at HQ to finding the mayor dead and being nailed as the one who did it.

Ashton stared at her. "And here I thought this had something to do with you and Leon."

"I wish." Relationship worries seemed like a walk in the park compared to murder.

Ashton raised an eyebrow at her.

"I didn't mean it like that," she said, slapping his arm. Her and Leon were nothing but a series of bad decisions.

Ashton sobered, watching her with his deep blue eyes. "What are you going to do?"

Maggie leaned back on the barstool, running a shaky hand over her head. "I don't know"

"You'll think of something." He walked around the breakfast bar and pulled her towards him.

"I can't even use any of my aliases," she said, leaning into his chest. "HQ know all the ones I use." An oversight on her part. Not that she could have foreseen something like this happening.

"Now that I can help with." Ashton's business endeavors weren't strictly legal. Not legal at all, actually. But no one could deny his ability to make things happen. Dealing with criminals provided him a wide and varied list of contacts to call upon, depending on what he needed. She didn't doubt his words.

Maggie looked up at him. "Can I stay here for the night?"

He tutted at her. "Like you have to ask."

"Thanks, Ashton." At least she could spend the night without having to keep one eye open. Maggie made sure to keep her friendship with Ashton secret from the Unit. He wasn't exactly on the best of terms with Bishop or the Director General. Not after his last and final mission as an agent.

"What are we going to do with you?" he said.

"I know." Maggie leaned on her fist. "Usually I'm the one getting *you* out of trouble."

His mischievous grin was back. "Trouble's my middle name."

Maggie pushed him towards his bedroom, smacking his rear as she did. "Well then, get back to your guest and cause a little more."

"You sure?" he asked, looking at his door. "I can sit up

with you if you want."

"No, I'll be fine," she said, sliding off the chair. "I'm knackered anyway."

Ashton kissed her forehead. "Don't worry too much. It'll all seem clearer in the morning."

And off he went.

Maggie helped herself to another whisky before heading upstairs. She chose the second spare room over the one she broke into. The cold from outside would have seeped in by now.

She took a long, hot shower, washing her hair twice to make sure it was free from blood and other mess, before wrapping a housecoat around herself and hopping into bed.

Despite being more tired than even the brutal first weeks of her training all those years ago, sleep never came. She tossed and turned in Ashton's Egyptian cotton sheets, going over every detail of what happened.

Was this a horrifically bad case of being in the wrong place at the wrong time? The assassin had checked himself into a room if the keycard was anything to go by. That was premeditated. She only got the assignment that morning, and for a hotel like the Baltic on a big conference night, rooms would have been scooped up quick. Weeks in advance even.

He attacked the mayor, not her. At least at first.

The woman from the CCTV footage was a mystery. Did the assassin have an accomplice? Or was the second killer simply someone who saw an opportunity and took it. Were there two different agendas at play, or just one?

And how did she, Maggie, play into all of it?

Who would want to get back at her? Maggie scoffed at the thought. That was a long list. You didn't do a job like hers without collecting a bunch of enemies along the way.

There were the remnants of the Rossi family, the Venetian mafia organization Maggie dealt with a while back. The militia group she stopped from blowing up parts of Paris a week after they bombed London. And those were just the tip of the iceberg. Since her first mission at twenty-one, Maggie had consistently made herself the potential target of revenge. Seven years of completing missions and leaving people with scores to settle in her wake.

But none of them knew who she really was. They never met Maggie, the Newcastle runaway trained by the best to infiltrate and eliminate the enemies of her country. They met Eva, the jet-setting model. Or Rebecca, the American drug smuggler. The ones who did learn of her real identity never lived long enough to share her secret.

That said, mistakes could have been made, either from her end or the people she worked with. Analysts, government officials with high enough clearance, other agents, supposed allies from every corner of the world, informants with questionable motives. Oh yes, it was possible.

Something could have slipped through the cracks. Maggie was trained to hunt down people hiding behind other names and personas. It would be naive to disregard the idea that the same could be done to her.

Yet that knowledge did little to narrow down her list of suspects. It didn't give her anything else to go on, and what she did have wasn't much.

Maggie stared into the darkness. Maybe she should hand herself over. Running only made her look guilty, and it would distract those investigating the case from discovering who really killed James Worthington.

Maggie had found herself in the middle of some sticky situations before, but this was a whole new level of complicated. There were too many questions and not enough answers.

Could she trust the Unit to find them for her? Or would she be taken out, labelled a mentally unstable individual gunned down while resisting arrest? It wasn't like that hadn't happened to people before. She'd heard the rumors. Knew enough to know that they weren't just wild speculations.

No, she couldn't take that risk. Not when her head was on the chopping block.

She could only trust herself to get the answers she needed to clear her name. Whether it was deliberate or not, the killers had placed her on top of the suspect list.

Someone had set her up, and she intended to find out who.

Chapter 7

21 MAY

fter an hour and forty minutes on the M11, Maggie and Ashton finally reached Cambridge.

Maggie's head pounded, and she gulped down two paracetamols with her coffee, strong and black to give her a much-needed boost after so little sleep. It was past four in the morning before she finally settled into an uneasy slumber.

Ashton's spirits were high as he sped through the traffic, weaving between cars in his Porsche 718 Boxster S type. The engine purred behind their seats, the sleek custom paint job making the car a blur of metallic gray as it flew past.

If Maggie wanted to be inconspicuous, she should have known better than to get in a car with Ashton.

Music blared from the speakers, the whole inside of the car vibrating as he sang along, loud and out of tune, to some guy screaming about his feelings over heavy guitar riffs. Maggie wished she hadn't planted her phone on the boy at the bus stop. They'd be chilling out to some nice indie bands instead of this poor excuse for music.

The screaming stopped and gave way to a perky country beat as Dolly Parton began her anthem on working nine to five. Ashton's taste was nothing if not eclectic.

Maggie would kill, literally, to have her main concern be a nine to five job. Sure, it might be boring and somewhat soul destroying, but at least her life wouldn't be in jeopardy all the time. For her, that was a constant twenty-four-hour shift, with no ten-minute breaks by the watercooler.

She leaned forward in her leather seat and turned off the music.

"Och," Ashton said, "we were just getting to the good part."

"How do I know I can trust your contact?" Maggie asked.

"Believe me, if the Unit came knocking at her door,

she'd have bigger worries than you. She's discreet. The best in the business."

"I hope so." Only the best could keep her hidden long enough to figure out what the hell was going on. And even then, it might not be enough.

Ashton stole his eyes from the road to look at her. "How are you holding up?"

"I don't know." Maggie tapped her fingers against the paper cup. She stared out the window as rain fell from the sky and ran down the glass.

She still couldn't believe the entire Unit, everyone she'd fought beside since she was recruited at the police station all those years ago, were hunting her down. Bishop. Director General Ms. Helmsley. Nina.

Leon.

They had to. All the evidence pointed to her guilt. From the CCTV footage to an eyewitness who filled in the gaps like a jigsaw puzzle with the wrong pieces. Faced with the same supposed facts, Maggie would reach the same conclusion: She was guilty. She'd turned her back on her country. On them.

The government's best agents would come for her. People who knew her, knew her strengths and weaknesses. Knew things about her no one else did. Things they would try to exploit.

Maggie gripped the edge of her seat. Let them try.

At least she didn't have a family they could use against her. Her mother died when she was six. She didn't have a husband or wife. Boyfriend or girlfriend. Even Willow the cat wasn't hers.

Aside from Ashton, she had no ties, no one to use as leverage. The Unit might know her, but she also knew them. She knew what made each agent tick. How they would try to find her. What their specialties were. By knowing them, Maggie could avoid them.

They continued seven miles north west of Cambridge to a small village named Oakington. According to the proud advert displayed next to the welcome sign, the town was famed for its tomatoes and idyllic rural homes. It was about as far from London as you could get.

Ashton turned down one of two main roads and carried on until they arrived at an unassuming detached house with a well-manicured garden and a parked family-sized SUV in the driveway.

Ashton opened the door for her and took a stuffed duffle bag from the boot.

A woman waited for them by the front door.

"Ashton." She smiled warmly. "It's so nice to see you."

Ashton wrapped an arm around her and gave her a squeeze. "Gillian, it's been too long."

Gillian was a plump woman in her forties with a bob of mouse brown hair and a kind face. She wore a floral apron over a knitted red jumper, dustings of flour scattered over the fabric like snow.

"Come in, come in," she said with a wave. "Can I get you both anything? Tea? Some cake?"

"Only if it's your famous lemon slices," Ashton said, stepping inside.

Maggie followed behind. Gillian's house was decorated in the same style as her clothes, knitted cushions on her mustard couch, clashing rugs, rose covered wallpaper, and oak furniture. Gillian most definitely had tea cozies.

"They're just out the oven," said Gillian, waltzing off to fetch them.

Maggie gave Ashton a look. "What's with the detour?" she whispered.

Ashton plopped down on the couch, arms resting over the back like he lived there. "What detour?"

"There we are." Gillian placed a tray of cups, saucers, lemon cake, and as expected, a tea pot covered in a striped cozy.

Ashton helped himself, stuffing a lemon slice in his mouth and talking while he chewed. "How are you, Gill?"

"Oh, same old," she said, pouring the tea and adding a cube of sugar to her cup. "Business as usual."

"And Howard and the kids?" Ashton reached for a second slice. For someone so tall and lean, Ashton ate like a horse. Maggie only had to look at the slices to feel them sticking to her thighs. She took one anyway.

"Let's see." Gillian placed her cup down with a dainty pinky finger sticking out. "Stacey's the top of her class in English, Tom started piano lessons last month, and Howard's fucking the bitch he works with."

Maggie almost spat out her tea.

Ashton shook his head, not seeming the least bit shocked. "Sorry to hear that."

Gillian laughed. "Don't be. It keeps him out of my hair." Her eyes settled on Maggie. "Who's your friend?"

"Sorry," said Ashton. "How rude. Gillian, this is Maggie. Maggie, Gillian."

"Nice to meet you," said Gillian.

"You, too." Maggie held up the lemon slice. "Ashton wasn't exaggerating about how good these are."

"Oh, you're too kind." Gillian blushed. "So, what's up, Ashton? Is there a problem with my last batch of–"

"No, they're perfect, thanks," interrupted Ashton, shooting a sideward glance at Maggie. He never liked to keep her too in-the-know about his business affairs, given that she still 'worked for The Man' as he called it. Except when he got in a little too deep and needed backup.

"That's not why we're here," he said. "Maggie's in need of a new identity."

Gillian nodded and took another sip of her tea. She placed it on the saucer and got up from her chair, ushering them to follow to the back of the house. "Step into my office."

Her 'office' was a conservatory looking out into the back garden. A flock of chickens clucked around in a pen next to an old swing set and a patch of soil in the back for growing herbs.

Maggie stepped over an old Labrador, who glanced at

her and Ashton with a grunt before settling back to sleep and snoring like a steam engine.

"Hmm..." Gillian studied Maggie from her computer chair, a state-of-the-art desktop buzzing to life in front of her. "I have three available that would fit you."

"One will be fine," said Maggie, taking a seat on a wicker chair next to a large printer and photocopier.

Ashton took the seat next to her. "She'll take them all."

Gillian studied them over her reading glasses. "They won't come cheap."

Ashton dumped his stuffed Louis Vuitton duffle bag on the table and unzipped it to reveal wads of notes tied into rolls. "That's okay."

"No." Maggie shook her head. "I can't let you buy them all." This wasn't some kind of early birthday present or a small gift among friends. Aliases started in the high five figures and only went up from there. If Ashton was right about the little housewife being one of the best, then they would be a lot more expensive than that.

Ashton brushed her off. "I know what The Man pays. These are on me. Plus, you can't transfer anything from your account. They'll be watching for signs of activity."

Maggie bit her lip. He was right. Even if she could afford the three identities, which she was pretty sure she could not, it wasn't like she could wire the money over to Gillian's account. Even if her account was in some suspect bank in the Cayman Islands.

The police, the Unit, and who knows who else would

be watching and waiting for her to access her accounts, expecting her to withdraw all her money and go off on the run. Any attempt to access her accounts, even logging in to check her balance, would give those hunting for her a breadcrumb to follow. Or at the very least, an idea of her location at the time.

"Fine," Maggie said. "But I'm paying you back."

Ashton nodded like they were fighting over who was paying the bill for lunch. "All three please." He slid the duffle bag to Gillian who put it in a cupboard under the stairs next to a mop and vacuum cleaner.

She had Maggie stand behind a white wall. "Say cheese."

Once the pictures were taken, all they had to do was wait.

Maggie and Ashton helped themselves to more lemon slices as Gillian worked her magic, photo-shopping the images into the depictions of the three different identities she chose. Maggie slipped the old Labrador a couple of slices on the fly, and he wolfed them down, his tail wagging.

"Finished," announced Gillian after a while. "And all done before I need to collect the children from school."

The school run. Maggie had lost count of the number of schools she attended—and got kicked out of—over the years. Just one of the many things she survived growing up in the system, moving from foster family to foster family. Never feeling at home or like she belonged. A place like

Oakington would have been nice. Picturesque, uneventful, and safe.

Maggie got up from the couch, her legs tingling with pins and needles from sitting so long. Counterfeiting and forgery took time as well as skill.

"You're a gem, Gill." Ashton stretched his long legs and reached up to the ceiling as he yawned.

"Thank you for doing this on such short notice," said Maggie.

"Anything for a friend of Ashton's." Gillian stroked his face with a motherly affection.

Even at twenty-six, Ashton could still turn on the boyish charm, like the annoying yet charismatic little brother she never had but always wanted.

"I've been building the names over the last couple of years. Everything you need to know about the backgrounds and movements of each identity is in this file. They'll all be recognized in the streets by those in similar occupations." Gillian gave her a knowing look.

Criminals, in other words.

She handed Maggie the documents.

They were good. Better than good. Maggie could find no flaws in the passports or the other ID cards, driving licenses, health insurance cards, and even a library card for one of them. The aliases the Unit provided her weren't any better, and they actually came from the official passport and DVLA offices.

Gillian threw in some credit cards with high limits for

free since they were buying in bulk. A nice and necessary perk if Maggie was going to pull off adapting herself to match these new aliases.

Ashton patted her on the shoulder. "Welcome to the wrong side of the law."

Chapter 8

Ashton pulled up behind the back of the Baltic Hotel and stopped the engine. He'd been quiet on the drive back.

Maggie knew what he was thinking, but she wouldn't allow it.

Ashton sighed and turned to her. "Let me help you," he said, confirming her suspicions.

"You've helped enough," she told him with a firm voice. He should know better than to try to change her mind. It wouldn't work, and she wasn't about to drag one of her only friends into her mess. If anything happened to him, she would never forgive herself.

"You don't need to do this alone," he continued.

Maggie smiled and kissed him on the cheek. "I do, but I love you for offering."

Ashton leaned back in his seat, his lip pouting like it

always did when he didn't get his way. The expression reminded her of Ashton as she'd known him back in training, when he was two years younger than most of the others, a wild and out of control fourteen-year-old who no one took seriously.

"Don't do anything I wouldn't do," he said, trying to mask his disappointment.

Maggie cocked an eyebrow at him. "That doesn't really leave much out."

Her words earned a smile, but his face grew serious again and he squeezed her hand. "Be safe."

"I'll try," she said, opening the passenger door and getting out the car. That was one promise she couldn't keep. She waved Ashton off and watched him drive around the corner before moving.

Most would call her plan reckless. Returning to the scene of your alleged crime wasn't the best strategic move in the world, especially when it was crawling with police constables, detectives, and from the look of the vans out front, forensic investigators. But it was her only choice. Her only hope of finding something, anything, that could help her track down the real killer.

Police presence was heavy out front, and reporters clustered near the entrance to give updates on the assassination. Maggie had checked the news on Ashton's phone; the police hadn't released any new information, telling the public it was an ongoing investigation of the highest priority.

She'd turned the news report off when it cut to Fiona, James's devastated wife and mother of their twin daughters, the girls too young to fully realize what was going on. They may not understand the impact of their father's death now, but they would throughout their lives. He would miss their first days of school, their first loves and heartbreaks. He wouldn't be there to wish them luck as they left for university. And he'd never walk them down the aisle as brides. Never live to be a grandfather.

He wouldn't be there to kiss them goodnight before bed, or to comfort them when they had a bad dream.

Someone had taken that from them.

And everyone, including James's poor wife, thought that person was her.

Maggie crept through the shadows along the wall of the hotel and walked towards a back door where a girl stood smoking.

She and Ashton had scoped out the hotel for an hour, and while the front of the building was busy with activity, the back didn't seem to be a priority. Two police constables patrolled the building every twenty minutes, giving her ample time for what she had in mind.

"Hey, can I steal a cigarette?" Maggie glanced past the girl and through the door she'd propped open with a chair while she stood outside.

"Sure." A little wary, the girl dug inside her cleaning uniform for the packet.

"It's my first shift tonight," Maggie said, taking the offered cigarette. "You on your break?"

"Yes, thank god," said the girl, fine now that she 'knew' who Maggie was. "Today's been hell."

The girl was about her size.

"When do you finish?" Maggie asked.

"I still have two more hours." She stubbed out her cigarette against the brick wall.

"It'll go quick," Maggie promised. Quicker than the girl knew. Maggie bent over for a light. She took a deep draw and blew the smoke into the air. "Nice uniform."

It didn't take long for Maggie to knock out the cleaner, deposit her safely in the back, and swap their clothes. The uniform was a little tight, but it would do the job. She wouldn't be long if she could help it.

Maggie walked through the staff area like she belonged there, her stride easy yet rushed, like she had to get back to work before the manager realized she was late.

It was a risk going back inside, but she had to find a lead. There was no way the assassin returned to his room after their run in. It was too dangerous, and police were crawling all over the place. Whatever he had with him before the job would be in his room. If he'd brought anything at all.

Maggie examined the keycard, reading the number on it for the hundredth time since picking it up the night before.

Room 303.

She travelled up the staff staircase, a bland and narrow set of stairs compared to the wide and lavishly decorated stairwells the guests used. A man was wheeling a trolley of room service into an elevator and Maggie ducked her head as she passed him, careful to hide her face.

The press hadn't released her image or name on the news, but that didn't mean the police or the Unit hadn't shown the staff and guests her photo during questioning.

Maggie reached the third floor without running into anyone else and made her way down the hall towards room 303.

Slipping in the keycard, she opened the door and entered, locking it behind her. Her gun was at the ready in the unlikely event that the assassin had risked coming back like she had.

It was a standard room, unlike the suite James and the drunk George Moulton had used. A double bed took up most of the space, a little desk to the side next to the built-in wardrobes and television unit. The bathroom was to the right, the door open and nothing but Maggie's reflection staring back at her from the large mirror inside.

The room was clear.

With no time to waste, Maggie searched the room from top to bottom. The wardrobe was empty, nothing but wire hangers, spare pillows, and an open, unused safe inside.

The bed was made, and there was nothing in the small waste basket under the desk. The drawers were vacant aside from a copy of the bible and some flyers for nearby tourist attractions. And the cabinet in the bathroom had nothing either, other than some wrapped bars of soap and small bottles of the hotel's complimentary shampoo and hair conditioner.

Maggie sat on the end of the bed and resisted the urge to trash the place. She was too late. The room had been cleaned.

So much for finding a clue. She had run into a dead end in less than twenty minutes. She leaned on her knees and looked around. Now what?

Her eyes lingered over to the room phone. She could call in right now, have Bishop pick her up and explain to him everything she knew. But that was part of the problem. All she knew was that she wasn't guilty and that someone else killed the mayor. She had no concrete evidence to back up her claims; she was up a shit creek the size of the Thames without a paddle. What she needed was proof, and she wasn't going to get it there. She had to move.

Standing, she pulled herself together and left.

Maggie closed the door to the room and came face to face with a man. She reached for her gun and almost pulled it on him before she noticed the matching uniform he wore.

"I already cleaned in there," he said in a thick Polish accent.

Maggie waited until her heartbeat calmed down to a

riot before responding. She was jumpy, and that led to stupid mistakes.

"A guest from the other night called and said he left some things behind in the room, but there's nothing in there."

"I put in lost and found," he said, watching her with dark eyes.

Maggie let out a breath. The assassin left something behind, something she could use if her luck was in.

"Oh, right." Maggie went to leave, spurred on by the news, then stopped. "You wouldn't happen to know where that is, do you?"

The man frowned.

"It's my first day," she explained. It had worked for her last time.

The man shook his head and spoke to her like she was an infant. "Any items found after guest checks out are put in back office of reception for thirty days. If no one claims them, they are up for grabs. I got nice pair of boots last month."

"Great," said Maggie, too excited to care about his condescending tone. "I'll check there."

"Hey," called the man. "Do I know you?"

Maggie shook her head and smiled. "I don't think so."

He narrowed his eyes. "You look familiar to me."

"I'd remember if we met before." Maggie laid it on thick and obvious for his benefit.

A smile tugged at his lips, and Maggie fought not to

shake her head at how easy it was with some men. "I'll see you around then," he said, watching her run off.

Back downstairs, Maggie walked out of the staff area and ventured towards reception.

Police were inside the foyer, talking to witnesses or pressing their phones to their ears to appear busy at work. The reception area lay right behind where most of them stood. Maggie hid behind the grand staircase and watched.

A porter was carrying a large cart of luggage, being harassed by an older woman.

"Would you get a move on?" she screeched. "And watch those bags, the contents are worth more than you make in a year."

Maggie seized the opportunity. She walked out, head low, and timed her pace with the porter, walking behind the cart and out of sight from the police. Maggie sent him a mental apology and nudged the pile of suitcases. They toppled to the floor, and the older woman shrieked, gathering the attention of everyone in the foyer.

Maggie hoped that she managed to break something inside the hag's cases.

She used the distraction and entered behind the reception desk unchallenged, echoes of the older woman demanding to speak to the manager filling the room.

A man in a manager's jacket hurried out from the reception room, and Maggie couldn't help herself. She stopped him in his tracks. "The woman walked into her own bags and they toppled over. I saw it happen, and now she's blaming the porter."

The man nodded, craning his neck out to the foyer. "Bloody Mrs. Sanderson," he muttered before marching out.

Coast clear, Maggie crept into the back office and found the lost and found area, a laminated sign helpfully pointing it out. There were more items than Maggie expected. Sorted by room number, the boxes contained everything from phone chargers and plug in adaptors, to hair straighteners and a rather intricate looking sex toy which someone had discreetly covered with a towel.

There was nothing for room 303.

Racks lined in rows beside the boxes like a department store for lost and forgotten clothes. Maggie searched through them, desperate for something, anything else that could help her.

Then she found it. A garment bag labelled 'Room 303: Mr. Ronaldo Vasquez.'

Maggie ignored the name, knowing it would be fake. Someone as professional as the assassin would never use his real name. She unzipped the bag and pulled out the contents.

It was a gray suit: tailored jacket, buttoned waistcoat, and trousers. Nothing else.

Chatter sounded from next door and was coming her way. Maggie frisked the suit, but the outer pockets were empty. She checked the inside pocket of the jacket and her fingers touched brushed against something. A business card.

No, not a business card, but a card to a private member's club.

Maggie tucked it in her pocket and exited out of the building undetected.

It was a long shot, but it was her only lead.

Chapter 9

Maggie dumped the contents of her shopping bag onto the bed. She'd paid for a single night in a small hotel room with one of her new credit cards. The payment went through with no issues, Gillian so far living up to her reputation.

A shabby hotel room next to a service station in outer London was one thing. The airport would be the real test.

The police would have issued an APW by now, her name and face plastered all over the major exit routes out of Britain. She considered crossing the Channel by ship and going to France, a place she was very familiar with thanks to the multiple missions Bishop had sent her on after displaying an affinity for the French language in her training. Though she would still have to find her way across the border to Spain, which would take some time.

A direct plane was riskier than a ship, but it was also

faster, and the longer she took to clear her name, the more time the people after her would have to track her down and stop her.

Maggie placed the card she discovered in the assassin's suit jacket along with her other items on the bed.

After a little digging in an internet café, she traced the location of the assassin's private club to Madrid. The Midnight Lounge didn't have a website or seem to publicize themselves in any way. They weren't found on any review sites or the local listings for the area. Even the card had nothing on it but the club's name, and a barcode. Maggie had to worm her way into the tax returns of the club to learn anything about them at all.

This told her a few things. One, exclusivity and discretion was important to the Midnight Lounge and their clientele. Two, they weren't reliant on tourists or locals for the substantial profits shown in their returns. And most importantly, they didn't want to be found.

Too bad.

Maggie knew the type of place. It was neutral ground. Establishments like the Midnight Lounge acted as both a social club and a place of business. Those with membership were provided with a safe place to carry out their illegal dealings without worry of interference, while also enjoying the privilege of easy access to whatever they considered fun. Booze, food, drugs, girls. Something more perverse. Whatever their dark little minds wanted, the clubs would supply.

It was the perfect place for an assassin to frequent. For all Maggie knew, the very deal to kill the mayor was made there.

Maggie sat on the bed with crossed legs and spread out the information for each of her new aliases, sipping a cup of bland instant coffee. She needed to change her appearance enough to get through airport security. They would be looking for a woman in her late twenties with long blond hair and blue eyes.

That eliminated Céline Delacroix, the French sex trafficker. There was the Russian arms dealer, Ekaterina Kovrova, but her very nationality could draw unwanted attention at customs.

Which left her with Felicity Greene.

Maggie pulled her hair out of its bun and ran her hands through the blond locks. Her natural hair had to go, and without access to her usual guy—who made her personalized, lace-front wigs made of real human hair—she had to settle for a store-bought do-it-yourself dye job.

She padded over to the bathroom, box of dye in hand, and got started.

Maggie leaned the file Gillian gave her against the mirror and began the process of transforming into Felicity Greene.

The first part was the look. That was easy.

Most people could change their image, even drastically. Yet they were still the same person underneath, with the same personality and quirks that make them unique.

Taking on an alias required you to strip all of that away, to become a blank canvas onto which you sketched out the basics of the new persona and then filled in the whole picture, brush stroke by brush stroke. You had to bury the person you once were until all that was left was a fully realized portrait of someone new.

It was a specialized skill set, and Maggie excelled at it. Bishop always joked that if she hadn't ended up an agent, she could have been a method actor.

Maggie mixed the dye and applied it to her hair, making sure to fully coat it before tying it up at the top of her head and letting it set in.

"Hello, I'm Felicity Greene," she said to her reflection.

Felicity was an English rose, pale faced and rosy cheeked to match her red hair.

Unscrewing a little bottle filled with liquid, Maggie fished out a set of contacts and popped them in her eyes, replacing the ice blue with a warm brown. She blinked them into place and smiled, bright and full, the way Felicity would.

The way she, Felicity, did.

"So nice to meet you," she said, enunciating her vowels more than normal. A girl like Felicity was raised with decorum; she had a regal air to her voice that came from money and influential parents.

Maggie went back to the bed and selected an over-priced dress, holding it up against her body and looking in the mirror. She tossed it back into the pile and chose a sleek and fitted Chanel skirt and top set with a pair of red bottom shoes. That was more like it.

Maggie sighed. "I'm so bored."

Being daddy's little princess wasn't all it was cracked up to be, and by the time Felicity was a teenager, it was suffocating. Most girls rebelled by getting a tattoo or a piercing, but not Felicity. That was far too obvious and bland. She needed something exciting. And dangerous.

"I read Art History at Oxford," Maggie said as she considered what to do with her gun. It couldn't go with her. She dismantled it into pieces, deciding to toss the separate parts away.

She walked back into the bathroom and read over the file again, making sure she committed everything about Ms. Greene to memory.

By the time she attended the University of Oxford, Felicity had become a well-known face in the underground scene, dating young men her father would despise and partying like any good socialite should.

Maggie giggled loud and lofty, titling her head back. "It's true what they say you know. Diamonds really are a girl's best friend."

Felicity had a thing for precious stones and jewelry. Her sticky fingers could always find the things that sparkled most. As she wrote her thesis on fine jewelry by day, she specialized in obtaining those very items at night.

Fast forward to today, and Felicity was the go to girl to

pull off the most intricate of jobs, her portfolio as a thief and black market trader extensive and well known.

Maggie read the files over and over again until she could relay the profiles for each alias out loud. Certain she had it all contained in her mind, Maggie set the files alight over the bath and let them burn to ash.

She couldn't leave anything behind. No trace to lead the Unit—or anyone else—back to her.

Maggie leaned over the sink and rinsed her hair. The red dye circled around the drain, bleeding into the water the same way the mayor's blood did in the bathroom at the bar.

The dye left a stain against the white porcelain, just like the stain left in her mind of the man she was supposed to protect. Of his dead eyes and shocked face.

Making sure all the dye was out of her hair, Maggie wrung it with her hands and flipped it back. The hair was a good match to the picture on her ID, a natural copper as opposed to a manufactured red.

She styled it with a comb and the hotel hairdryer, letting it fall over one shoulder. Then, she put on the skirt and top and looked at herself in the bedroom mirror.

"I'm Felicity Greene."

The terminal was packed later that night. Heathrow Airport was the second busiest airport in the world, and it suited Maggie just fine.

"Would you get a move on?" she snapped at the member of airport staff she coerced into helping her with her suitcases. "And watch those bags. The contents are worth more than you make in a year."

A woman dressed in a tracksuit that matched the ones her family wore watched them pass. Maggie gave her a knowing shake of the head. "You just can't get good help these days," she said as she whisked passed, her heels stomping on the floor.

Maggie slapped her passport on the check-in counter.

"Good evening," said the woman working the desk.

"Is it?" Maggie snapped.

The woman stuttered at her response. "Where are you heading?"

Maggie slid her ticket over to the woman and the pay-as-you-go phone rang in her designer handbag, the alarm going off right when she'd planned. "Felicity Greene," she said, holding the phone to her ear.

She waited a moment, then loud and as obnoxious as she could she said, "Oh, Alexandra, how sweet to hear from you."

"How many bags?" asked the check-in woman.

Maggie clicked her fingers at the man, and he hoisted

the bags onto the conveyor belt one at a time to be weighed and tagged before they were carried away to be packed on the direct flight.

"Yes," Maggie said, speaking to her phone, "I'm headed there now. Can you believe the plane doesn't have a first-class section? It's an absolute nightmare."

"Anything else I can help you with?" said the man through gritted teeth, a hand pressed against his back.

Maggie handed him a folded note and shook her head, not stopping her fake conversation on her phone. "What do you mean you're not coming? Did Ollie not invite you to the party?"

The man held the money in his hand with a look of clear insult, but Maggie turned from him and by the time she looked back he was gone, and so was the money.

Checked in, Maggie breezed her way through airport security, complaining the whole way in her role as Felicity, hiding in plain sight.

Chapter 10

MADRID, SPAIN
22 MAY

Maggie arrived at the Madrid-Barajas Airport in the early hours of the morning. She checked into the Hotel Villa Magna, an elegant five-star hotel on Paseo de la Castellana befitting of someone like Felicity. Maggie was a perfectionist, maintaining her alias until she was alone and safe inside her room.

All the executive suites were unavailable, which Felicity was not happy about, but the manager had sedated her with a choice of the junior suites. Once inside, Maggie had kicked off her shoes, thrown off her clothes, and crawled into bed, leaving the do not disturb sign hanging on the door handle until she roused hours later.

The weather was a far cry from the rain slicked streets of London. The sun was pinned high into the clear blue sky, its rays shining through her window and coating everything inside the room with brilliant light.

Maggie grabbed the pillow at the other side of the bed and covered her face with a groan. Though well rested now, the temptation to close her eyes again and sleep the day away was strong. She would kill—almost literally—for the chance to curl up under the sheets and pretend that none of it was real. To pretend she was finally taking the vacation everyone seemed to think she needed.

It was a role she could play with ease. One where her life wasn't complicated and all she had to worry about was what to order from room service for breakfast and which of the city's sights she would visit first. One where she wasn't wanted for murder and forced to hide while she tried to find out why.

Maggie had travelled all over the world, and yet she had never spent much time seeing what the places had to offer, discovering the history and searching for places where the locals ate so she could sample their authentic regional dishes.

The sights Maggie saw on her trips were a lot different from most tourists. She'd witnessed the darker sides to the places many travelled to for pleasure. She'd seen the pain and corruption happening under their noses, smelled the vile stench of greed and evil as it infected beautiful locations like poison, seeping into the very fabric of the community and rotting away all that was good and pure.

Just the thought of it left a bitter taste in her mouth.

Yes, she could pretend. Allow herself to spend the day like the other guests in the hotel. She could be a normal girl off on an adventure, or just looking to spend some time on her own for a while in a different city, away from the stresses of daily life. Even if it was just for a day.

But sooner or later, Maggie would have to return to reality. The clock would strike midnight, and she would have to leave her fairytale behind and step back into the real world.

Maggie sat up in the bed and stretched her arms, releasing a yawn that sounded more like a growl. She had work to do. Her vacation could wait.

Getting up, she padded to the window and looked out into the city. Cars whooshed past on the streets below as people perused the shops and enjoyed the sun.

She requested a room at the south side of the building on the eight floor, overlooking the beginning of Calle de José Ortega y Gasset, and not just because it held a spectacular view of one of Madrid's nicest streets with the skyline behind it. It also happened to be the street where the Midnight Lounge was located.

Hauling over one of her three suitcases, one of which was purely for show and weighed down by things Maggie found in the hotel by the service station, she dug inside and brought out a pair of binoculars. She bought them at a camping store in Islington when out for hair dye and other supplies.

She returned the suitcase, leaving all her things packed inside. The last thing she needed was for the staff to discover her multiple passports or other items when sprucing up the room.

Configuring the settings to get a closer look, Maggie aimed the binoculars at the private members' club.

The front entrance was nondescript, giving the appearance of a residential five-story building, surrounded by designer retailers and nestled between a bank and a coffee shop. But Maggie knew better. The street number on the tax forms pointed to that exact address, and no matter how twisted the figures were on the balance sheets, that was one thing the owners could not lie about.

There were no signs of life or activity from the outside, though it was hard to tell much more. The club had reflective glass for windows that blocked her from getting a visual inside. It was still early, though, and most of those types of clubs didn't open until night.

Maggie went to the bathroom and took a shower before getting dressed and ordering room service. Her food arrived thirty minutes later, a selection from the lunch menu due to her long lie in. The waiter rolled in a tray and left her to it.

Maggie moved the tray and wheeled it in front of a comfortable cushioned chair she had positioned by the window. The smells emanating from under the tray covers filled the room, and her mouth watered.

She dined on a selection of Spanish meats on thin crispy bread, a seasonal green salad, spicy potatoes in a truffle aioli sauce, and a fresh fruit salad including local oranges to finish it off. She leaned back on the chair, stuffed yet regretting none of it.

A freshly ground coffee in one hand and her binoculars in the other, Maggie set her sights on the club.

Stake outs and recon work were never her favorite parts of the job, but they were vital. She hunkered down and prepared for a long and boring day.

Three days, in fact.

Maggie paced the imposing confines of her hotel room, ready to climb the walls. For the hundredth time, she considered if she was making the right move.

Not that she had many options.

Going back to London was a definite no. Unless she wanted to hand herself over, Maggie couldn't return until she could prove her innocence. Like it or not, the only way to do that was to use what little information she already had, and the single lead the assassin had left behind in the Baltic hotel was across the street.

Yet so far, the Midnight Lounge had proved to be nothing but a dead end.

Maggie pinched the bridge of her nose and forced herself back to her seat. For three whole days, she hadn't left her post, save for bathroom breaks and to stretch her legs every now and again before they cramped.

She couldn't do a fourth day of sitting around and waiting. She'd sampled the entire room service menu, guzzled down enough coffee to last a lifetime, and grew antsier by the hour.

For all Maggie knew, the people after her were closing in. It was never a good idea to stay in one spot too long. Especially when you were wanted for murder.

Something had to give.

Time was already a precious commodity when on the run, and the thought of wasting so long to end up with nothing drove her mad.

Patience was never a virtue she possessed, and the added pressure of her situation only made things worse. The clock was ticking, and it niggled at her like an itch she couldn't scratch.

Maggie decided there and then to give herself one more day. If the assassin didn't show, then she would pack up and move on. To where, she had no idea, but staying in Madrid was getting her nowhere fast.

The day dragged on like the ones before it, and it was five in the afternoon before anything caught her attention.

A man in his forties walked down the street and

stopped at the front door of the Midnight Lounge. He knocked with three short raps and someone answered from the other side.

Not for the first time, Maggie tried to get a glimpse of who answered or what lay beyond, but her view was limited by the angle of her room. The man handed over a purple card like the one she possessed and then was let inside.

More people arrived after that, the club coming alive each night as the shadows grew long and the sun set over the horizon. Members never arrived more than two at a time, and Maggie kept count. Sixteen women. Twenty-one men. None of them the assassin.

Three hours passed and no one left.

Just after eight o'clock, a black Bentley pulled up outside. A wide and muscled man came out from the driver's seat and opened the back-passenger door. A man stepped out, and Maggie zoomed in as close as she could, the nighttime affecting her vision.

Her heart leapt and she held her breath, desperate for something, anything, she could work with. The man turned to look down the street, and she caught sight of his face.

It wasn't the assassin, but he was familiar. Maggie had never met the man before, but she knew of him.

Daniel Church.

Maggie put down her binoculars once Daniel entered the Midnight Lounge and got dressed. She might not be able to access the private club yet, but she could follow the man back to his hotel when he got out.

Relief flooded her as Maggie shoved on all black clothes. Finally, something she could use.

He may not know it, but Daniel Church was her way inside.

Chapter 11

25 May

Maggie stifled a yawn, glad for the large sunglasses hiding the bags under her eyes.

She arrived back at the hotel at three thirty in the morning and was up and out again by seven, not wanting to miss her target if he chose to get up early after his long night at the Midnight Lounge.

Following him back to his hotel in the Centro district hadn't been hard. She sat across the street from it now, outside in the sun at a little restaurant where she enjoyed a breakfast of pincho de tortilla, a delicious and light Spanish omelet, along with a nice strong café con leche.

Now all she had to do was wait for the opportune moment to run into him.

Daniel Church was a British trader of fine art, paintings mostly. Known for sourcing some of the rarest pieces around and selling them to the black market, Daniel was the ideal person for Maggie to exploit to gain access to the members' only club.

He and Felicity would get on like a house on fire.

Maggie had never met him before, but his name and face had come up in a particularly difficult mission in Vienna where she had to learn a thing or two about oil paintings. The Unit believed he could be helpful and had set up a meeting, but before Maggie could attend, he slipped out the country after selling a knockoff to someone who didn't much appreciate it.

Mr. Church's escapades weren't a threat to national security, and he was too low level for the Unit to take any interest in his underhand dealings at the time, but Maggie had a keen interest in him now.

She needed a way into the club, and Mr. Church was going to get her there.

Like casinos and the keycard she used to access the Unit HQ, Maggie was certain the assassin's card would bring up his image when the barcode was swiped. She may be quite the chameleon, but she wasn't good enough to fool anyone comparing her to the picture they held on file for the man.

Maggie couldn't see a way to break into the club

without drawing too much attention to herself. The club made a lot of effort to go unnoticed, and Maggie suspected their security systems would be air tight. In a normal mission, the computer whizzes at the Unit could take care of any electronic security measures inside, but this was no normal mission. She could no longer rely on the Unit for help.

Which meant she would need to discover another way through the front doors.

Just over an hour later, a bright eyed and bushy tailed Daniel stepped out of the hotel as the black Bentley from the night before pulled up outside. Instead of getting in the car, he waited for his large chauffeur to get out from his seat and walk around the car to hold the door open for him.

Pretentious arse.

Grabbing a second coffee to go as he eventually got into the car, Maggie set off.

She jumped into the taxi she had waiting for her, the driver only too happy to comply when she handed over fifty euros for the privilege. "I need you to follow that car," she said.

The driver stared at her through the mirror, his hands hovering over the keys of the ignition. "Follow the car?"

Maggie handed him a hundred euros. "Yes."

The driver shrugged, tucked the money into his shirt pocket, and pulled out, leaving a few cars between them and Daniel. Maggie sat in the back, leaning forward in her seat and never allowing her eyes to lose sight of the Bentley. They drove for six minutes and then the car stopped, parking in front of a strip of stores.

It seemed Daniel was in the mood for shopping.

Felicity loved shopping.

Maggie had her driver park down the street a bit from the Bentley, and she watched Daniel exit the car, his chauffeur taking off down the street. He wasn't planning on going back to his hotel anytime soon then. Maggie got out of the taxi and thanked the driver before sending him on his way, too.

As soon as she got outside, Maggie was replaced with Felicity, and she did exactly what a girl who loved diamonds and the finer things in life did. She went shopping.

By the time she approached the clothes shop where Daniel had disappeared, she held six bags of different shapes and sizes plus her coffee from the restaurant.

She steadied her pace in line with Daniel's, watching him through the glass windows as he made to leave. Then, right when he was walking out with his nose in his phone, Maggie stepped forward.

Daniel collided right into Maggie. A harmless bump, but Maggie made the most of it, squeezing her coffee cup so hard the lid fell off and the lukewarm coffee spilled down her white playsuit. At the same time, she dropped her bags in the apparent shock of their unfortunate crash and tumbled backwards, falling to the ground with a shriek.

Daniel looked up from his phone, and his eyes widened.

"I am so sorry," he said, shoving his phone in his pocket and rushing to help Maggie back to her feet.

Maggie plastered a look of sheer shock on her face, holding her arms out and looking at the great brown stain all down her pristine white outfit.

"Are you okay?" Daniel reached for her as his cheeks reddened to match the sunburn on his forehead.

"I think so," she said when he hoisted her up from the street floor.

Daniel looked around at a loss for what to do, fidgeting with his tan summer jacket. A man in his mid-thirties, he had the look of aristocracy about him, from his casual yet expensive attire to his quaffed blond hair and long nose.

"I am so sorry," he repeated, gesturing back to the collision point with his hands. "I didn't see you. I wasn't looking where I was going."

"That's clear, isn't it?" Maggie let Felicity's shock subside. She ran a hand down her sodden playsuit. "Look at the state of me."

Daniel handed her over a handkerchief from his jacket pocket.

Maggie simply stared at it.

"Please, allow me to buy you a new outfit," he said, returning the handkerchief. "I feel terrible."

"I have something I can change into," Maggie said as Daniel collected her scattered bags and put her things back into them.

"Please, I insist." Daniel held her bags in some sort of chivalrous attempt to make up for knocking her over.

"Fine." Maggie kept her voice sharp.

Daniel smiled anyway. "Thank you. Is this place okay? I don't mind going elsewhere if you'd prefer."

Maggie shook her head and walked into the shop. "No, it will have to do. I'm not walking around like this."

"Let's find you something nice." Daniel stole a glance at her from the side. "A beautiful girl like you doesn't deserve this."

No one deserves pick-up lines as bad as that, Maggie thought but stopped herself from saying. Instead, she merely walked away from him, glancing through the clothes.

The shop assistants fussed over her once they saw the mess and led her into the dressing rooms, leaving Daniel out on the shop floor to stand around like a spare part.

Maggie tried on a few dresses the girls brought to her, making Daniel stew a bit. A woman like Felicity wouldn't grab the first thing offered to her. She liked to have choices, and besides, all the attention was on her. She'd make it last.

Choosing a blue day-look maxi-dress that hugged her curves in all the right places, she stepped out of the dressing room and returned to her target.

The dress worked like a treat.

Daniel licked the corner of his lips as he watched her walk his way, a tell that would lose him a lot of money if he played poker.

"Much better," he said, taking her in.

"You don't have to pay." Maggie picked up her other bags. "I have my own money."

"I've already settled the bill with the girl at the register," said Daniel.

"Thank you, um..." She trailed off, waiting for a name.

"Daniel Church," he said, holding out his hand to her.

Maggie conceded and held her hand out for him, which he held for a few seconds too long. "I'm Felicity," she said. "Felicity Greene."

Daniel straightened at that. "*The* Felicity Greene?"

"The only one I'm aware off." Maggie allowed a smile, Felicity savoring the way he said her name with an almost awe-like reverence.

Intrigue sparkled in Daniel's watery gray eyes. "In that case, I must say your reputation proceeds you, Ms. Greene."

"Oh?" she said.

He leaned towards her and lowered his voice. "I'm a trader of sorts myself."

Maggie nodded her head in acknowledgement and touched his arm. "And here I thought you knew me from Oxford."

"I'm a Cambridge man myself." Daniel's gaze lingered where her fingers had brushed his jacket.

"A pity," she teased, flipping her hair. "So tell me Mr. Church, what are you doing in Madrid?"

"A bit of this, a bit of that," he said, trying too hard to sound mysterious. "How are you liking the city?"

"I just arrived yesterday," she lied, letting false embarrassment turn her gaze to the floor. "I don't really know anyone, so I mostly stayed in my hotel."

Daniel seized the moment, just like she wanted him to. "Now we can't have that," he said, leading her out of the shop. "Allow me to show you the town."

Maggie turned to him, the sun gazing down at them. "I don't know."

"Come on," he said, standing a little too close to her. "As a way of apologizing."

Maggie bit her lip. "Well..."

"Where are you staying?" asked Daniel.

"The Hotel Villa Magna."

"Perfect," he said, a look of triumph spreading across his features. "I'll pick you up at nine this evening."

Maggie giggled. "Will you now?"

"I promise you'll have a good time."

Maggie cocked her head a little to the side to act coy. "I'll see how I feel. I might be busy."

"Staying in your room all night?" he said.

Maggie placed a hand over his toned chest. "Goodbye, Daniel Church. Perhaps I'll see you around."

And without another word, Maggie walked away.

"Nine o'clock," he called, watching her go.

She didn't turn around or reply, knowing that it would keep him keen to see her again, especially from the way he looked at her. Unlike Maggie, Daniel was unable to mask his true feelings.

At nine o'clock that evening, Daniel would be in the lobby of her hotel, anxiously waiting to see if she would turn up.

And Maggie would be there alright. She'd be there with bells on.

Chapter 12

Maggie kept Daniel waiting, confident he wouldn't give up for at least half an hour. Men like him knew what they wanted and did what was necessary to get it. Though Daniel would consider the possibility that she'd stand him up, that flash of worry would make him all the more pliable when she did show.

Daniel Church would want to seal the deal like any good trader, and he'd do all he could to impress her.

The tactics Maggie used in these situations were less than ideal. She much preferred to punch her way to the truth and break down doors rather than play the slow, manipulative game, but there was no denying it was effective.

When she was first recruited, Maggie and Nina had a teacher who taught them about men and how to use them.

All agents had their own areas of expertise, and when their teacher was an agent herself, she displayed an affinity for seduction and became well versed in honeypot missions, seducing intelligence targets for information or blackmail, and killing enemies in their beds when they least expected it.

Bishop didn't send Maggie on those missions. While she didn't think anything bad of people who excelled at them, like Nina and their teacher, Maggie couldn't bring herself to take it that far, as she learned her very first time out in the field. It was one role she couldn't play. One part of herself she wouldn't give to the job.

But there was more than one way to skin a cat, and Maggie was nothing if not resourceful. She'd play the game, but only to a point.

After a shower to get the smell of coffee from her skin, Maggie selected a dress for the evening, longing for the day when she could return home and live in pajama trousers and warm oversized jumpers for a week, binging some of the television shows she never got around to finishing.

When Daniel left her earlier that day, Maggie had continued her shopping spree and bought herself a nice switch blade. It was only fair to buy a gift for herself if Felicity got to put her new credit card to good use. Maggie tossed it into her clutch bag with her phone, ID, money, and perfume, concealing the weapon in the inner lining of the bag which she had sliced open for that very reason.

Giving herself a final once over, Maggie left her room

and made her way down to meet her mark and date for the night.

Daniel Church leaned against the wall next to the elevators, raising his head from his phone whenever the noise of heels clacked on the tiled floors. He did a double take when he spotted Maggie, then quickly returned his expression to one more cool, calm, and collected.

"I knew you'd come," he said, taking her in. "You look breathtaking."

Maggie appraised his tailored navy suit and slicked back hair. "You scrub up rather well yourself."

It wasn't a lie. Daniel was handsome, if you like that sort of thing. Maggie preferred men more on the rugged side, but she could see why Daniel seemed accustomed to getting his way with women.

"Where are we going?" she asked.

Daniel tucked his phone away in the back pocket of his trousers and gave her his full attention. "There is a great little place in Chamberi where all the locals go to eat."

Maggie sighed. "A restaurant? I thought you were taking me some place fun?" Felicity was a party girl, after all.

"It really is quite lovely," added Daniel, his eyes wary at her response.

"I want to go somewhere exclusive." Maggie stepped close, pressing a finger into his chest, letting it trail down to just above his belt. "Somewhere for VIPs like you and me."

Daniel thought it over for a second before Maggie saw the idea coming to him, his eyes lighting up. "I know just the place."

"You do?" She looked up at him through thick lashes.

"Yes," he said, opening the front door of the hotel and holding it open for her. "And it's just around the corner."

Maggie suppressed a smug grin. "Perfect." She wrapped her arm around his and allowed him to lead the way to the Midnight Lounge.

"Is this it?" Maggie showed Felicity's clear distain at the nondescript facade. "You're not taking me to a friend's apartment, are you?"

Daniel laughed. "Not everything is as it seems," he said, and rapped on the door with three sharp knocks.

The door unlocked with a click, and a man stood before them, wide enough to block the view further inside. His face was dark and unamused.

Daniel dug inside his suit pocket and handed the man a purple card, matching the one the assassin had dropped.

The man blocking the entrance took the card and turned it around so the bar code faced up at him. He brought out a handheld scanner and hovered it over the card, the barcode registering with a beep. Maggie glanced at the scanner to see a picture of Daniel appear on the little screen alongside his name.

The man looked between the screen and Daniel, brows burrowed then said, "And you, madam?" His English was much better than Maggie's Spanish.

"She's with me," said Daniel, before Maggie could respond.

"You'll need to sign her in." The man turned his attention to her. "Do you have ID?"

Maggie opened her clutch and handed him Felicity's passport.

"I'll hold on to this until you leave," he said, once he seemed satisfied that the passport belonged to her. It wasn't a request.

Daniel signed Maggie in on a guestbook and then stood with his arms out. The man ran a metal detector over him, giving his arms and legs a frisk like they were at the airport.

The man moved to Maggie, only using the metal detector this time, which was just as well. If he thought he was frisking her, then he had another thing coming. And that thing was a punch to the throat.

The detector bleeped at her hand and the man stared at her clutch. Maggie sighed and opened the bag. "It's the cap on my perfume," she said, showing him the bottle.

The man examined the bottle, taking another look in the bag. The knife was hidden, but if he rummaged around he would find out soon enough.

Maggie held her breath, keeping her cool and displaying Felicity's impatience.

The big lump of a man seemed satisfied and returned the perfume to her, finally allowing them to pass. The hallway led them further into the heart of the building until they arrived at a set of wide doors. Daniel held them open for her, playing the part of the perfect gentleman, and Maggie entered.

The décor of the Midnight Lounge was true to its name. The room was dark, the seats and walls a deep purple, the tables and wooden floor a rich mahogany. Overhead lights illuminated the room in an opaque glow, like little moons looking down upon them. Smoke hung in a thick mist, the scent of Cuban cigars and alcohol dominant in the air.

Though finely furnished, the place had a seedy quality to it. A long bar filled one entire wall at the back, separated from the private booths filling the rest of the room. The dancefloor sported circular stages at each corner, silver poles sprouting up from their centers and climbing to the ceiling.

While not to Maggie's taste, she was sure it made most of the clientele feel right at home.

A maître d' was by their side in a heartbeat, his arms open. "Ah, Mr. Church. It's a pleasure to see you again."

Daniel shook his hand. "Hello, Emanuel."

Emanuel was a man of around forty, and Spanish from his dark features. His suit was immaculate, his face clean shaven and thinning hair swept back with gel.

"Same as last night, sir?" Emanuel asked.

"Perhaps later." Daniel shared a masked smile with the maître d'. "For now though, I think a spot of dinner."

"Of course, of course."

Emanuel led them across the room, and Maggie scanned her surroundings. The place was quiet, only two of the many booths occupied, one with an older man sitting by himself, and the other by two women who seemed far more interested in each other's lips than they were with their meals.

Emanuel led them across the room to a private booth nestled in the corner. While perfect for privacy, it was less than ideal for scoping out the room and the people in it.

Maggie stopped and tapped her lips, looking around at the other booths. The two men halted when she didn't follow.

"Could we sit at that one?" Maggie pointed to the booth two spaces down. It looked out into the dancefloor and had a great view of the door if she sat to the right side of the table.

"As you wish, Miss..." trailed off Emanuel.

"Felicity Greene," said Maggie.

"Nice to meet your acquaintance, Miss Greene." Emanuel ushered them to her chosen booth and handed out menus. "Welcome to the Midnight Lounge. Can I get you both something to drink first?"

"A French Martini." Felicity enjoyed cocktails. "I like it with a lot of foam at the top, enough to hold a little straw, but not one of those tacky bendy ones. And add a splash of champagne on top. Not the house stuff. A nice vintage brut will do."

"I'll have one of those Spanish beers you gave me last

night," Daniel told Emanuel, who whisked off to fetch them.

Daniel turned to Maggie. "I love a woman who knows what she wants."

Maggie shook her head towards Emanuel. "I hope he makes it right, otherwise I'm sending him back to try again."

Daniel moved his eyes around the room, gesturing with his hands. "Is this exclusive enough for you?"

"It's nice," Maggie lied, peering up from her menu. "Do you come here a lot?"

Daniel draped an arm over his seat like he owned the place, his Rolex sparkling under the dull lights. "When I'm in town. It's only open to members, for people like us."

People like us. Maggie was nothing like the members of this place. Nothing like Daniel Church.

"Yes, I gathered that from the brute at the door," she said, going through the menu. Everything sounded delicious and her mouth watered as she read the descriptions of Spanish specialties.

"You've never heard of this place before?" asked Daniel with a quizzical frown.

"I don't find myself in Madrid that often," Maggie replied.

"They have them in other cities, too. You should consider joining. They are very..." Daniel considered his words. "Accommodating."

Maggie wondered what the club had 'accommodated'

for Daniel. While Felicity might be fooled by his charm and chivalrous ways, Maggie was under no illusion about who she sat beside. Daniel Church was a con artist, and no matter what kind of mask he wore, Maggie knew what lay behind was much darker. Though how dark, she wasn't sure.

Emanuel interrupted their little chat, placing their drinks in front of them. He took their order for dinner, Maggie choosing a spicy roast pepper soup to start, and a mixed seafood paella for her main.

"It's not very busy," commented Maggie. She knew it would get busier within the hour, if the last three nights were anything to go by, but Felicity didn't know that, and she liked a lively atmosphere. Quiet and intimate wasn't her thing.

Daniel raised his bottle, and Maggie clinked it with her glass. He took a drink from his beer and smacked his lips in pleasure. "Give it an hour and the room will fill up. I know you like to party."

"Oh, really?" Felicity tried and failed to play coy.

"So I've heard." Daniel brushed her leg with his under the table.

Maggie fought to keep her leg where it was, which Daniel took as a sign to go ahead and rub his foot against hers. "And what else have you heard about me, Mr. Church?" she asked instead of jabbing her blade into his thigh like she really wanted.

"I know you obtained the prized lot in the Fleur Estep

auction mere hours before it was due to go under the hammer. Diamonds that have yet to resurface in the market, black or otherwise."

Maggie sipped her cocktail and glanced at him over the glass. "Diamonds are a girl's best friend."

"I also know that you come highly recommended, yet no one seems able to pin point you to many other jobs, meaning that you're discreet and don't like to brag. Which tells me you're one of the best."

Maggie nodded her approval. Gillian's handiwork was yet again proving itself. If Daniel had heard of all this, then so had everyone else in the same line of work. The name Felicity Greene was known, just as the little house-wife had promised.

"You appear to be well informed." Maggie twirled the little straw in the foam of her drink.

Daniel shrugged, yet appeared pleased with himself. "It's part of my job to know things."

"Oh really?" Maggie leaned forward and nodded her head to the old man alone in his booth. "What about him over there? Tell me about him."

Daniel followed her gaze and leaned forward, his voice low like he was sharing a secret. "That's Edgar Cannon. He's a banker with a knack for laundering funds to offshore accounts. I've used him a couple times. He's very good, if a little expensive."

"And the two women near the door?" continued Maggie.

Daniel stole a casual look over his shoulder to get a glimpse at them then turned back. "The brunette is Rowena Trent, wife of Nathaniel Trent, the infamous racketeer. Rowena's companion is her mistress Yvette Lewis, an investment banker from Jamaica who's in business with Nathaniel."

"Scandalous." Maggie wondered if Ashton knew Nathaniel. Her best friend had a knack for solving the problems of criminals. What they didn't know, however, was that Ashton often created those problems in the first place.

"Not really," said Daniel, bringing Maggie back to the conversation. "Nathaniel knows."

Emanuel returned with their food and conversation led to the arts, jewelry, and then paintings which were Daniel's area of expertise. He enjoyed talking about himself, which would have been a real turn off had the dinner been a real date, but in this instance, it was ideal. Maggie let him talk and yammer on about how good he was at this and how much he made selling that.

All the while, more people arrived at the Midnight Lounge. A trickle at first, but soon a much larger crowd, filling the room up to almost capacity.

A hum of chatter floated in the air, and the gentle dining music which played when Maggie and Daniel arrived gave way to more modern songs, the volume getting louder with each tune.

As the crowd became rowdier, Daniel grew drunker,

the monologue of his greatness continuing with no intermission in sight. Maggie tuned out most of it, enjoying her soup and delicious paella, the fluffy rice spiced with saffron and the seafood perfectly cooked.

From her spot in the room, she had a visual on every face that entered the club. Some were somewhat familiar, most complete strangers, yet none of them were of the man she was hoping to find. He hadn't turned up the last three nights either, and there was no guarantee the assassin would show tonight. In the days since the murder of the mayor, he could have gone anywhere. If it were Maggie, she'd be on another mission by now.

But he was not Maggie. Like Leon said back at the Unit HQ, most people would take some time out after a job. Most people would spend a few days living their lives a bit. And what better place for the Spanish assassin to spend his downtime than the private club he cared for enough that he brought his card all the way to London. If he was planning on going out and enjoying a night in the city, then this was the place he'd go. All Maggie could do was sit, wait, and have a little hope.

Then she saw him.

The door opened, and in slinked the man whose face she had imprinted to memory. The killer, and the one who played a part in framing her for the mayor's murder.

The assassin.

Chapter 13

Maggie clenched the handle of her knife. The metal dug into her palm, and she placed it at the side of her plate along with the fork, the edge of the dull blade clinking with the plate.

It was him.

Maggie took a deep breath, Daniel still babbling on about something as her gaze followed the assassin across the room to the bar where he ordered a drink.

"You weren't lying when you said it would get busy," Maggie said, interrupting whatever story Daniel was in the middle of telling.

"Yes," he said, peering out at everyone there. "A couple of hours and things will get pretty wild in here." Daniel wiggled his eyebrows, the effects of his beer beginning to show.

Maggie laughed, tossing her hair. "Sounds fun. Who's that man by the bar?"

Daniel's face soured. "Oh, him? He's one of the Handler's men."

"The Handler?" Maggie inquired. The name wasn't familiar.

"He runs an agency, of sorts." Daniel gave a flippant wave of his hand, seeming uninterested in any discussion that didn't center on him.

Maggie kept a close eye on this assassin, his back to her while he drank clear liquid from a glass. "And what type of service does this agency provide?"

Daniel shrugged. "Assassinations."

Maggie gave Daniel a shocked look, an air of excitement in Felicity's voice. "The man over there is an assassin? What's his name?"

"Who knows. Sometimes he's José Garcia, and the next time he's calling himself Ronaldo Vasquez. I doubt he even remembers his real name any more."

Maggie stared at the assassin's back. She knew what that was like. To go by so many different names for so long that you began to lose sight of who you were among it all. The lines between fiction and reality blurred until they bled together. In some ways, Maggie felt like she knew her aliases better than she knew herself. Take away the aliases and the missions, and Maggie wasn't sure what would be left behind. Perhaps a part of her was scared to discover what lay underneath it all in the end.

She never stopped long enough to find out.

"Why are you interested in him?" There was a dark edge to Daniel's words.

"I'm not." Maggie sipped from her drink, still on her first glass. "He just seemed to stand out."

Daniel's eyes narrowed. "In what way?"

Maggie scrunched her face towards the bar. "He looks like a weirdo."

Daniel said nothing, only watched her. The air had changed between them. Daniel clearly wasn't used to women paying attention to another man while in his company. He was like a toddler with a new toy, jealous and unwilling to share.

A minute passed in awkward silence, Daniel snapping his fingers for Emanuel to deliver another beer. The assassin remained at the bar, nursing his drink and speaking to no one.

When he had drained his glass, the assassin left some money on the bar and headed for the door.

Maggie took her clutch bag and stood up from her seat. "Excuse me. I need to visit the little girl's room."

"It's through the doors and to your left," Daniel said, finishing off yet another beer and slamming the bottle down on the table. The assassin left through the very same doors and disappeared out of sight.

Maggie went to leave when Daniel grabbed her wrist. His grip was too tight, his eyes glazed with alcohol. Daniel Church's mask was slipping.

Amateur.

"What shall I order you for dessert?" he asked, tightening his hold.

Maggie tensed her arm, fighting the urge to break each finger that held her. She leaned down and spoke in his ear, her lips brushing his cheek. "Why don't you get us something we can share."

Daniel relented and released her, temporarily satisfied. Maggie's hands itched to slap him. Instead, she straightened her dress and made for the door. The assassin may have slipped her once, but it would not happen again.

Through the doors, the hall was deserted. A noise came from the left, and Maggie snapped her neck to it, only to discover a drunk woman stumbling out of the bathroom. Maggie passed her and pressed her ear to the door of the men's room. The noise from the lounge didn't help, but Maggie couldn't hear anything beyond.

Prying the door open a few inches, she glimpsed inside for any sign of movement. Water trickled from a set of unoccupied urinals at the back. Slipping inside, Maggie crept to the stalls at the other end to find the doors open and unlocked.

Damn it.

She returned to the hall, anticipation tingling in her stomach. He couldn't have gone far. Maggie walked to the front door where the same bouncer stood chewing on a piece of gum with his arms folded.

"Did a man just leave?" she asked. "I think he dropped his wallet inside."

The bouncer shook his head. "No one has left in the last hour."

Maggie moved to the guestbook and fussed over the pages as the man turned back to the little TV behind the desk. With his back turned, Maggie reached into the cabinet where the man had put Felicity's passport and returned it to her clutch bag. Backtracking, Maggie trudged down the hall, her new shoes digging into the back of her heels.

A clattering of metal came from somewhere to her right, and Maggie rounded the corner and arrived at the kitchen. The large room buzzed with activity. Bright orange flames burned under pots and pans, the smell of sizzling meat and spices filling the air. Chefs milled around, weaving between each other, chopping vegetables and serving up dishes onto plates with military precision, a woman yelling orders as she scrutinized their offerings.

Maggie stepped further inside.

She was about to ask the head chef if anyone had passed through, when something collided into her from behind.

Not something. Someone.

Maggie stumbled forward as the assassin forced her deeper into the kitchen, his arms wrapped around her waist. Her clutch slipped from her hands and slid across the tiled floor.

She crashed into a storage unit and metal shelves dug against her ribs.

The kitchen staff backed away and headed for the fire exit, no one daring to interfere.

Maggie grabbed the first thing that came to her hands and brought it down on the assassin's head. The bag of flour burst and exploded over him and she kicked him away from her, right in the solar plexus.

He stumbled back a couple of paces, the flour dusting off from his shoulders like smoke as he charged at her.

Maggie lunged out of the way and rolled across the floor. The assassin recovered and gave chase, aiming a right hook to her jaw as she got to her feet. Maggie pivoted to the side, the wind from his missed attack brushing past her face as she aimed a knee for his groin.

It wasn't a fair move, but Maggie didn't play fair. She played to win.

The assassin doubled over and leaned onto the nearest counter, writhing in pain and frustration before throwing himself at her with a predatory growl.

The glint of silver caught in the light as he approached, the kitchen knife long and deadly sharp. Maggie ducked, and a wisp of red hair floated to the ground beside her like blood against the white tiles, cut with the blade's edge.

Maggie swept her leg across the floor, knocking the assassin's feet out from under him and sending him falling back.

Gripping the counter, Maggie pulled herself up and wrapped her hand around the handle of a chrome pot. She swung hard and smacked the assassin in his temple. Boiling water spilled from the pot and burned her skin. Maggie swore as she dropped the pot.

The assassin staggered from the blow but recovered quick. The pain seemed to fuel him, and he caught her in the face with a jab, startling Maggie long enough for him to grab her by the hair.

He yanked her back, throwing her to the floor. She screamed as her hair tore from its roots to hang in his clenched fists.

Maggie's heart pounded and drummed in her ears.

Someone called from the door leading to the hall, and the assassin was on them. The bouncer from the entrance wasn't fast enough to see the attack. He stared at his chest, where the kitchen knife was buried deep between his ribs, a look of surprise spreading over him before he dropped to the ground with thud, his gun still clutched in his meaty fist.

Maggie didn't waste the distraction. She crawled across the floor and found her clutch, snapping it open and bringing out the switchblade.

Charging towards him, Maggie raised the knife and prepared to plunge it into his leg. She needed him alive, and she needed him to talk.

The assassin must have heard her coming. He spun on

his feet, kicking with the momentum of his spin, and hit her square in the chest.

Maggie reeled back, fighting to keep balance, but she fell over the counter. Air rushed from her lungs, leaving her gasping for breath. Her chest burned as she struggled for oxygen.

The assassin grabbed her arm and twisted it behind her back, pulling her up towards him.

"I'm not here to kill you," she rasped.

"You shouldn't have come here at all." He panted in her ear, almost as out of breath as she was. But that didn't stop him from pushing her face towards the orange metal rings of the burner above one of the ovens.

Maggie threw her free hand out and gripped the edge of the counter, using every bit of strength to stop the assassin's downwards momentum. But he was stronger and Maggie's head moved inch by inch towards the searing metal.

The heat kissed her skin, sweat beading down her brow as panic threatened to take over.

No, she couldn't let it.

A drop of sweat fell from the tip of her nose and landed on the metal rings with a hiss.

Maggie's mind raced for a solution. Something, anything to stop the inevitable. Talking had gotten her nowhere. The assassin didn't want to hear it. He wasn't going to stop until she was dead.

Mere seconds before her skin touched the burner, it

came to her, and Maggie dropped to her knees in a dead weight.

The move was unexpected, and the release of tension sent the assassin careening forward. Maggie reached up and grabbed the back of his neck and pulled down with all her might.

The assassin screamed as a hissing sound filled Maggie's ears, the sickening smell of cooking flesh sticking to the back of her throat.

Maggie held her grip on the writhing assassin, his whole body shaking. He threw himself back, breaking her hold, and roared.

Angry char marks covered the side of his face, dark blood coagulated in the heat with beads of bright red that dripped from the wound like tears. Maggie cringed at the sight, bile rising in her throat at the cooked smell surrounding them.

The assassin opened his eyes and charged at her. Maggie was too slow to move, held in place by the shock of the man's grotesque face, and she braced herself for impact.

They fell to the floor in a mess of tangled limbs, the assassin sprawled on top of her. He wrapped his strong hands around her throat, but the grip of his fingers never came.

A muffled squeak escaped his lips as warm liquid soaked into the fabric of Maggie's dress.

The assassin stared at her with his dark eyes, and

Maggie was close enough to see his pupils dilate. Blood trickled out of the corner of his mouth, and he sputtered, like his brain hadn't quite caught up with what happened.

Maggie wriggled out from under him, the switchblade slick in her hand and covered in the man's spilled blood.

The assassin rolled onto his back and ran his fingers over the entry wound in his stomach. His light blue shirt was saturated in blood, and it spilled out between his fingers, his chest heaving up and down on the floor.

Maggie sat beside him, every part of her sore and limp with fatigue. "Who hired you to kill the mayor?"

The assassin blinked and turned his head to her, like he had just noticed she was there. His face was pale. "I wasn't hired to kill the mayor," he said, his voice soft, almost gentle. "I was hired to get you away from him."

The assassin released one last sigh and then was gone. The light left his eyes, and before anyone found them there, Maggie gathered her things, collected the bouncer's gun from his dead grip, and left the Midnight Lounge behind.

Chapter 14

26 May

Maggie allowed the hot water to run over her tight and aching muscles, eyeing the bruises that had appeared overnight as she slept.

Last night, she'd snuck inside the hotel, avoiding the cameras as best she could by taking the service stairwell. After a quick shower to wash away the blood and other mess, she forced herself to stay awake to observe the club. When she was certain no one was coming for her, she collapsed into dreamless sleep.

Thankfully, no one had seen her return, but they would see her today. A purple mark covered her jawline where the assassin struck her, the force behind his professional fists leaving their imprint. The ones on her arms, body, and legs could be hidden with her clothes, but her face required make-up—and a thick layer of it.

Steam rose and misted the bathroom, Maggie's skin red from the intense heat. She closed her eyes and leaned into the jet of water. Her stomach growled, empty and neglected since last night. Maggie hadn't even been able to keep her meal from the Midnight Lounge down, the attacks on her body making her shake and convulse once the adrenaline stopped flowing. The ordeal left her shivering in a ball on the bathroom floor.

It had been a close one. Too close.

Maggie was trained in combat, but it wasn't every day she faced a professional killer; someone just as deadly, if not more so, than she was.

The tips of her fingers shriveled from the water, and Maggie dragged herself out from the heat and into the air-conditioned bedroom, wrapping a towel tight around her. She winced as she bent to sit down, too tired to dry herself off.

Last night had been a bust.

She didn't go to the club to kill anyone. If the assassin had been willing to talk, Maggie would have taken what he told her and left, no hard feelings. After all, the man had only been doing his job, and she had bigger fish to fry.

Maggie grimaced at the thought, the smell of the assassin's charred flesh clawing onto her senses in a memory no shower could wash away. Some things just stuck with you.

Just like the last words to leave his lips before he took his final breath.

They replayed in Maggie's mind over and over again. Someone had hired him to distract her and lure her away from James Worthington. And she'd fallen for it, doing exactly what he wanted. She chased him through the hotel when she should have been protecting the mayor.

She could kick herself, but the assassin had already kicked her plenty.

Maggie didn't expect the trail to end with the assassin. She wasn't a chess player, but she knew a pawn when she saw one. And she figured she was a long way off from figuring out who she was playing against. If only she knew enough to plan a few moves ahead, then maybe she could cross the board for the final checkmate. But to get there, she would have to go through the knight.

Daniel had referred to him as the Handler. It was an ominous, if not obvious, title for someone in his line of work, but it paid to advertise, and the Handler did exactly what was labeled on the tin. And the ones he handled were no joke.

Forcing herself to her feet, Maggie began the painful process of getting ready and packing her things. She couldn't linger in Madrid. Word would already be out about last night, and while Felicity may not be impli-cated, her presence would have been noted along with everyone else at the private club. And her absence. If he didn't already know, the Handler would soon learn he was a man down. Assets like that weren't easy to find, and the resulting death would cost him money. A lot of it.

As far as Maggie knew, she had never come across The Handler or any of his assassins before the Baltic Hotel. She couldn't recall any mission involving him or his people, and she made a point to try and remember everyone she ever dealt with in her career. Forgetting a face or name could get you killed.

That meant someone had taken out a contract with the agency. As she suspected, the murder of the mayor was planned, and planned well. Maggie mused over the assassin's role in the death, trying to connect the pieces to an unknown puzzle. Was he paid to distract the mayor's guards, which happened to include her? Or were his words more literal, meaning Maggie specifically? And if he didn't kill the mayor, who did?

The assassin could have been lying. Maggie had just dealt him a fatal blow, after all. One last fuck you before he died to mess with her head. He had enough time to circle back downstairs and get to the mayor before she arrived to discover his throat slashed.

But that didn't explain the video footage Bishop sent her.

Maggie let out a deep sigh and fell back into the chair. Thanks to her own hands, she had to find someone else who could answer those questions for her.

She stared out at the sun-kissed street, people milling

up and down and walking by the entrance of the Midnight Lounge without a second glance.

When Maggie had watched from her bedroom window the night before, the Midnight Lounge had carried on as inconspicuous as ever. No ambulance had been called, no police sirens wailed out front to go in and see the crime scene.

The deaths had been contained, the two bodies most likely long gone by now through one means or another. Perhaps it was even one of the 'accommodating' services the club provided its members.

Daniel had stumbled out in the early hours, and the same bulking driver as before helped him into the back of his car. Maggie would be long gone from her hotel should her date rouse and decide to pay her a visit. His ego would be bruised if he thought she abandoned him. Then again, his day would most likely be spent hugging the toilet and tossing back painkillers. He was certainly drunk enough to warrant a killer hangover.

Maggie called the front desk and arranged to have the staff help with her bags. Felicity didn't carry luggage, and besides, Maggie's aching muscles could do with a break.

By the time they arrived at her door, Maggie was dressed in a silk long sleeve blouse and trousers to hide her wounds. A pair of designer sunglasses covered most of her face. She walked out of her room, the staff following dutifully behind her, and made her way down to the front desk.

"Your car is waiting for you, Madam," said a woman at the front desk after checking her out.

A light breeze brushed by Maggie as she stepped out into the morning sun, and she got into the back of the car as the staff packed her luggage into the boot. Maggie closed her eyes and leaned back into the headrest.

"Where to?" asked the driver.

"The airport," she replied. It was too early to return to London. She couldn't go back until she learned more. Until she had enough evidence to clear her name. Where she would find said evidence, she didn't know, but there was nothing left for her in Madrid.

The doors locked, and Maggie felt the car pull out as she settled in to catch some sleep on the short journey.

"Going anywhere nice?" asked the cabby, interrupting her plans of slumber.

It was only then Maggie noted the voice.

She snapped her eyes open and shot a glance at the dark brown irises looking at her through the rearview mirror.

Her heart plummeted to her stomach.

Leon.

Chapter 15

Leon.

He'd found her. *They* had found her.

Maggie grabbed the door handle and pulled it back.

It didn't budge.

She was locked in.

Her heartbeat drummed against her ears in a crescendo of panic, like a foreboding symphony that played with the same intensity as her rushing thoughts. Each worry, each fear collided into the next, making it hard to concentrate on the man before her.

"Let's have a little chat, shall we?" Leon's deep voice was as familiar as her own.

"Stop the car." Maggie slammed her hand against the pane of glass separating her from the man she once loved. The man who was there to kill her.

Maggie knew the Unit would send their own after her, people she had fought beside for years, but she never thought they'd send Leon. Or that Leon would agree to hunt her down.

Not after everything.

Leon was an undeniable part of her history, woven into her marrow and bones, and now he was there to put an end to her future.

The Unit must have issued the hit. Maggie expected as much; she was too big a threat to national security to be given a fair trial. To be brought in and allowed to speak to the police, or stand before a judge to insist her innocence. For the public to see her face in the newspapers and to have her life excavated by the media. They needed to silence her before she could speak. Before she said too much. The Unit wasn't even supposed to exist. They couldn't allow a rogue agent like Maggie to blow their cover. She had to be eliminated.

All of this she knew, and all of it she'd accepted. All of it, but Leon.

"What's going on, Maggie?"

Maggie stared at him, unable to tear away her gaze as memories flooded her mind. The day she first laid eyes on him when she arrived for training, both still kids who thought they knew everything. The day she realized she loved him, more than anything or anyone in the world. A world full of darkness and despair that he somehow made beautiful. Of Venice, and the night they fell into each other's arms, not their first time, but most certainly the last. Of knowing they could never be together, and the pain that came with that knowledge. Of her life after him and the consequences of their actions.

So many memories. Each of them a chapter in her life that Leon was about to end.

"Let me out," she said, a quiver lacing her words. Water misted her eyes, and she willed the tears back. He would not see how much he hurt her.

"You know I can't do that," he said, each catch of his eye in the rearview mirror a stab in her gut.

Maggie's walls were solid. Impenetrable. They had been for most of her life, ever since her mother died and left her alone in the world. It made her good at her job, and kept the real her nestled away where no one could see it. Leon was the only one who knew which parts of the wall made the bricks crumble. Only he could tear them down. Only he saw the real Maggie.

They both knew it. As did the Unit.

She cursed the director and Bishop under her breath, cursed all of them for putting her in this position.

"Fine." Maggie reached into her bag and brought out the gun she took from the dead bouncer the night before.

Leon raised his eyebrows, unflinching and calm, like it was easy for him to be there. For her to be his mission. "You going to shoot me?" he asked, taking a left and merging into the M-30.

Maggie hesitated, her knuckles bone white on the

handle. She bit her lip, knowing what she had do to. Knowing that she could never forgive herself once she pulled the trigger.

Leon rapped on the glass. "It's bulletproof."

Despite her situation, a wave of relief washed over Maggie. She thrashed the feeling away, knowing it was wrong. He was there to kill her, and no matter their ties, she was not about to let that happened. Even if that meant ending him.

Maggie studied the thick glass. Leon wasn't lying. She took a moment to slow her breathing and focus. She reviewed every detail of her situation, allowing her training to overthrow her emotions.

She couldn't reach Leon through the transparent barrier. Which meant he couldn't reach her, either. Traffic whizzed between them, the motorway especially busy for the time of day.

Leon was taking her somewhere. Most likely somewhere secluded that wouldn't draw attention. She could bide her time and try to escape when he pulled her out the car, but that assumed he wouldn't just torch the vehicle with her locked inside. It was too risky to wait until they reached their destination.

Which meant she needed an exit route. Now.

Maggie pushed herself across the back seat and aimed her gun. The glass might be bulletproof, but the door wasn't.

With three strategic shots, she blasted the lock apart

and kicked the door open. Wind swept into the cab and made her hair dance in front of her face as the car sped along the motorway.

"Don't be daft," began Leon, hitting the brakes but unable to stop due to the line of cars speeding behind them. Whatever he said next, Maggie didn't hear.

Without a second thought, she leaped out of the moving car. She landed in a roll, breaking the force of the impact as her body hit the gravel tarmac.

She rolled three times before tensing her muscles to stop herself.

The gun slid from her grasp and skidded into the middle of the next lane of the motorway, lost to her now amid the rushing traffic.

Ignoring the pain pulsing over her, Maggie stumbled to her feet and darted across the road, weaving between speeding cars that swerved around her and honked in anger as she passed.

The sound of screeching tires carried in the wind from down the road, and Maggie spotted Leon making a U-turn over four lanes of traffic. The engine roared and the car sped towards her at full speed.

Maggie, glad to be wearing flats for once, raced across the road, propelled by the deep-seated animal instinct to survive.

Leaping over a metal barrier at the side of the road, Maggie ran through a patch of bushes and snarling trees and headed down the steep hill. Brakes screeched behind her, and then a door slammed shut, but she kept moving. No looking back.

Another road barrier lay at the foot of the hill and Maggie hurtled over it, landing at the edge of a city street. She crossed the road and made it to the pavement, her lungs burning.

Shops and little cafes lined the street, but Maggie couldn't find her bearings. She reached for her phone and swore. Her bag, along with the rest of her belongings, was in the car.

A few pedestrians watched her with suspicious eyes. Maggie frowned, but then stared down at her dirt covered clothes, the arm of her blouse ripped open and stained red.

Maggie didn't even feel it. Checking over her shoulder in case Leon followed, she picked up her pace and slipped down a side alley.

Light on her feet, she weaved through the narrow streets, passing behind rows of townhouses and apartments, not allowing herself to stop until she was far away from the motorway.

The heat of the sun loomed over her. Sweat trickled down her back and beaded on her forehead. She sped around the next turn, and a cluster of private parking garages blocked her in. A dead end. Maggie drew back to return the way she came when she stopped.

It was quiet. Too quiet.

Her senses twitched, but it was too late.

Strong, forceful hands grabbed her shoulders and spun her around.

Maggie used the momentum to add power to her punch and managed to catch Leon across the face. His head snapped to the side upon impact, and he sucked in a breath. She aimed another, but he was ready for her this time. Leon caught her fist in a vice grip, his big hand completely covering her own.

Maggie brought up her knee to ram his crotch, but Leon knew her tactics too well and took a step back, dodging the blow.

"Stop," he warned.

Maggie twisted in his hold, trying to break free, but he was far stronger and the speed she normally used to counter superior strength was gone. Between the impact with the pavement, the frantic escape, and last night's run in with the assassin, her body had nothing left to give.

But that didn't stop her from trying. Maggie threw her elbow into Leon's forearm with what little strength she had left, her chest heaving and body aching in complaint as she tried to break his hold.

Leon huffed and yanked her by the arm, shoving her into the near wall and bringing her off her feet. "Calm down."

Maggie stopped fighting, and her body slumped in his grasp. She looked at the man she once trusted with her life and willed him to hear her. To listen.

"I didn't do it, Leon. I didn't kill him."

Leon's face softened, a trickle of blood slipping between his lips from where she caught him. For a split second his mask dropped, and he was her Leon again. The Leon who couldn't hide anything from her. Who never wanted to hide anything from her. His hold on her relaxed. "I know. We're here to help you."

Maggie slid down the wall, and her feet met the ground again. Relief slowly travelled through her, calming her rattled nerves as Leon's sincerity stared back at her. He wasn't there to kill her. She fought the urge to place a gentle hand on Leon's face and wipe the blood from his full lips. Lips she'd tasted, in another life.

Maggie gave herself a shake and frowned at Leon's choice of words.

"We?" she asked.

Chapter 16

Maggie returned with Leon to the abandoned car on the edge of the motorway. Thankfully, the police hadn't arrived to investigate, so her multiple passports and identities remained safe and sound where she'd left them before she dove out the back seat.

The gun was lost though.

Leon drove down the motorway and turned off a slip road twenty minutes later, leading them through the outskirts of the city. Maggie tried to get Leon to fill her in on everything, but he refused.

"It'll be easier to go through everything once we're all together," he said.

Maggie groaned. Spies could be so enigmatic. She blamed Ian Fleming.

Five minutes of awkward silence later, Leon pulled up

to a private villa hidden between lush green trees and walls covered in blossoming ivy. A man waited for them by the door, leaning casually against the frame and biting into an apple.

Leon tried to open Maggie's door for her, but she shooed him away. "I think I can open a door on my own," she said, sharper than she meant, with a nod to the three holes in the now beat-up passenger door.

"Maggie." The man greeted her like they were meeting up for a spot of lunch.

"Ashton." Maggie shook her head. She should have known he was behind this.

He wrapped one of his arms around her and eyed her appearance. "Are you okay? You look like you've been wrestling a wild badger."

Maggie cocked an eyebrow. "Thanks. The badger won."

Ashton ran a hand over her hair. "Clearly."

Maggie caught a glimpse of herself in the reflection of the glass door. It wasn't an exaggeration. Felicity would have had a melt down by now. She looked like roadkill.

"You're supposed to be staying out of this," Maggie said, shoving off Ashton's arm and walking into the villa. "I'm in some deep shit here, and I can't have you getting caught in the crossfire."

"I was never any good at doing what I was told." Ashton flashed her a boyish grin. "You should know that by now."

In typical Ashton fashion, he'd spared no expense on accommodations. It was a modern building with large glass walls that looked out into the private pool outside beside the large and secluded garden. The scent of lemons and new leather filled the room, the heat from outside covering everything it touched with a comforting warmth.

Maggie went to the sleek kitchen and filled a glass with water, gulping it down her parched throat. "I'm serious, Ash," she said. "You can't get involved."

"Och shoosh," Ashton waved her off. "Like I'm really going to let you do this on your own."

"He's right," Leon said, coming in from the car with her bags. He placed them on the floor and tossed the keys to the car on the counter.

"I'll get to you in a minute," Maggie warned, still pissed at him for not starting their meeting with a heads up that he wasn't there to kill her.

Ashton smiled. "It's just like the old days. The gang's back together."

"No, it's not." Maggie's patience had worn to nothing. Jumping out a speeding car and fearing for your life would do that to a girl.

But even she had to admit, it *was* strange for all of them to be in the same room together. These days, Maggie made a point to avoid Leon as best she could, the pain of being around him too much to bear.

As for Leon and Ashton, they hadn't been around each other for years. Not since one of their early assignments. They were all still green, too green, and Ashton had left the Unit—and everyone in it—with a bang. Literally.

Everyone, but Maggie.

She took in the feel of the room, noting the subtle tension between the two men, who had once been as close as brothers. Leon felt Ashton had betrayed them, and he never forgave him for that. Maggie didn't hold the same grudge. She knew Ashton wasn't cut out to be an agent, though not for lack of talent.

Despite the years that had passed, neither of the men attempted to heal their severed friendship. Leon used the excuse of following the Unit's orders not to associate with known criminals, while Ashton preferred to act like none of it ever happened, through what Maggie suspected was a sense of shame.

It said a lot, them both being there. She wondered who made first contact.

A glass of something strong hovered under her nose, returning her from her thoughts. "Drink?" Ashton asked, his own glass in hand.

Maggie blinked. "It's ten in the morning."

"It's five o'clock somewhere." Ashton shrugged. "Besides, you seem like you need one."

Maggie pushed it away. "No, thanks."

"Suit yourself." Ashton downed his glass before moving on to hers.

Maggie pinched the bridge of her nose. "How did you

even find me?" she asked, aiming the question at her friend. Even still, she felt Leon staring at her.

Ashton scoffed. "Give me a little credit, Mags. All it took was a wee search for each of your new names on the outbound flights at the airports. Felicity Greene, one way ticket. I've got to say, I never would've guessed you'd pick Madrid as a place to lay low. Though it is gorgeous this time of year."

"I'm not laying low," Maggie corrected. "I'm following a lead."

"What lead?" Leon asked, stepping toward her.

Maggie betrayed herself and faced him. Her gut churned in a mixture of butterflies and dread. Leon had a way of ruining her cool exterior, like his mere presence somehow caught her off balance, even after everything they'd been through.

"Not yet. I'll get to that," she said, trying to focus. "First, I need to know what's happening back home."

Leon and Ashton shared a look.

"Tell me," Maggie said, setting her jaw. Whatever it was, it wasn't good. She straightened and set her shoulders like she was bracing herself to take a punch. In some ways, she was.

Leon cleared his throat and rubbed at the back of his neck the way he always did when he had bad news, or when something was stressing him out.

"The Unit got the lab results back on the murder weapon. It had one set of prints on it. Yours."

"Of course it had my prints. I picked it up when I discovered the mayor's body, and—" Maggie tried to continue, but Leon held up his hands.

"You don't need to explain yourself. I know you didn't do it."

"But the Unit thinks I did." It wasn't a question.

"With the prints and the CCTV footage, they have no reason to look for anyone else."

Maggie ran a hand through her hair. "Fuck."

"Bishop's livid. He knows you didn't do it."

"He does?"

"Of course, Maggie. We know you." Leon made to reach for her, but stopped himself and curled his fingers into his palm.

"I don't see him doing anything about it," Ashton spat.

Ashton never got along with authority figures.

"His hands are tied," Leon explained, his focus on Maggie. "The Director's made up her mind, and the evidence against you doesn't give Bishop any ammunition to argue otherwise."

Maggie nodded. She'd seen the video with her own eyes. Bishop was likely the only one still at the Unit who believed her. Faced with hard evidence like that, she didn't blame the others for thinking her guilty. In their position, she'd based her opinion on the facts.

Fact: All evidence pointed to Maggie.

Fact: She'd run instead of turning herself in.

Fact: Only Bishop and Leon believed in her innocence.

She was thoroughly screwed.

"It's official, then?" Maggie hugged her arms around her waist, waiting for confirmation of what she already knew in her bones to be true.

Leon nodded. "The Director's given the kill order."

Maggie let out a deep, shaking breath, rubbing her clammy palms on her thighs. She knew it would happen. Knew it the moment she saw Leon in the car. It was procedure. Yet hearing it from Leon made it real. The Unit wanted her dead. As far as they and the government were concerned, she was public enemy number one.

"They think you're hunting me down like the others?" she asked.

Again, Leon nodded.

"Who else have they sent?"

"Everyone not on assignment. They pulled a few out of their covers, too."

The weight of his words pressed down on her, making it hard to breathe. They were coming for her. Some of the best agents in the world had their sights set on tracking her down. For all Maggie knew, they could be close.

Maggie bit on her thumbnail, moving away from the large glass walls and out of range by sheer habit as paranoia niggled at the edge of her mind. She was a wanted criminal. Hunted.

She let it all sink in, trying to accept it for what it was.

She couldn't change anything that had happened, but she could sure as hell try to prove her innocence before the Unit caught up with her. She wasn't dead yet, and she wouldn't let the Unit—the only family she had left—be the cause of her demise. Most agents didn't live past their thirties; it was part of the job. One of the many risks involved in protecting her country. But she refused to go down branded a traitor and a murderer.

And she refused to bring those she cared about most down with her.

Snatching the keys from the counter, Maggie headed for the door at a run.

"Whoa, whoa," yelled Ashton. "What are you doing?"

Leon was fast, his arms wrapped around her waist before she even got close to the door.

Maggie squirmed in his hold, digging her nails into his arm. "Let me go."

"Not until you calm down." Leon tightened his grip as she tried to twist around.

Maggie went to kick him, but Ashton saw it coming and caught her legs, hoisting her off the ground. "Don't make me hurt you both," she warned, dangling in the air between them.

Ashton tried to pry her fingers open. "Give me the keys."

"Get off me." Maggie fought and freed her legs, slipping through Leon's hold. She spun on them, panting. She didn't want to fight her way out, but she would if she had to. "Don't you see?" she shouted. "I'm a wanted criminal."

"Who isn't?" Ashton said, standing between her and the front door.

Leon gave Ashton a side eye before turning to her. "You're not a criminal. You did nothing wrong."

"It doesn't matter," replied Maggie. "They think I did, and they're coming after me. If anyone so much as catches a glimpse of us together, they're going to jump to conclusions. They'll think we're working together."

They'd be two more deaths on her hands. The mayor was already one too many. She couldn't let them risk their lives for her.

"Then we don't let them see us," Ashton said, like it was that simple.

"You know these people," Maggie countered. "It's only a matter of time before one of them finds me, and neither of you can be there when they do."

In two swift strides, Leon closed the gap until they were mere inches apart, his large frame towering over her. "There's absolutely no way I'm leaving you on this."

Ashton stepped closer, too. "Let us help you, Maggie. For Christ's sake, you've gotten my arse out of plenty situations before."

"Not like this." Maggie craned her neck up to meet Leon's gaze. "I appreciate you both running here for me, I do. More than you'll ever know. But I can't let you get involved. If anything happened to either of you—"

She stopped before her voice broke, the lump in her throat almost choking her as she tried to hold it together.

"Remember Venice?" Leon asked, the heat from his body radiating over her cold skin. "Things were bad then. We thought we were done for, but we made it out. We always do." He placed a hand on her cheek, and her eyes betrayed her. A tear slipped down to meet his finger, and he wiped it away, peering straight into her eyes.

"Please, just let me go," she said, her voice a whisper.

He gave her a rare smile; one she hadn't seen in a long time. "Not a chance."

"I can do this on my own," she repeated, weaker this time.

Leon laughed. "I know you can. If anyone can make it through this, it's you. But when will you learn you don't *need* to do everything alone?"

Maggie didn't respond. Relying on others had never come easy for her. She'd spent so much of her life alone, first through a string of foster families and then on her own in the streets of London where no one could be trusted. She had learned that lesson the hard way. And no matter how much her life had changed since Bishop offered her a new start, no matter how much she cared for someone, she was still very much the same homeless orphan who didn't need anyone but herself.

"He's right, Mags," Ashton said, rubbing her back.

"See?" Leon nodded toward Ashton. "I'm agreeing with this nutter, and I'm pretty sure that hasn't happened in ten years. We're here for you, so tell us how we can help."

Could she do it? Could she be selfish enough to accept their help? Could she allow them to risk their lives for her?

"We know what we're getting into," Leon assured her, as if reading her thoughts.

"Plus, you know we'll just follow you wherever you go anyway," Ashton added, a smug smile on his face. "You might as well just accept that we're tagging along."

Maggie looked between them both. Her thoughts flitted back to London, to Bishop. He was always telling Maggie she needed to learn to work with others. Three minds were better than one, and her own mind was coming up empty. She didn't know what her next move should be, especially now that she knew the Unit planned to terminate her from their employ in the most literal sense.

Yes, she was skilled, but Leon and Ashton had strengths she didn't. Strengths that could help her get to the bottom of everything before it was too late.

Maggie didn't like it, didn't want to admit it out loud, but she could use their help. If their roles were reversed, there was nothing in this world that could keep her from helping either of them. She closed her eyes and sighed, resigning herself to the idea, even if she hated herself for doing it.

She allowed herself another moment of tears before swiping them away. "Okay," she said. "But I don't want either of you doing anything daft or unnecessary to protect me. We treat this like any other job."

Except it wasn't any other job. This was one mission she couldn't fail. Not if she wanted to make it out alive. And now, she had two more lives to worry about. Two more people who could end up dead because of her.

"Anything you say, boss." Ashton gave her a salute, sharing a look of triumph with Leon.

Leon ushered her to the living area. "Tell us what you know."

Maggie settled down on one of the sofas and filled her companions in on everything that happened since the night the mayor was murdered, going over some of the earlier events Ashton already knew about for Leon's benefit.

She briefed them like she would any other agents on a mission, her tone void of emotion, her facts void of speculation.

"Ah, the Midnight Lounge," Ashton said once she'd finished.

"You know it?" Maggie asked.

"Of course." Ashton scoffed, like he was almost offended.

Maggie rolled her eyes. "Please tell me you're not a member."

"I'm not," he said, like butter wouldn't melt. "They barred me for life a while back."

"Why am I not surprised?" But his antics brought the

ghost of a smile to Maggie's lips. "Anyway, it doesn't matter. I can't go back there after what happened."

"What about this Handler?" Leon, who had remained silent on the opposite sofa through her run down of events, leaned toward her with his elbows resting on his knees. "I've never heard of him."

"Me neither." Maggie sat back against the soft cushions, letting her heavy eyelids fall shut. "But I need to track him down. It's the only lead I have."

"The only lead *we* have," Leon corrected.

"Well," Ashton cut in, "that one is easy."

Maggie and Leon stared at him.

Ashton stood up and clapped his hands. "Pack your bags, kids, we're going to Moscow."

Chapter 17

MOSCOW, RUSSIA

It was a five-hour flight to Russia's capital city. It had been a couple of years since Maggie last visited, but little had changed. Russia was old school, and its proud, yet tumultuous history ran deep through its veins.

Despite her racing mind, Maggie managed to sleep most of the journey, her body bone tired. She learned early in her line of work to sleep when the opportunity presented itself. You never knew when you'd get another chance. A tired body led to a tired mind, both of which could get you killed if you weren't careful.

They arrived at their hotel, a nice yet much less extravagant local than Ashton would have preferred, but Maggie put her foot down. They needed to go unnoticed, and a simple hotel in the heart of the city filled with tourists was ideal for blending in.

Maggie booked them adjoining rooms on the top floor, overlooking the city skyline. The onion shaped domes of Saint Basil's Cathedral and the unique architecture of the historic Red Square stood out like festive gingerbread structures amid the tall, modern buildings.

Night blanketed the city, giving it a dark, ominous presence, the lights like leering yellow eyes. Watching. Waiting. Maggie shuddered and closed the curtains, turning to Leon and Ashton.

"Anything?" she asked.

Leon slammed his laptop closed and leaned back in his chair, rubbing at his eyes. "Nothing. Whoever this guy is, he's a ghost."

"Relax." Ashton stood and put on his coat. "From what I hear, the Handler is strictly off the radar. He doesn't leave a paper trial, and is extra cautious about concealing his whereabouts."

It made sense. His business would have earned him many enemies; a problematic yet unavoidable outcome when you ran an agency of contract killers. "Then how did you know to come here?" Maggie asked.

Ashton shrugged. "I hear rumors."

Maggie raised an eyebrow as he headed for the door. "And where are you going?"

"Off to see a man about a dog."

"I'm coming with you." Maggie grabbed her jacket. Despite summer being on the horizon, a winter chill carried through the air, making it colder than usual for the time of year.

"Now, now, settle down." Ashton blocked her view of the door. "An acquaintance of mine might know how to get in touch with this guy, but I don't plan on spooking him with a pair of spooks at my side."

Maggie folded her arms, ignoring his ridiculous pun. "You don't want us knowing who this acquaintance is, you mean?"

"A good businessman never reveals his contacts." Ashton opened the door. "Plus, you may be wanted for murder, but you technically still work for The Man."

Before Maggie could protest, Ashton was out into the hall, and the door swung closed behind him.

Leon groaned, brows burrowed in disapproval. "He's a loose cannon."

"Perhaps." Maggie plopped herself down on the couch across from him. "But he's also the only one of us who has any chance of finding out how to reach the Handler."

"I don't like it."

"You mean you don't like *him*," Maggie countered.

"He can't be trusted." Leon tapped a hard finger on the armrest.

Maggie sat up from her slouched position, prickling at his words. "I trust him with my life."

"You never could see sense when it came to him."

Maggie huffed. "He's my friend, and once upon a time, he was yours, too. No matter what you might think of him now, he's good at what he does. He'll find out how to make contact."

Leon picked up his laptop and opened it again, like Maggie's words had done nothing to change his mind. He was just as stubborn as she was.

"I'm going to get into character," Maggie told him, getting up from the couch. If things went well with Ashton's contact, they could come face to face with the Handler that night. She had to be ready.

"Felicity again?" Leon asked, not looking up from the screen.

"No. She could have drawn too much attention in Madrid. I don't want the Handler to hear she's in his territory, too. It'll put him on guard."

Maggie still couldn't be sure that Felicity got away with the assassin's murder. Even though no one came looking for her after, the chefs in the kitchen saw her before they ran off. They could have mentioned her to anyone who came asking. Maggie only hoped they had learned to see nothing in their time working at the Midnight Lounge.

"Rebecca Sterling? She came in handy for the Venice job."

"I can't use her. The Unit has a list of all my known aliases." Mainly because they were the ones who came up with them for her. All her usual personas were blacklisted for the time being.

"Right."

An awkward silence enveloped around them, the tension heavy in the air. Venice was their last mission together, and the mention of it brought up memories Maggie had worked hard to block from her mind.

Almost a year had passed since then, and she could count the number of times she'd seen Leon with one hand. Maggie opened her mouth to speak, but instead, she turned around and went to her room, closing the joining door between them.

She leaned against the door and tilted her head to the ceiling. There was so much she could say to him, so much she wanted to say. But there was no point. Relationships between agents were frowned upon. Over the years, they'd tried to make it work, keeping things a secret. They were both good at secrets.

At first it was exciting, hiding it from their colleagues and meeting up for secret trysts in the middle of the night, or running off for the weekend together.

Bishop eventually found out and warned them to end it. Their superiors—and the Director in particular—would have separated them the instant they found out, sending them on assignment to opposite ends of the world. Neither of them listened to him, of course, but he never mentioned it again.

Maggie suspected that Bishop made sure he was the

only one who ever knew about their relationship. Maggie and Leon were two of his best, and he wouldn't want to lose them.

Even without the risk of being found out, they never managed to make it work. At first it was because they were young and drunk in love, the kind of love that could never last. As they got older, and their love deepened, the job got in the way. There was a reason most of the agents in the Unit found themselves single or divorced. Bishop's wife left him after years of late nights and last minute 'conferences' abroad, not knowing if he would be gone for a couple of days or weeks at a time.

Venice had been a moment of weakness for them both, high off narrowly escaping death and needing to feel the touch of another living, breathing person.

It was a mistake she couldn't make again.

"My name is Ekaterina Kovrova."

Maggie sighed as she took in the state of her newly died hair. Felicity's red needed to go. If she made it out of this mess alive, then she was going to have to take her ruined hair to the salon and pray they could fix the damage she usually avoided by wearing wigs.

So dark it was almost black, Ekaterina wore her thick hair iron-straight and draped past her shoulders. The photo on her passport also showed her sporting a blunt fringe which gave a severe look to match Ekaterina's serious personality and ruthless reputation.

Her reputation.

After the dye had settled and was rinsed clean, Maggie trimmed her hair to match the photos, going over in her head the history of her new persona from the detailed file Gillian had provided for the second of her three new aliases.

"I fucking hate tourists," spat Maggie, letting the Russian roll off her tongue. It had been a while since she'd spoken the language, but the nuances didn't take long to come back.

Ekaterina was born in Suzdal, a historic town in Vladimir Oblast, around a hundred and forty miles east of Moscow. Part of the Golden Ring, Suzdal attracted a horde of tourists by the busload throughout the year, and was the town's main source of income.

Her mother and father owned a humble gift shop, full of tchotchkes and any other piece of overpriced crap they could get their hands on and sell to unwitting tourists. It was there Ekaterina first learned the art of trading.

"That seems like a fair deal," she said as she dried her hair.

Using her pocket money, Ekaterina bought some of her parents' stock and sold them to people from a little cart as they milled around the town, going from church to church—Suzdal had no shortage of those. She charged twice, sometimes three times as much, for each piece.

"Idiots," Maggie said, opening her make-up bag.

Ekaterina was a few years older than Maggie, and a fan of cosmetics. Maggie covered her face in a thick layer of foundation before going in with black eyeshadow to create a smoky eye. Filling in her eyebrows to match the color of her new hair, Maggie then smeared her lips with a bright red lipstick. She finished off the look with a beauty mark on her cheek.

Maggie kissed the mirror to remove the excess, leaving a print on the glass. "Much better," she said, staring at herself and making sure her face was perfect. There was no need for contacts, like with Felicity. Ekaterina had blue eyes like her own, which stood out like crystals of ice against her dark hair.

Walking to the closet, Maggie considered what to wear. Ideally something that could conceal a gun.

"I can get you fifty Vityaz-SN submachine guns by tonight. They're lighter than the Ak-47 and are favored by the Russian military. The nine millimeter Lugers will cut through body armor like butter."

It didn't take long for little Ekaterina to learn that the profit margins were much higher for items that were rare or difficult to obtain. Even more so when they happened to be illegal. As she got older, she carried on with her fledgling business, graduating from selling trinkets to tourists to eventually selling weapons on the black market.

Maggie smirked and thinned her lips. "Do we have a deal?"

Ekaterina's stock came at a high price, but she had a reputation for discretion and her products were always of the highest quality. From simple handhelds to militarized grenade launchers, Ekaterina's supply was very much in demand.

"Don't make me ask you again," she snapped, her words as sharp as blades.

Like her weapons, Ekaterina wasn't dangerous until she took her safety off. Whispers floated around the city of the unfortunate fate of those who had tried to deceive her, and rumor had it, she was not afraid to pull the trigger.

Satisfied with her work, Maggie returned to the adjoining room in the hopes that Ashton had returned, but there was no sign of him. Leon stood alone by the window, staring off into the city. He turned when he saw her reflection approaching him.

Maggie held out her hand. "Ekaterina Kovrova."

"Ah," Leon said, shaking her hand. "A Russian makes sense."

"How do I look?" she asked, handing him Ekaterina's passport before spinning around.

Leon's voice was somber. "Beautiful."

Maggie stopped her spinning. "I didn't mean..."

"I'm sorry." Leon handed back the passport and rubbed his neck. "I shouldn't have said that."

"No, it's fine." Maggie stumbled over her words but didn't know what else to say.

He was beautiful, too. She'd always thought so. His looks never went unnoticed when women were around, and some men, too. His skin was a rich brown, with eyes like midnight and a short, groomed beard that encircled his full lips. Even in his simple t-shirt, there was no hiding his physique, his biceps taught against the white fabric.

They stood there for a moment, caught in each other's gaze.

"Would it be wrong of me to say I've missed you?" Leon asked after a while.

"Not if it's the truth." Her words came out a whisper across her lips.

He reached out and entwined a finger with hers. "You know it is."

She did. She knew because she missed him, too. Missed how he could make her laugh, even after they'd argued over their doomed romance. Or how safe she felt in his arms, able to sleep through a whole night without being visited by nightmares of the things she'd seen and done. Of how he somehow made the best cup of tea in the world, and how he'd hold her hand for no other reason than he wanted to be close to her.

She missed all of that, and so much more.

Time and time again, they circled back to each other. The undeniable draw between them was second nature. Yet each time, when the inevitable happened and they went their separate ways, a piece of her would break. Each time, it took a little longer to heal.

After Venice, a part of her broke that she didn't think would ever mend itself.

Leon inched nearer, but Maggie took a step back, their linked fingers disconnecting as Ashton came barging through the door.

"We're on," he said, his face alight with the thrill of an impending chase.

"When?" Maggie asked, forging a gap between her and Leon that might as well have been miles long instead of a few feet.

"Tomorrow morning."

Chapter 18

27 May

Maggie sat waiting in the rental car, going over everything one last time with Ashton and Leon.

"Everyone know what they're doing?" she asked, keeping an eye outside as more people began to line up.

"Yup," Ashton said, busy fiddling with the device in his hands.

"Yeah," confirmed Leon at the wheel before turning the engine off. The tension from the night before was still there between them, but Maggie couldn't let it distract her. It was game time, and they couldn't afford any slipups.

"Okay, then let's move." Maggie exited the backseat

and left the boys to their task as she crossed the road and joined the back of the queue where it rounded the corner to the adjacent street. Ashton had not been exaggerating when he said the Handler liked to stay off the grid.

A couple of old women gossiped in front of her as the line slowly moved forward, more joining the queue in a production line of hungry customers. The early morning air was crisp, and the buttery scent of pastries and fresh bread led an enticing trail to the front door of the bakery.

The sign above the Abramov Brother's bakery was decorated to emulate the famous architecture of the city and reminded Maggie of the gingerbread house the evil witch from the fairytales used to lure children.

She hugged her coat closer to her chest and stepped inside.

The tantalizing smell of freshly baked goods made her empty stomach growl with longing and her mouth water. Rows and rows of Russian delicacies sat behind glass counters, each looking more delicious than the last. There were so many items to choose from, and Maggie would have loved to sample them all, but she had come with a very specific order in mind.

The little store was filled to capacity, servers collecting cakes and breads from each of the counters, following orders from eager fingers pointing out their chosen baked goods. A little girl danced between the horde of customers, ignoring the calls from her mother as she dug into an iced bun, most of the compote filling dripping down her chin and staining her jacket.

Maggie gave her a smile as she waited, quickly hiding it and setting her expression back to one of unimpressed boredom. Ekaterina didn't like children.

A large man stood at the back of the bakery filling a tray of eclairs with pastry cream, his solid arms covered with old-school tattoos that appeared faded against his tough and weathered skin. He held each of the dainty little confections between two thick fingers with a surprising gentleness for a man of his size and appearance, taking great care to delicately place a pair of choux wings at either side of the puffs along with a long-necked head to create the appearance of a swan.

"Can I help you, Madam?" asked a red cheeked server, her hair coming out of her hairnet.

Maggie stepped forward and began the order Ashton's contact described, the girl scribbling down each item on a little notepad. "A dozen pastila, a large kalach, four slices of ptichie moloko, and three of your choux swans."

"Anything else?" asked the girl, already tallying up the bill.

"Yes," said Maggie. "I need a Prague cake for my daughter's birthday party."

The girl's pen stopped, and she glanced up at Maggie. "A Prague cake?"

Maggie huffed. Ekaterina hated repeating herself. People needed to learn to listen. "That's what I said."

"And what age will your daughter be?" stuttered the girl, peering over her shoulder.

Maggie followed the script. "Six."

The girl held up a finger and said, "One moment, please," before shuffling off to the back.

She spoke to the large man with the tattoos for a moment, both staring back at Maggie with scrutinizing eyes. Maggie arched an eyebrow at them, unblinking under their stare.

Then, the man abandoned his station, taking a large box from a pile on the counter, and began to fill it with Maggie's order.

When he was done, he walked over to Maggie and slid the box across the counter.

"Name?" he asked, his voice gruff as he took her money and counted change from the cash register.

"Ekaterina Kovrova," said Maggie, unsure of what happened next.

The man gave her a handful of coins and with that, he left her and returned to his swans without another word.

Maggie hovered by the counter, but the next customer stepped in front of her with an annoyed expression and called for service. Maggie took the box and left the bakery.

Leon and Ashton were waiting in the car when she returned.

"The bug is in place," reported Ashton, the location of the baker's car blinking at them from the map on the tracking device's screen.

Leon turned in his seat. "How did it go?"

"I must have done something wrong." Maggie went over the order in her head. She was sure she got it right.

"Look in the box," Ashton suggested.

Maggie untied the string and opened the lid. On the back of the cardboard was a neatly written message. *Your order will be ready for collection tomorrow.*

Maggie took a cake from the box and sunk her teeth into it. She'd be ready.

Chapter 19

Maggie sat with folded legs on top of a small wall in Red Square. She wrapped her fingers around a steaming cup of tea and savored the warmth. Beside her, Leon and Ashton sat with their long legs hanging off the edge as they watched people discover the sights of Moscow for the first time while others seemed to return to the city as if they were visiting an old friend.

The number of selfie-sticks was quite disconcerting.

It always seemed odd to Maggie that people were more concerned about taking pictures than enjoying the experience of being there. She followed the sightseers as they took in the magnificence of the square through a camera lens, barely looking up from their phones.

She said as much out loud. Leon tended to agree, but Ashton just rolled his eyes.

"You sound like an old grouch." Ashton yanked her close until she fit in the frame of his camera phone and snapped a photo.

"I look like a Bond villain," she said, peeking at the screen.

"Hey, stop hogging the goods." Leon reached out for the half-eaten box of cakes. The Abramov Brother's bakery may partake in some shady extracurricular activities, but the bakery was still legit. The Russian pastries were unbelievably good.

Leon took the box from between her and Ashton, and dug into one of the choux swans.

Maggie laughed.

"What?" he asked.

"You've got cream on your nose." Without thinking, she reached over and wiped it off with her finger.

He shot her a smile, and she found the edges of her lips tugging upwards despite herself.

Maggie cleared her throat and changed the subject. "I haven't been in Moscow for about three years." Her last assignment in Russia had led her to Saint Petersburg. Even then, that was almost two years ago. "I forgot how beautiful it was."

Moscow was one of those cities where the past lived and breathed on every corner, almost like a presence. It could be felt when walking down the very same streets as people from centuries ago, or staring at the dark red walls of the Kremlin, its bold color like a symbol of its proud and bloody history.

Leon dusted his hands free of icing sugar. "I prefer Vegas."

"Now there's a place I haven't been to in forever," said Ashton.

It struck Maggie how different the two places were, one ancient with a macabre air to it, the other a synthetic pleasure resort. "I haven't been back since the time Bishop took us."

Ashton snorted and almost spat out his tea. "You mean the time you broke his nose? Oh man, that was the best."

Maggie's temper had always been a problem, particularly in her younger years as an agent. "I'm lucky he never broke my neck for that one," she said with a grin, the moment replaying in her mind.

Leon nudged her with his arm. "Well, you get away with a lot when you're the favorite."

"Bishop doesn't have favorites," she retorted, not for the first time.

The men laughed, sharing a look like they used to back at the academy, usually when they teased her for excelling in their training. It only lasted a moment, but Maggie caught it. Perhaps there was hope for the boys' friendship yet.

That was one battle she'd let them hash out on their own.

Maggie glanced across the square to the Monument to Minin and Pozharsky. The bronze statue was covered in a layer of patina thanks to time and the elements, giving it a turquoise façade. It stood before the cathedral, a commemoration to the prince and his friend who had gathered an army to put an end to what was known as The Time of Troubles.

Maggie's own time of trouble was far from over, her meager army consisting of the two men beside her. But she was a soldier, and she never backed away from a fight, no matter the odds.

A beeping came from Ashton's pocket, and he brought out the tracking device. "Looks like our tattooed master baker is on the move."

"Are you sure you don't want us to come with you?" Maggie asked, for the tenth time.

"Nah." Ashton jumped down from the wall. "No need for three of us to go on a one-man job. And besides, the last thing we need is the baker to realize the bond villain from earlier is following him."

"Be safe." Maggie didn't like the plan, even though it made sense. She had to stay under the radar until tomorrow.

"And if you can't be safe, be careful," Leon added, getting up to toss his empty cup into a nearby bin.

Ashton nudged his head subtly towards Leon and gave Maggie a sly wink.

Maggie glared at Ashton before he spun on his heels

and left, blending in with the busy crowd and vanishing out of sight.

"He hasn't changed a bit," Leon said as he watched Ashton leave.

"He has, actually." Maggie shivered as the wind picked up across the wide expanse of the square. "He just doesn't show it."

There was a lot Ashton didn't show. In some ways, his care-free exterior was more of a fortress than the heavily guarded Kremlin towering above them.

"Let's go for a walk," said Leon. "My legs have gone stiff."

"You're getting old," she teased, hopping down from the wall. Leon was only two years her senior.

"I definitely feel it sometimes," he said, zipping up his bomber jacket. "I even found a gray hair last week."

"Where?" Maggie searched his head, though she was far too short to see much.

Leon flattened a hand over his hair like it was sticking up with the wind, even though it was cropped down to military regulation bristles. "I plucked it out," he admitted.

They headed east, sticking close as they weaved through the crowd of tourists and made their way across the arched Bolshoy Moskvoretsky Bridge at a leisurely pace. They had the rest of the day to kill while they waited for their trip back to the bakery the following morning.

Maggie stopped mid-way across the bridge and leaned

over the edge to see the boats sail under on the Moskva River.

"Thanks," Maggie said, keeping her gaze on the water below. "For coming to help me, I mean."

"Of course." Leon stood next to her, the heat of his body warm against her side amid the cold wind.

"How did you know I didn't do it?" Everyone else believed she was guilty. Based on the evidence against her, it was almost foolish not to.

"You're many things, Maggie, but a traitor isn't one of them."

Maggie ran an absent hand over her stomach. She didn't deserve his blind faith. While she never lied to him, she wasn't entirely honest either.

"It all feels so surreal," she said as clouds crept over the sun and left the sky a dull gray. "I keep expecting to wake up and realize it's just a nightmare."

It was in a way, she supposed. A living one.

"We'll get through this," Leon said with that unshakeable certainty he carried with him. "We always do."

It was true. No matter what they'd faced, each time they pulled through. But this time felt different. Bigger. More dangerous. It was funny how much your life could change in only a few short days.

"Weren't you supposed to be out on assignment?" Maggie asked, recalling their meeting in the elevator at headquarters before everything went to shit.

"I was at the airport when they called me in. You spared me a trip to Peru."

"Well, in that case, I guess we're even then."

Leon hated long haul flights. Any type of flying really. He once told her it was why he joined the army instead of the RAF after he left school. When Bishop caught wind of his aversion at the academy, he forced Leon to take flying lessons.

Phobias could get an agent killed.

They were quiet for a time, the sounds of the city playing around them. The sky reflected off the surface of the water, distorted by ripples as boats passed by.

"You've been avoiding me." It wasn't a question.

Maggie began to deny it, but she stopped herself. It was pretty obvious what she'd been doing. "It's easier that way."

"Perhaps for you." His words were thick with emotion, and the rawness tugged at Maggie's heart.

She realized how close she was to him and moved away. "It's better this way."

Leon took her hand in his, and she left it there. "I miss you, Maggie."

"I miss you, too," she admitted, squeezing his hand, "but we can't keep doing this to ourselves."

She couldn't do it again, not after last time. She'd promised herself she would stay away. Yet the temptation to go back to their old ways was there. It would be so easy to fall into his arms, to allow her heart to open fully to him again. They'd become experts at ignoring the realities of their situation. So much so that when the same problems arrived, they came as quite a shock.

"We can still be friends, though." Leon's voice was soft, but there was a desperate urgency to his tone. "Even if we're not together, I want you in my life."

Maggie closed her eyes. She wanted him in her life, too. His absence was like a physical hole, a missing piece that she couldn't fill. Her attempts to move on never worked, no matter how great the people were that she dated. No matter who they were or how they made her feel, no one compared to Leon. They weren't him, and that was the problem.

"I can't just be your friend, Leon. I can't." Her voice broke, and she hated the weakness she heard in her words.

"Why not?" His eyes were wide, his face filled with the boyish innocence the Unit had somehow been unable to destroy despite all he'd seen and done.

"Because it hurts too much to be around you!" Her voice came out louder than she meant, earning them a few stares from passersby.

The idea of Leon being with another woman made her recoil inside. She felt it like a serrated knife digging into her chest and ripping out her heart. And yet, she wanted him to find someone. Someone who could be there for him when he needed them. Someone pure and untarnished, who hadn't been forever altered by the darkness in the world. By the deeds they had committed. He deserved to be with someone worthy of his love, to be touched by hands that hadn't killed.

Maggie didn't even know the number of lives she had taken anymore. Didn't want to sit down and try to count them. But they were many, and each one took a piece of her soul she could never get back. She believed in the Unit and all it stood for, but carrying out the work came at a price for her, a price she wasn't prepared to let Leon pay.

"What if we tried again?" he said. "Things could be different this time."

"We've been over this. There's no future for us. How can there be given what we do, who we are?"

Each time one of them left for a mission, Maggie said goodbye like it could be their last. She agonized for days, sometimes weeks at a time without hearing from him, unable to contact each other during a mission. They couldn't tell each other where they were going or for how long. It left her constantly on edge, dreading each time the phone rang in case it was the one call that would shatter their world.

It was no way to live.

Even the idea of starting a family was absurd. Their lives were unstable and extremely dangerous. Together they had garnered a list of enemies longer than the phonebook, and the risk of past deeds catching up with them was too high to consider any sort of normal life together.

Her current predicament was proof enough of that.

"I'm not saying it would be easy, but isn't it worth

trying?" Leon persisted, pointing between them. "Isn't this worth fighting for?"

Maggie placed her free hand on his chest, the beat of his heart strong and willful. "We've tried, and it never works," she replied. "You know that."

"But, I lo–"

"Stop." She pulled away, breaking their connection. "Please don't make this harder than it already is." Those words might break her if she heard them, and she couldn't fold. They were better off apart, no matter how hard it was.

Leon clenched his jaw, a wet gloss coating his eyes. "I'm sorry."

"I am, too." Maggie bit her lip. It pained her to see him upset, but she couldn't yield.

"We should head back." He turned to walk back to the hotel.

Maggie followed along in silence, her hair blowing in the wind like spilled ink.

Above, the sky rumbled with the promise of an approaching storm.

Chapter 20

28 May

The Abramov Brothers bakery was just as busy as the previous morning. Maggie lined up as before and waited to be served, tempted to buy a few more of the choux swans.

"I ordered a cake yesterday," she said when it was her turn. "I'm here to collect."

The server, a different girl from yesterday, took Ekaterina's name and disappeared through the back.

Maggie checked over her shoulder to the car waiting outside. Ashton leaned back in the passenger seat, stifling a yawn. He'd gotten in late after tailing the tattooed man, but it paid off. Maggie now had some much-needed ammunition for her role as weapons dealer.

If the bakery reported back to the Handler, they would assume her companions were hired muscle under Ekaterina's employ. A woman like her would need good security, a fact Maggie intended to exploit as part of her cover.

Leon sat in the driver's seat, his attention focused on the surroundings. With the kill order on Maggie's head on top of everything else, extra vigilance was needed. All of them were on edge, expecting an attack to come any moment.

Neither of them spoke much after their conversation on the bridge. There wasn't much to say after that. Nothing could change their situation. Leon spent the rest of the day in his room, as did Maggie, ordering room service and pacing the floor until Ashton returned.

The girl arrived a minute later carrying a string-tied box, and Maggie waited until she was back in the car before looking inside.

Café Pushkin, two o'clock.

The Café Pushkin was located on Tverskoy Boulevard, and Maggie arrived ten minutes early to scope out the place.

Famed for its theatrical recreation of an old aristocratic mansion, the restaurant offered their diners the option of several themed rooms. Maggie was greeted with a warm welcome, and her coat was promptly taken and hung away in the cloakroom. Leon kept his on, playing the role of bodyguard for the meeting.

"I'm meeting someone for lunch," Maggie said to an older gentleman at the front desk, "though I'm not sure which room."

"That would be the Library, Madam. Please, follow me."

The Library was aptly named, and a rather impressive sight upon entry. Great walnut bookcases reached high up to a Baroque-style ceiling, filled with antique books and vintage carriage-clocks. She weaved through the tables at the behest of the old man, passing a large globe of the world, yellowed with age. There was plenty to look at in the unique dining room, but it was all the empty tables that caught Maggie's attention. Only one of them was occupied.

The Handler was already seated and waiting for her.

A row of four burly men stood behind him, their broad shoulders linking them together like a brick wall that blocked the sunlight coming in from the nearest window. Maggie spotted another lackey by the door, and two more at opposite ends of the room.

Two against eight, assuming there weren't more lurking out of sight.

The Handler himself remained seated upon her approach and gestured for her to sit.

Maggie straightened the jacket of her tailored black suit and sat down, Leon pulling out the seat for her before settling behind her to play a game of faceoff with the Handler's guys.

Their boss looked to be in his late-forties, early-fifties, and had a full head of salt and pepper hair which was slicked back with too much gel. Clean shaven with a prominent jaw, the Handler examined her like someone would a piece of meat in a butcher's shop, clasping his hands in front of him.

Maggie spotted the white scars over his knuckles, which together with the toned body beneath his expensive charcoal suit, suggested the man was no stranger to getting his hands dirty.

"Ms. Kovrova," he said, his green-eyed stare intense as he scrutinized every minute action she made.

"Thank you for meeting me." Maggie kept her back straight and her expression deadpan the way Ekaterina did when about to talk business, ignoring the sweat forming under her arms.

A young waiter arrived with wine and busied himself filling their glasses with shaking hands. He wore an old-school chemise and long sideburns that framed his pockmarked face.

Even if the man across from Maggie stayed out of the limelight, it was clear the Handler was someone of influence, and not the legal kind. The men behind him did little to hide the guns on their belts, their heads shaven and faces hard as stone.

"I'm intrigued to know how you learned to contact me," he said when the waiter gladly scampered off. "From someone who has used my services in the past, I presume?"

"Now, Mr. Fedorov," Maggie said, taking her napkin and spreading it over her lap, "I don't know about you, but I for one do not discuss my confidential clients in conversation with potential ones. It's bad business."

The Handler's eyes narrowed at the mention of his real name, but he recovered quick. The waiter returned to take their order before he could respond.

"Try the côtelette de volaille," said Viktor Fedorov, with just the hint of annoyance to his voice. "It's the chef's specialty."

"Very well." Maggie handed the menu back to the waiter.

Viktor took a cigarette from his suit jacket and placed it between his lips. One of his men leaned forward with a lighter and he took a deep inhale, blowing tendrils of smoke towards her. "So, what brings you to me?"

Maggie was certain the restaurant did not permit smoking inside, but none of the staff seemed to be in a hurry to correct him.

"I have a situation with one of my suppliers which may go hostile, and I plan to make the first move," she said, keeping it concise. Ekaterina despised dawdlers. "I need someone taken out and protection in case of retaliation."

Viktor turned his gaze to Leon. "You already have protection."

"I need more than one personal guard, and, from what I hear, your assets are the best."

"They are," he replied without a hint of arrogance. It was a simple fact, one Maggie could attest to. He took a drink of his wine. "You appear very well informed."

"I like to know who I'm dealing with before I do business with them."

"As do I." Viktor studied her with a piercing gaze. "From what I understand, you and I are rather similar. Though I assume supplying weaponry is much simpler than supplying people."

"How so?" she asked.

"You don't have to dispose of a body when your product becomes faulty."

"Ah, but I do have to dispose of the person who supplied the faulty product." Maggie sipped on her wine, which was a bit too dry for her taste.

Viktor raised his eyebrows at her comment, earning her a smile which revealed a set of rather pointed teeth between his thin, tight lips.

Their meals arrived, a modern take on a Russian classic that on any other occasion Maggie would have gladly savored. Sitting with the man before her turned her stomach. There was something about him she didn't like, something twisted and deeply dangerous.

Maggie had developed an intuition for that sort of thing, having had the displeasure of meeting so many unsavory people over the years. Viktor Fedorov made her uneasy.

He stared at her plate for a moment longer than necessary, given that he had the same order. "Ladies first," he said with another smile.

Maggie gripped her fork and hovered it by the plate.

"Something wrong?" Viktor asked, stubbing out his cigarette on the linen.

Maggie cut the chicken and placed it in her mouth, staring straight into Viktor's eyes the whole time she chewed. It was moist, strongly flavored with garlic butter, and she took another bite before smiling back at her host. "Delicious."

Viktor reached for his knife.

Maggie caught Leon moving just a fraction in the corner of her eye, shifting his weight to the balls of his feet. She motioned with her hand for him to relax, hiding the gesture behind her end of the table so as not to alert Fedorov's men. They needed to play it cool.

Viktor picked up his roll and sliced it in half, dolloping a generous amount of butter onto it and smearing it slowly.

"So, do we have a deal?" Maggie asked, unable to eat any more.

Viktor sighed. He abandoned his roll, tossing it and the

knife onto the plate with a clang. "Normally, I would think so, but you see, there's just one problem."

Maggie tensed. "And that is?"

Fedorov leaned forward over the table. "I admit, your Russian is flawless," he said, switching to English. "But you see, I also know who *you* are, Maggie Black."

Chapter 21

Maggie didn't flinch.

She had always planned to reveal her identity at some point. Ekaterina was merely a tool to set up the meeting. Viktor knowing who she was just sped things up a little.

"Well," Maggie said, dabbing the side of her lips with her napkin and tossing it over her uneaten chicken, "you're not as stupid as I thought."

It was a lie. Viktor Fedorov was no fool, but it threw him off, clearly unused to being spoken to in such a manner.

The Handler sneered at her like an angry wolf. "You killed my Spaniard."

Maggie shrugged. "It wasn't my intention, but yes."

A vein protruded from Fedorov's neck, bulging against his shirt collar. "He was one of my finest."

"I wasn't that impressed." Another lie. Maggie kept her hands under the table and rested them on her thighs, keeping eye contact with the man. People like Fedorov were predators. He would catch any sign of fear or unease radiating from her, the lure of it like the smell of blood to a shark. Backing down would only excite him, and Maggie willed her tense muscles to relax, reminding herself that she wasn't some helpless lamb before a lion.

She was a predator, too.

Maggie leaned back in her chair now that she didn't need to keep up Ekaterina's rigid posture. "Here's what's going to happen. You're going to tell me who hired you and where I can find them. Then, I'm going to walk out of here and never see or hear from you, or any of your remaining assets, again."

Viktor laughed, seeming genuinely amused. He waved a hand around the room. "Look around you, girl. You think you're getting out of here alive?"

Leon inched his hand into his jacket where his Glock rested, ready to move at a moment's notice.

A smile tugged at Maggie's lips. "I know I am."

The Handler studied her with a severe and pene-trating stare. "I admire your bravery," he said after a moment, "even if it was stupid of you to come here. But this is one fight you will not be walking away from."

Viktor gave the slightest nod of his head and his guards lunged forward. Leon had his gun out and pointed at Fedorov before they took a second step.

Maggie held out her hand at the men. "Oh, we're not fighting, gentleman," she said, turning to their boss. "In fact, you're going to let me leave here untouched."

"Even if I liked you, which I don't, I would still need to end you." Fedorov didn't even flinch at the gun pointed at his face. His men pointed their own weapons at Maggie and Leon. "You killed one of my men, and for that, you must pay. I have a reputation to uphold, Ms. Black, and the Handler cannot allow some little bitch to undermine his operation."

"The Handler needs to stop referring to himself in third person." Maggie shook her head.

Viktor sneered. "I'm going to enjoy ripping off your head."

His words sent stabs of ice down Maggie's spine, the hairs at the back of her neck standing on end. For men like the Handler, threats weren't metaphorical.

They were promises.

The air was thick, the tension around the room palpable and electric. Something had to give, and Maggie pulled out the big guns.

"That's unfortunate, Viktor. Truly." Maggie let out a seemingly concerned sigh. "If you do that, then I won't be able to make sure nothing bad happens to Galina or little Klara."

The blood drained from Viktor's face, and he shot up from his seat, knocking it back to crash on the floor. "Lies!"

He grabbed the gun from the guard nearest him and aimed it at her.

Leon was by Maggie's side in a heartbeat, his finger on the trigger and ready to fire if Viktor even thought about trying to shoot her.

Maggie stayed in her seat. Across from her, Viktor breathed heavy as he loomed over the table. A tremor ran through his arm, causing the barrel staring down at her to shake. The predator within had burst from its tailored suit and all but snarled at her.

But there was something else there. Something that hadn't been there before.

Fear.

A bead of sweat ran down Maggie's back as blood coursed through her veins, her body itching for action, but still she didn't move. Their little power play had taken a significant shift, and Viktor knew it.

The Handler's men stood around him, stationary with their weapons drawn. Confusion mapped across each of their faces as they waited for their next order.

"You're lying," Fedorov yelled again when Maggie remained quiet, his voice echoing through the empty dining room. She let the reality of the situation sink in deep before responding.

"I thought you might say that." Maggie held out her hand and Leon passed her his phone. She checked the screen and slid it across the table.

Viktor stole a glance at the screen, keeping his gun on her.

Ashton waved at them from the live video. He discretely repositioned his phone, allowing the viewers to get a good picture of where he was and, more importantly, who he was with.

A little girl sat beside him at a kitchen table, no older than four years old. Klara Fedorov giggled as they played with her toys, Ashton making dinosaur noises as he bobbed a T-Rex around her dolly.

Viktor sucked in a breath, his attention glued to the screen.

A woman came into view carrying a tray of tea and pastries which she sat down before Ashton and the little girl. "Thanks again for letting me call the breakdown service," Ashton said in broken Russian, accepting a cup of tea which he sweetened with some traditional cherry syrup.

"Of course." Galina Fedorov flashed him a kind smile. "We can't have you standing out in the cold. It's a bad place for your engine to die, being so far out here."

Galina was younger than her husband by about twenty years, the young mother wiping jam from the side of her daughter's cute little face.

Maggie slid the phone back, breaking Viktor from his stunned stupor.

"If you hurt them, I –"

"Shut up," Maggie snapped. "And get that gun away from my face."

Viktor's eyes shifted, and Maggie could see the temptation to blow a hole in her head flicker behind his hateful stare.

"Theirs too," Maggie ordered.

The guards held their positions until Viktor motioned for them to stand down. Leon did the same at Maggie's request, though from the look he gave her it seemed like the last thing he wanted to do. Viktor was on edge, but she knew he wouldn't try anything. Not with his wife and daughter at stake.

Viktor thought his family was safe, secret, but finding them was simple.

The tracker they'd placed on the tattooed baker's car led Ashton straight to the secluded farmhouse an hour outside of the city, the visit to his boss's home triggered by Maggie's order. All Ashton had to do was follow the GPS signal to the location, take out the security Viktor had placed outside the perimeter, and weasel his way inside the house under the guise of a stranded tourist looking to see more of Russia than just the sights of Moscow.

Piece of cake for a man who used his charm and boyish innocence like a weapon. Not that Ashton planned on laying a finger on mother or daughter. None of them were in the business of hurting innocents, but Viktor didn't know that.

Maggie told Fedorov to sit, and he obliged like a well-trained pet, his pride and bravado evaporated by the threat to his family. He gripped onto the edge of the table, his knuckles bone white. The vice grip caused the table to shake, the wine from their glasses sloshing over the brim and bleeding out onto the crisp white tablecloth.

"No one needs to get hurt," Maggie said. "Not if you give me what I ask."

Viktor clenched his jaw.

"Who hired you?"

"You're going to regret this day," he growled. "That, I promise you."

"A name," pressed Maggie.

Client anonymity was a vital component to the Handler's agency, but Maggie had him by the balls. Viktor let out a deep sigh. "Herman Vogel."

"And where might I find Mr. Vogel?" Maggie ran through her history of missions and the people who would want her dead. She didn't recognize the name.

Viktor closed his mouth in defiance, but Maggie tapped the mobile phone to remind him his cooperation wasn't voluntary.

"He owns a business in Frankfurt," Viktor spat.

Maggie rose from her seat and tucked the mobile phone into her breast pocket. "I think it best if Mr. Vogel doesn't know I plan to pay him a visit. The last thing you need is for people to hear you're leaking client names. You wouldn't want to put your family in that kind of danger."

Viktor Fedorov said nothing as she turned to leave with Leon by her side.

Maggie stopped at the door and looked over her shoulder. "Pleasure doing business with you," she said in Russian.

Chapter 22

Frankfurt, Germany
30 May

Herman Vogel.

In the two days since the Handler had first uttered the name, Maggie racked her brain trying to place it. They must have crossed paths at some point given that he'd hired an assassin to frame her for murder. But when? Where? She went over mission after mission, face after face, but nothing came to her.

Finding the man proved much easier than remembering him.

The corporate headquarters for Vogel Enterprises—a large, multinational construction company—was located in the central business sector of Frankfurt, known as the Bankenviertel, where its ten story building nestled among towering skyscrapers belonging to some of the world's most dominant financial titans. The buildings cast far reaching shadows across the city, the Commerzbank Tower like a clawed, pointed finger reaching for the sun.

Maggie had completed a few missions in Germany over the years, but had never visited Frankfurt before. And given her current reason for being there, she doubted she'd get the chance to see much of the city. They'd arrived at Frankfurt Airport yesterday afternoon and had been working surveillance from the back of a nondescript van rental ever since.

"Can we put the air conditioning on?" complained Ashton from the driver's seat. "I'm roasting in here."

The windows were down, but that did little to battle the humid heat that hung in the air. Summer had arrived in the city, and the sun bore down on their metal prison, creating a pressure cooker inside.

Maggie wiped her forehead with her arm, her t-shirt sticking to her as she worked from her spot in the back. "We can't have the engine running while we sit here. It would look suspicious," she said.

Outside, workers wore suit jackets over their shoulders, the rigid uniform of the finance industry unchanging regardless of the weather, the men's shirt collars buttoned to the neck with strangling ties.

"Vogel's back," said Leon, sitting next to Maggie. His

eyes were glued to the screen of his laptop, which showed the live feed from the camera placed on the van's roof, masking as an aerial. It was positioned towards the entrance of the building across the street from them, the glass walls of the bottom floor giving them a clear view inside the lobby of Vogel Enterprises.

A car pulled up outside and three armed guards exited, closely followed by the tall and slender Vogel. The sun glinted off his balding head as he went into his building, eyes covered with dark sunglasses. The female guard hovered by the entrance and stared at the van for a few moments, eyes narrowed. Then, she turned her attention to the rest of the cars in the area before going inside, their disguise as an electrical contractor blending in like they had hoped.

In the four sightings since they arrived, Vogel was always surrounded by hired muscle. They were highly trained, their movements indicative of ex-military or special forces. "Vogel must have earned some enemies if he needs a detail like that to follow him around," Maggie noted.

"Either that, or he's paranoid," countered Leon.

Maggie dug her nails into her palms. "He should be."

The whole mess was Vogel's fault. He was the reason Maggie was on the run. He was the reason a death penalty hung over her head. And while she may know the answer to *who* set the wheels in motion, the *why* still niggled in her mind. It burrowed deep in her brain, consuming her thoughts like an incessant itch she couldn't scratch.

Why would a stranger set her up to take the fall for James Worthington's death?

"Right, I need to get out of this van for a while," Ashton announced, reaching for the door.

Maggie nodded, giving the go ahead. Lunch time was fast approaching. Soon the surrounding streets would be filled with workers breaking free from their offices to enjoy the weather. "Bring back something cold to eat." She groaned. "Or even just a bag of ice."

"And take all the time you need," called Leon over his shoulder as Ashton left. "The longer the better."

"I heard that," Ashton said in their ears.

Leon took out his earpiece and replaced it with a finger, wiggling it around.

Maggie suppressed a sigh. While she and Leon were perfectly capable of sitting for hours on end with the patience of a trained spy, it was increasingly apparent said patience did not extend to Ashton.

Ashton had never been good at sitting around. He needed to keep busy, boredom a common symptom of his over-stimulated brain. He had once described his mind to Maggie as a computer with hundreds of tabs open and running all at once.

Perhaps having the boys in close confines wasn't such a good idea.

"Ash," Maggie said, "take position on the roof when

you're done. See what Vogel's up to upstairs." The roof of the building across the street gave the perfect view into Vogel's home.

"Got it, boss," came Ashton's voice before checking out.

Vogel lived in the penthouse of the building, never more than a floor away from his business. It struck Maggie as an odd choice, considering the man had the means to live anywhere he wanted. Vogel Enterprises had experienced consistent growth since its conception and showed no signs of stopping.

It could be a display of power, the king living at the top of his castle, watching over his subjects as his empire grew.

Maggie would burn his kingdom to the ground if she had to.

"Still no idea why this guy wanted to frame you?" Leon asked.

"Whatever I did to him, I can't remember." Assuming she did do something to him. Maggie had combed through her past and she couldn't recall a point in her life when she and Vogel crossed paths. Her official files were unobtainable, back at Unit HQ, but she was certain she wouldn't find a link in them either. At least, not a direct one.

"Think the Rossi family has anything to do with this?" Leon asked, his thoughts going a similar route to her own.

Maggie shook her head. "I considered them, but I don't see a connection." She was sure there was a missing link in the equation, but she doubted the Rossis were the answer.

"They have business here." Leon stretched his long legs out before him, his t-shirt tight in all the right places.

"They have business everywhere." Everywhere but Britain, thanks to her and Leon. And while Maggie was certain the remnants of the Venetian family were thirsty for revenge, she didn't think they were involved. Their gripe was with Rebecca Sterling, an American drug lord, not with Maggie herself. As far as she knew, the cover of her alias was never blown. At least not to anyone who lived to tell the tale.

Herman Vogel knew who she was. Knew her real name.

"It's been a while since we've been like this." Leon's voice was quiet in the cramped confines of the van, his body so close it brushed against hers. "On a mission, I mean."

"Venice." A lot had happened since then; their last mission together had changed her forever. Yet in some ways, she was still the lost teenage girl sitting next to the boy who made her feel at home. Still the new recruit he confided in, telling her his hopes, his fears. The mistakes he'd made and how desperate he was to make up for them.

"If only all missions were as easy as that one," said Leon wistfully.

"Easy?" Maggie laughed. "We almost died."

Leon shrugged. "I had it all under control."

"Was that before or after we were left to drown?" countered Maggie.

"All part of my plan." Leon's lips curved into an infectious grin she never could resist.

Maggie smiled. "You and I have very different recollections of that mission."

A shiver ran through her at the memory. They had come so close to death. Said things they would only admit in their last moments on earth.

"I didn't want to go back home once we were done." Leon stared at her, and the longing she saw in his gaze made her crumble. For a man with so many secrets, so many defenses set in place to be good at his job, he was never anything but open with her.

"Neither did I," Maggie admitted, heat rushing over her as a very different set of memories resurfaced. The rush that came from narrowly escaping death. How they clung to each other with the yearning to feel alive, their passion feral and hungry. It was a need rather than a desire, an animalistic urge that left them spent and fully content in each other's arms.

Sweat glistened over his skin, highlighting the grooves and contours of his muscled physique. His masculine scent filled the confined space, mixing with the woody tones of his aftershave and the mint infused soap he liked to use. It was so familiar, just as the lines of his face and the sound of his deep, graveled voice.

His mere presence, and the memories that came with it, sent tingles through her body, heading south.

"Did I do something wrong?" Leon asked, turning his gaze from her like he couldn't bear the answer.

Maggie sat up and cupped his jaw, the bristles of his beard tickling her palms, and made him face her. "No."

Leon placed a hand on her leg, hands that knew the map of her entire body. Hands that were strong and capable, yet gentle when they touched her. "Then what happened?"

It was Maggie's turn to look away. She stared at her lap, her hair falling in a curtain between them.

Leon tucked her locks behind her ear, so close she could smell the mint from his breath. "Talk to me."

"I can't," she said, the words catching her throat. "We can't."

"We can." Leon leaned down to rest his forehead against hers. "If you want to."

Maggie wanted him. She wanted him forever.

But there were so many other things she wanted. Things that would never happen. Fantasies of getting out of the Unit and having a normal life. A superbly mundane life with Leon, one where they would grow old together. Where they'd never worry about people coming after them. Where Maggie wouldn't have to kill for the greater good anymore.

Yes, she wanted to talk to him—to be with him—but she couldn't fool herself into thinking it was anything but a fantasy, a dream that would never be.

"All right, kids, I have eyes on Herman," came

Ashton's voice through her earpiece. "Nothing to report, though he does have an alarming number of mirrors for a guy whose face is perfect for radio."

Maggie cleared her throat and sat back from Leon, the moment slipping away like sand through fingers. "Roger that."

"How are things up front?"

"Lunchtime rush." Leon's focused returned, and he was all business. He'd re-inserted his earpiece and maneuvered the camera over the lobby.

Maggie watched the screen, careful to not get too close to him, the tension thick in the stuffy air.

"Wait." Maggie tapped at the screen. "Zoom in on him."

The man in question was one of the security staff stationed at the front desk. He watched a set of screens as workers spilled from their offices, the call for food and a much-needed break beckoning. They lined up and exited one-by-one through sets of glass doors, hovering their passes over a scanner to release the lock before it closed again, waiting for the next staff member to show their ID.

Leon set the camera on the target and narrowed in for a better look.

The security man was white, fair headed, and reaching his late thirties. He watched people walk through the glass doors with the glazed expression of someone who would rather be anywhere but there. He opened his drawer and took a swig from a thermos, wincing as the liquid hit the back of his throat.

"Something tells me that's not coffee in there," said Maggie.

The man confirmed her hypothesis a few minutes later. After the last of the employees exited the building, he left his post to one of his colleagues and walked down the street to the nearest bar.

"Drinking on the job," said Leon when the man came back out the bar thirty minutes later, looking a little worse for wear. "Naughty boy."

Ashton scoffed in their ears, still in position on the roof. "Nothing wrong with a liquid lunch."

"Not in this case," agreed Maggie. It didn't matter how tight security was. Every set up had a crack, a weak spot to exploit. And Maggie had found Herman Vogel's. "He's the one. He's our way inside."

Chapter 23

Addicts were predictable. Like any good alcoholic, the front desk security guard headed straight to a dingy watering hole after his shift ended. The bar was in Bahnhofsviertel, Frankfurt's red-light district. Its neon sign winked at passersby, the paint on the front doors chipped like nail polish.

The streets didn't have the manicured look of the financial district. Skyscrapers and office buildings gave way to strip clubs, casinos, and questionable establishments offering peepshows to satisfy the kinks of lonely businessmen.

Maggie's target had disappeared into the bar four hours ago, gallantly continuing his all-day binge like a true professional. She watched him through the dirt-covered window, pretending to smoke under the designated shelter outside. Like back home, Germany had banned smoking in public places.

Maggie took a draw of the cigarette, the smoke catching the back of her throat before she had the chance to blow it back out. She had been a solid twenty-a-day girl at the sweet age of sixteen when Bishop found her. He soon rid her of that little habit, among others.

She twirled the little glass vial in her jacket pocket, the only flaw in her plan. The dealer said it was strong enough for her purpose, but it's not like the woman would admit to selling an inferior product. Maggie would have to take her chances. Time was a precious commodity when you were being hunted down. She'd already wasted too much.

Allowing her cigarette to burn down, Maggie watched people as they passed, searching for signs of trouble. Ever since she learned about the kill order against her, Maggie felt like she was being watched, two eyes on her back along with the laser of a sniper rifle. If only she were being paranoid.

A light breeze whisked by, ash falling around her feet. Ashes to ashes, dust to dust.

The night was warm, but Maggie hugged her arms together as a cold chill ran down her spine. She stubbed out her cigarette and slipped into the bar, making her way to a vacant chair. Spinning to face the patrons, Maggie noted how busy it was. An empty bar would have caused more troubles, but the crowd meant there many potential witnesses. Stealth was a necessity.

There were two exits, the main entrance and the door behind the bar that lead out into an alley. Maggie checked the corners of the ceiling for cameras. Like she assumed, the bar had no CCTV. She doubted the place had toilet seats.

Maggie wore tight denim jeans, a thin leather jacket, and a low-cut tank top for effect. Anything too nice would stand out, and she needed the security guy to feel comfortable in his place of worship rather than intimidated.

The man in question stood right next to her, waiting to be served. His head turned to get a better look at her, but Maggie ignored him, keeping her eyes on the rest of the patrons. Allowing the target to approach you was a vital lesson from her training. If they initiated first contact, they were less likely to get suspicious.

"Kann ich dir ein Getränk kaufen?"

Maggie turned as if just noticing he was there. "Sorry, I don't speak German."

"Thankfully, I speak English. I'm Johan."

"Eva." Maggie shook Johan's hand. He reeked of booze, the alcohol escaping from every pore.

"Beautiful name for a beautiful woman. Can I buy you a drink, Eva?"

Maggie smiled. "A rum and coke please."

She would have much preferred a whisky, but Eva didn't like the taste. Not that Maggie was fully adopting her model alias for the job. It wasn't needed. Not when

Johan wouldn't remember meeting her. Still, old habits die hard, and she clinked her rum with Johan's beer.

"Cheers," said Johan.

"Why don't we find somewhere to sit?" said Maggie, already off her seat and walking towards the line of booths at the back.

Johan followed like a tail-wagging puppy, eager footsteps clumsy in the familiar dance of those well-past drunk.

They passed two men, one of whom nursed his beer while the other made up for it, knocking back a chaser and slamming it on the table with calls to the bar for another round. Maggie chose the vacant booth next to them as a young couple left the seats.

Johan sat down first, and Maggie slid in beside him rather than sit across the scratched table. Johan's eyes lit up, a willing captive, taking the move as come on instead of an imprisonment. Most men had a habit of assuming women were coming on to them. A polite smile like a sex whistle only they could hear. An exasperated 'fuck off' at their unwanted advances seen only as 'playing hard to get.'

Regardless of how drunk or unappealing Johan was, it would never occur to him that Maggie wasn't interested. He did most of the work for her, like a fly entangling itself into her spider's web.

"I like a man in uniform," Maggie said, peering over her glass.

"I just got off from work."

"You must be someone very important."

"I'm head of security for a very successful businessman."

"You're his bodyguard?"

"His head bodyguard," lied Johan. "I look after all his security matters."

"That sounds dangerous." Maggie did her best to seem impressed, and he drank it right in.

"I know what I'm doing."

Maggie bit her lip. "Of course. A big strong man like you must know how to handle himself."

"All part of the job," said Johan, like he was Superman and had just saved the day. Though the only thing he'd defeated was his beer.

"Same again?" she asked.

"I'll get it."

Maggie placed her hand on Johan's chest and pushed him back against the seat. "No, no, it's my round, Mr. Head Bodyguard. Let's have one more drink before we head out of here."

There was no disagreement from Johan after that little comment. Maggie purchased another round, skipping the rum in her coke. According to the dealer, she only needed a few drops of the liquid rohypnol to knock Johan on his arse. Maggie tipped the whole vial into the beer and stirred it in with her finger.

"Bottoms up," said Maggie, clinking glasses again. Johan took a deep drink and smacked his lips, the threads of her web spindling tighter around him.

It didn't take long for the drug to do its job, the effects hurried by the alcohol in Johan's system. His eyelids grew heavy, and his movements were slow as he reached again for another drink of his spiked beer.

"Are you working tomorrow?" Maggie asked.

Johan nodded and slurred, "Eight to six." His eyes rolled to the back of his head, and he slumped forward, drooling as he snored.

Maggie yanked the sleeping man by his collar and positioned him in the corner of the booth, out of view of the other drinkers.

"He's out," said Maggie.

Behind her, the two men in the adjoining booth got up and joined her. Ashton brought his beer with him and tutted at the comatose Johan. "Some people can't handle their drink."

Maggie unclipped Johan's security pass from his waistband and pocketed it. "Let's get out of here. We have an early start tomorrow."

Ashton spoke to the man behind the bar, the German flowing fluently from his lips, and pointed a thumb at the booth. The barman gave a weary shake of the head, like it wasn't the first time Johan had passed out there in a drunken stupor.

They walked out of the bar like strangers in the night, never to be seen again.

Tomorrow, Johan would wake up with no memory of the English woman who called herself Eva, or of anything else that happened that night. Left with nothing but an empty bed and a debilitating hangover.

Chapter 24

Maggie lay wide awake in the bedroom of the rental apartment. She never really slept the night before a job. You could plan everything to the last detail, and still something could go wrong. Things happened. Unforeseen problems arose.

When those problems meant the difference between life and death, it was hard to clear your head and drift off. Pre-mission nerves never went away, no matter how many assignments she completed. She'd lost count of the sleepless nights she endured, due in part to the nightmares that followed once her work was done. Maybe if she remembered, she could count them instead of sheep and manage to get some shut eye.

Cursing herself for not picking up something to read, she kicked off the covers and went in search of tea. She padded barefoot into the kitchen to discover the light on.

"Can't sleep?" asked Leon, standing by the kettle.

Maggie shook her head.

"Me neither. I forgot how much Ashton snored." Leon huffed, though Maggie caught the glimmer of amusement there, too. "Even in his sleep he's loud."

He took out another cup and teabag, not needing to ask how she liked it. Leon was good at remembering the little things.

"Everything okay?" he said.

It was such a loaded question, Maggie didn't even know where to begin. "Fine," she said, averting her eyes. While she wore a pair of baggy pajama bottoms and a t-shirt, Leon wore nothing but boxer shorts that clung around his strong legs and hung low at the waist.

"I know what 'fine' means," he said, handing her a cup with milk and no sugar.

They went into the little living room, looking out the sloped attic windows that offered a view of Frankfurt's green belt. Maggie hadn't expected the city to be surround by so many parks and gardens.

Leon sat on the sofa and stayed quiet, the way he always did when he knew she needed to talk. Not pressing her, simply there to listen when she was ready.

Maggie leaned her forehead against the cool window. "I don't think I can do this anymore."

The realization had simmered under the surface for a while now, hidden away like her emotions and anything personal she didn't want to deal with. Yet no matter how much she tried to ignore it, to keep it submerged, the truth fought to break free. To be heard. She couldn't do it anymore.

"Do what?" Leon asked.

"Any of it."

"I know things are bad now, but we'll get through this."

"It's not just being framed. It's everything." Maggie sighed and flopped on the sofa. "My whole life is a fucking mess. I go from place to place, doing things I can't talk about. Things I don't *want* to talk about. Then, I get home and can't stop thinking about what I've done, so I go off on another mission to forget about it."

In a lot of ways, her aliases helped her cope with what she did. Maggie didn't kill people and risk her life. Felicity the thief did. Or Ekaterina the arms dealer. Or even the American drug smuggler Rebecca. The aliases distanced her from the job. Distanced her from herself.

She glanced over at Leon, her voice coming out small and tired. "I don't know who I am anymore. Outside the job, I'm no one."

After Venice, Maggie left for a perilous mission in New York. Having then come home to some bad news which changed everything, she had worked non-stop, running away from her problems. Paris one minute, Toronto the next. Sydney. Tokyo.

Leon took her hand.

He held her gaze, and Maggie saw him as he was the first day they met. Young and desperately determined to make up for his wrongs. Maggie wasn't like that. Even back then she adopted an alias, one where she didn't give a shit about anything. One where she didn't need anyone by her side. A wild and reckless girl trying to hide how broken and lost she was inside.

Maggie may have lost much of her identity, but she knew she was still very much that broken girl. She constantly doubted herself and her worth. Over the years, Leon had picked away at her constantly evolving masks, searching for the truth beneath. When she doubted herself, he believed in her. When she thought it was over, he made her see another way through. Where she saw walls, Leon showed her doorways.

Yet years of fighting on a frontline invisible to the public had taken its toll. When she first joined the Unit, she was more than willing to pay that price. It was a small, necessary cost to take down Britain's most dangerous enemies. To be a silent warrior in a war most people didn't even know existed.

But now she was running on empty.

She had nothing more to give.

"I know who you are." Leon traced his thumb along the back of her hand. "You're the bravest person I know, Maggie Black. You're stubborn, and hot headed, and you throw yourself in harm's way to help others without a second thought."

Maggie bit back tears.

"You're loyal to a fault. You can't make a decent cup of

tea to save your life, and you have a mean right hook on you."

Leon drew a gentle thumb across her cheek, wiping away her tears as she laughed.

"You're my favorite person to be around, more intelligent than you are beautiful, which believe me is saying something, and I lo–" Leon stopped himself. "And I admire you very much."

Maggie sat there, stunned into silence. Her chest swelled at his words, knowing he meant every one of them. He never lied to her. Their magnetic pull couldn't be ignored any longer. Part of her felt like she didn't deserve someone like Leon, someone who acknowledged her flaws yet embraced them anyway. He saw things in her she could never see in herself. He was heartbreakingly good for her. A great man whom, no matter how much she tried to ignore it, she loved more than anyone else in the world.

Maggie loved him so much it could destroy her. Destroy them both.

But Maggie needed Leon now. Craved him. She needed to feel something real. Something to ground her in the moment and remind her she was alive.

She closed the gap between them and straddled his lap, taking his arms and wrapping them around her waist. His calloused and capable hands brushed over her skin, sending trills through her entire body.

"Are you sure?" Leon asked.

"I'm not sure about anything," Maggie said, heat rising

within her. "Except that I need you, need *this*, right now." She searched his gaze, her heart pounding loud in her ears. "I can't make you any promises, but can we have tonight?"

Leon drew Maggie towards him and answered with a kiss.

Maggie sank into the rhythm of the kiss, at once familiar yet new and exciting. She bit his bottom lip, drawing a moan from deep in his chest. The sound of his desire sent heat pooling between her thighs.

Off went her t-shirt, her bottoms following close behind, abandoned on the floor as Leon explored the curves of her body, each brush of his lips and tongue sending pulses of electricity to her core.

Leon gathered her in his arms, and they were a flurry of kisses as they moved across the apartment back toward Maggie's room. When a wall stalled their escape, Leon pressed her tight against it and shimmied out of his boxers, neither of them willing to wait a second longer.

Maggie traced the roadmap of raised lines on his back, scars earned over the years, each with a story to tell. She suppressed a cry of pleasure as he entered her, afraid of waking Ashton.

Every time they gave into their desire for each other, it was like coming home. Maggie arched into Leon's touch and let herself get lost in the moment. As her inhibitions melted away, so did her quiet. Sounds of pleasure hummed in her throat, and they knocked into the side table, spilling tea and shattering Leon's cup on the floor.

Neither of them stopped to clean it up.

Slowly but surely, they made their way to Maggie's bedroom and stayed there for what felt like an eternity, reacquainting themselves with every part of their bodies.

When they were both utterly spent—exhausted and bone tired—Leon stayed. Maggie didn't mind. His presence made her feel safe and content in a way she hadn't for long time. She molded herself into him and closed her eyes.

"I still love you, Maggie," Leon whispered in her ear as she fell asleep in his arms. "I've always loved you."

Chapter 25

31 May

The financial district was a hive of activity the following morning. Workers buzzed through the streets, some yawning and bleary eyed, others alert and eager to start their day. The stock market wouldn't open for an hour yet already brokers marched like soldiers to their stations, yammering on phones or guzzling coffee like it was their lifeblood.

Vogel Enterprises was no less busy than the surrounding businesses. A constant flurry of staff used their passes to unlock the glass doors and disappear into the offices within. The front desk was occupied by two members of security, and Maggie was pleased to discover that neither of them were Johan.

The unfortunate drunk would be hugging a toilet right about now, hating himself for drinking his way to a blackout. Maggie imagined Johan at home, trying to time the call into work between heaves and wretches. Last night would be a blank for him, and any impression Maggie might have left now lost to his alcohol soaked mind. Gone without a trace.

The sun was still in the early stages of its daily commute across the sky, yet it was already hotter than yesterday. Maggie tugged at her blouse collar, her suit jacket removed and hanging over an arm to conceal an electronic device no larger than a cellphone.

"All in position?" she asked, searching the crowd from a bench outside the building.

"Sitting pretty, boss," came Ashton's voice.

Maggie leaned back to see him parked further down the street, waiting for her to give him the go-ahead.

"Ready when you are," said Leon from his place across the street, sitting inside their stuffy surveillance van. While none of them were half as good as the Unit techs, they were still proficient enough to get the job done, and Leon was the strongest hacker among them. Maggie never had the patience for it in training. She preferred breaking through actual doors, rather than finding virtual ways to slip past them.

"Roger that." Maggie scanned the crowd for a target.

She weaved between the rushing workers like a shark with the scent of blood in the water. Timing it perfectly, she walked past a woman with flushed cheeks and knocked into her with a shoulder.

The woman spun around to see who had clipped her and shot Maggie an accusing glare.

"I'm so sorry," Maggie said as she slipped the device into the woman's bag. "I wasn't watching where I was going."

Shaking her head, the woman muttered something in German before trotting off into the building. So far so good.

Maggie returned to the bench, keeping her eyes on the woman as she passed through security and stepped into an elevator. The doors closed and Maggie counted to thirty. "Okay lads, the package is in range."

"Initiating." Leon's voice preceded the clacking of keys.

Maggie hadn't talked with him about last night. When she woke that morning, Leon was already up and ready with a breakfast of local sausage and eggs prepared for the three of them. If Ashton had heard them, he didn't mention it, which Maggie assumed meant he slept through their antics.

They would need to talk, though. She couldn't allow herself another moment of weakness like that. Maggie promised herself she'd step away from him, allow them both to get on with their lives. They had no future together, and the longer they pretended like they did, the more painful the final separation would be.

Memories of his touch came to her as she waited for the device to get up and running. Leon was an anchor amid the crashing waves of her life, holding her steady as her world spiraled out of control. But she couldn't let him get washed away in the tide.

"Device activated," Leon confirmed. Inside Vogel Enterprises, the phone and internet connection systems went haywire.

"I love my phone lines scrambled in the morning," Ashton said.

Maggie brushed away her troubled thoughts and got her head back in the game. She took out her phone and smiled at the screen as it trembled in the frame, rendering the thing useless.

Scrambled indeed.

One of the security guards stationed at the front desk picked up the phone and listened to what should be a series of static noises. Returning the phone, the guard ventured into the belly of the building to investigate.

"Turn the phones back on and then off again," said Maggie after ten minutes had passed, by which time confused and frustrated workers had travelled down to the foyer to make inquiries.

Leon repeated the process a couple more times, thoroughly disrupting the entire building and everyone with an electronic device within a six-block radius.

Everyone but them, of course. Leon had rigged their earpieces to withstand the scrambler's effects, allowing them to be in constant contact throughout their mission.

"Let them call IT in now," Maggie ordered.

Leon complied, and the next time the front desk tried the phones, they were online.

"They're ringing," Maggie warned.

"Rerouting your way, Ash," said Leon.

Ashton put his phone on loudspeaker so it played through their earpieces.

"Guten Morgen, A1 Telekom," he said.

A quick search online had been enough to track the name of Vogel's internet provider. They supplied the whole street. From there, they got the address, and all it took was a little hotwiring, and Maggie had procured a call-out van before A1 Telekom opened for business.

Maggie didn't understand what the security guard was saying, but his tone indicated he was annoyed about something. She made a mental note to learn at least some German in case she found herself back there in the future.

Ashton responded to the man in a placating tone and then hung up. "Told them I'd be right out."

"I'll reactivate the device in case they try to call out again." Leon was always one step ahead.

"Good," said Maggie, "that should keep them distracted." They would need all the distractions they could get if their mission was to succeed.

A1 Telekom held offices ten minutes away, fifteen in

traffic. Ashton waited the allotted time before driving down the street and parking right out front, showing the emblazed logo painted across the side of the van. He whistled as he walked past Maggie, neither of them acknowledging the other.

Kitted in red polo shirt and an A1 Telekom's hat he found in the back of the van, Ashton entered the building and approached the front desk. He spoke for a moment and then one of the security guards led him through a set of doors behind the desk where the mainlines must be located.

"He's in," Maggie said aloud for Leon's benefit.

Ashton made what she assumed was small talk with the guard, and was then left to do his job. The security guard returned to his spot at the desk and spoke with the office workers who waited around for the phones and internet to come back on.

"Talk to me, Ashton," said Maggie.

"I'm looking for the lines to the CCTV. There's bloody wires everywhere, it's like spaghetti junction in here."

"Focus," hissed Leon.

"Aye, awrite big man. Calm down," said Ashton. "There, found it."

Maggie mentally reviewed their plan as Ashton carried it out. Once he located the camera's control center, he had to connect it to a portable router, allowing Leon to access it remotely and hack into the system.

"I'm in," said Leon.

Now that Leon had access to the cameras, he needed to locate each angle that crossed the path from the entrance to the elevator leading up to Vogel's penthouse. Then, he'd make a recording for each camera feed and play it back on loop. The loop would then allow Maggie to enter unnoticed.

"You're up, Maggie," Leon said once the video loop was in place.

Maggie squared her shoulders. She walked straight into the building like she had done so a hundred times before, making sure to walk behind the group of workers clustering between her and the security desk. She used their cover to pause and take in her surroundings. She was twelve paces from the glass doors.

Ashton came out from the room behind the desk and spoke with the guards, distracting them further. Maggie slipped free from the crowd and headed for Vogel.

At the glass doors, Maggie hovered Johan's security pass under the scanner. The doors clicked open, and she walked through undetected. A row of elevators lined one wall, and Maggie pressed the button to summon the nearest. Leon should have already looped the elevator's CCTV footage so she could arrive on Vogel's floor with the element of suprise.

Her unexpected arrival would give Maggie the advantage over Herman's hired muscle. From their observations, he only kept two stationed on his floor, the additional men used only when he had an outing. Maggie clenched a fist as she waited for the elevator. She could take them no problem.

"Hello, stranger," said a voice through her earpiece.

Maggie's heart lurched, and she stopped dead as the elevator doors pinged opened.

It was Nina.

Chapter 26

"Nina."

Ashton was still talking with the guards, their conversation scattering through Maggie's racing thoughts as she tried to concentrate and remain calm.

Nina was there.

Somehow, she'd managed to gain access to their private feed. Which meant she had to be close enough to stay in range of the signal. Maggie scanned her surroundings, throat tight as she took a few steps forward, peering out into the foyer and examining each face. She could be anywhere. Masking as a worker inside the building or a tourist wandering around the street outside.

Or a sniper on the roof.

"Can everyone hear this?" Maggie asked, her entire

body locked with tension. She examined the roofs across the street, checking for hints of metal reflecting through open windows. The glass walls made her a sitting duck, and Nina wouldn't need a second shot.

"Leon's asleep right now," Nina replied.

The blood drained from Maggie's face.

Nina hadn't intercepted their feed. She was talking through Leon's line.

Maggie spun on her heels and abandoned the elevator, all thoughts of Vogel tossed to the side. Leon was in trouble.

"If you've hurt him, I swear—"

"How about instead of swearing, you come show me?" Nina's voice was calm, like this was just another mission.

Maggie was already on her way. Using Johan's pass again, she went through the security doors and strode to the exit, forcing down the impulse to run. She couldn't make a scene. Not if she wanted her friends to get out of this alive.

Ashton and the guards weren't there, but their voices continued in Maggie's ear. He seemed oblivious to Nina's presence, as if his feed was blocked, but Maggie didn't go to him. Alerting Ashton could only put him in more danger.

Outside, Maggie's eyes latched onto the van across the street, and she headed straight towards it. Her heart thumped in her chest, strong beats growing with intensity like the drums of war. The growing fear inside her spiked, and she couldn't wait a second longer. Maggie darted across the street.

Brakes screeched and horns honked as she sped across the road, paying the passing cars no mind. Panic rose with each step, threatening to drown her.

Maggie made straight for the back of the van.

She reached for the handle, but the door swung open and collided into Maggie, smashing her face. The impact knocked her back and Maggie fell to the ground. She snapped her gaze to the side as a car barreled towards her at full-speed, the front wheel on course to run over her head. Maggie ducked as the vehicle whizzed past, missing her by inches and trampling over the ends of her hair.

A figure stepped out of the van.

Nina lunged for Maggie and raised her arm, a flash of light glinting off the silver blade in her hand. Maggie caught Nina's wrist as she plunged the blade towards her heart and made note of the knife's serrated edge. Blades like that did more damage coming out than going in.

The women struggled, each fighting to gain another inch. Maggie held tight to Nina's wrist then tugged her arms down and to the side, the shift in pressure sending Nina sprawling forward.

It wasn't enough to floor her, but it was all Maggie needed. Using the split second's advantage, she bounced to her feet and raised her fists, careful to block her body and vital organs with her arms.

Nina regained her balance, and they squared off with a line of parked cars between them.

A few passersby stopped and pointed at the commotion while others rushed away in the opposite direction.

"I didn't do it, Nina." Maggie sniffed and tasted blood as it ran down the back of her throat.

Nina huffed. "I've seen the footage."

"It wasn't me. I've been set up."

"That's not what the Director thinks. She sent me to kill you, by the way, in case you thought I had any intentions of bringing you in alive. It's too late for that."

Nina stepped to the left and Maggie stepped right, keeping a safe distance from her friend, a woman she had trained with, laughed with, and fought beside for years. Nina might have orders to kill Maggie on sight, but if Maggie could only make her see she wasn't to blame for James Worthington's death, perhaps she could change her mind.

The real killer, through his use of assassins, sat only ten stories above them.

"Bishop knows I didn't do it," Maggie said, playing off Nina's immense respect for their boss.

"Bishop never could see reason when it came to you, his little favorite. But I can." Nina scrunched her face in disgust. "How could you?"

"I know this doesn't look good, but you have to believe me. Please, Nina." She needed more time. If only Nina had come a day later, when she had concrete proof to counter the damning footage of the blond murdering the mayor. She needed Nina to trust her, but would she? Could she? If their roles were reversed, Maggie wasn't sure she'd be willing to listen.

Nina stepped closer, bridging the gap between them. "You might have been able to trick your boyfriend, but you can't fool me."

Maggie stole a quick glance into the van. Leon lay motionless on the floor.

"He's not dead," Nina said. "Though he might be once the Director learns he's been helping you."

Maggie winced at Nina's dark expression, betrayal etched into every inch of her face. Nina believed they'd betrayed her—and the rest of the Unit—which meant there was no getting through to her. Nina made up her mind before she'd ever left London.

"Leave him out of this." Maggie fought the panic rising within her. Her life was one thing, but Leon's... "You're here for me."

"He's a traitor, just like you," Nina spat.

"Nothing has to happen here. We could walk away and pretend we never saw each other."

"That's not going to happen."

"I don't want to hurt you," Maggie warned, but she would if she had to. For Leon. For Ashton.

For herself.

Nina let out a guttural yell, clearly done with words, and charged forward with a swing of her knife.

People on the street shrieked as Maggie leapt back, the tip of the blade barely missing her face. Onlookers pulled phones from their bags and pressed them urgently to their ears.

Maggie couldn't risk the police turning up. Not on Vogel's doorstep, with Leon out cold and Ashton still in the building. If they were going to do this, then it had to be out of the way.

Dodging another attack, Maggie ran down the street.

Nina followed close behind. "Coward!"

Up ahead, Maggie noticed a gap between two buildings and darted down the narrow street between them. Another left and they were in a dank alleyway used for storing industrial-sized trashcans, tucked away behind the surrounding businesses to keep the streets clean.

The pain from her impact with the van door settled over her, and Maggie wiped the blood from her nose, spitting out a mouthful of red. She turned to face Nina as she caught up, her friend not remotely out of breath.

Maggie would be a fool to underestimate Nina. She was a skilled fighter with a vicious streak that made her one of the Unit's most accomplished cleaners. She approached Maggie like a lioness ready to pounce, hungry and predatory.

A gun would have been handy, but thanks to the security at Vogel's, Maggie was unarmed. She would need to stand toe to toe with Nina, something she hadn't done since their training days.

Back then, they were an even match. Maggie had no idea what the odds were now, but like it or not, she was about to discover the answer.

Neither of them spoke, their focus homed in, watching for the slightest twitch that could signal an attack.

Maggie eyed the blade in Nina's capable hands and made it her top priority to keep far away from it. Nina had a thing for knives, and Maggie knew the blade's edge would be laced with poison. Even the smallest nick of the sharp steel would kill. Eventually. It was better to let her end you in one fell swoop.

Not that Maggie had any intentions of that.

"What's going on?" Ashton asked in startled English, his voice loud in Maggie's ear.

The panic in his voice distracted Maggie, and Nina seized the opening, lunging for her. She went low with the knife, aiming for Maggie's thigh.

Maggie pivoted out of the way and thrust her knee into Nina's chin.

Nina's head snapped back, and Maggie pressed forward, connecting a wicked round house with Nina's hand that sent the blade flying out of her grasp.

Maggie winced, hating herself for causing her friend pain, but at this point it was either her or Nina. She went for another blow.

Nina was ready this time, and she caught Maggie in

the gut with a fist that sent the air from her lungs. Winded but still standing, Maggie landed an uppercut on Nina's already sore chin. The skin blossomed red with the promise of a morning bruise.

Maggie sucked in air and gasped as her lungs burned.

"Hello?" came Ashton's voice again. "I don't know how long I can keep this up. They're asking questions."

Shit.

Like a rabid animal, Nina was on Maggie again. She grabbed Maggie's jacket and yanked her back, sending her into the side of the metal trashcan.

Maggie stumbled, swaying on her feet as the echo from her collision bounced off the close walls and reverberated through the alley.

"I never understood why you were Brice's favorite," Nina said as she punched Maggie across the jaw. "Maybe now he'll realize he has others more capable. People who are loyal to him."

"Careful, Nina. It almost sounds like you have a thing for the man." Maggie lashed out with a back fist.

Nina stepped back and fell over a pile of trash bags, the contents clinking upon impact.

Ashton spoke through the earpiece, more pressing this time. "Guys, where are you? I've got company, and they don't look happy."

Maggie wriggled the earpiece. "Ashton, can you hear me?"

Something hard collided against Maggie's skull, and

shards of green glass fell over her head like emerald rain. Nina was up and swinging faster than Maggie had expected, and she spun as Nina aimed the broken bottle for her.

Nina was too fast, and all Maggie could do was try to block her face. She yelped as the jagged splinters of glass pierced her skin and dug deep into her forearm.

"Code red," cried Ashton, his voice screeching in her ear.

Something was wrong.

Another yell escaped Maggie's lips as Nina yanked back the bottle and made to stab her again. Maggie was ready this time and dodged the bottle as the sounds of a scuffle filled her ears.

Nina wasn't playing fair, and Ashton needed her. Maggie swiped Nina's leg from under her and sent her to the graveled floor. She rushed to the piles of trash and searched for something, anything to give her an advantage.

"Get the fuck off me," shouted Ashton over a sound-track of fists against flesh and bone.

A frustrated growl came from behind Maggie as Nina charged for her. Maggie grabbed an item from the trash and counted two whole seconds before she swung, waiting for just the right moment as Nina approached.

The metal pipe swung true and struck the side of Nina's neck with a hard smack.

Nina landed with a thud beside her, unconscious before she even hit the ground.

Maggie dropped the metal pipe and left the alley. "Ashton, hang on. I'm coming."

A voice yelled in pain, one Maggie didn't recognize. Ashton was holding his own.

Then more voices chimed in, footsteps growing louder.

"Fuck," hissed Ashton before all that was left was the sound of trading blows.

"Ashton, come in," said Maggie, fiddling with her earpiece to no avail as she headed back to Vogel Enterprises.

The fighting seemed to have stopped, German voices coming through the feed.

"Ashton, do you copy?"

A moan came through, and Maggie felt like Nina's knife had stabbed her in the heart. She recognized the whimper.

It was the same one she heard when consoling Ashton as a boy, angry at the other kids for not taking him seriously in training. He at least two years their junior and scrawny to boot; puberty hadn't yet paid him a visit.

Maggie surged on, as fast as her feet could carry her, blood tricking down her arm and staining her white blouse a garish red.

From down the street, Maggie saw people exit Vogel Enterprises, carrying someone between them. Ashton. He was limp in their arms, feet dragging behind him as a car pulled up to meet them.

Vogel's guards hauled Ashton into the boot of the car.

Maggie chased after them, ignoring the pain each step caused her, but the car sped off down the street and out of sight before she could reach them, leaving only the smell of burned rubber behind.

"Ashton. Ashton!"

The line went dead.

Chapter 27

Maggie heard the police before she saw them. Their wild sirens grew louder and louder as she stood dumbstruck in the middle of the street, gazing down the road where Vogel's men had taken Ashton.

Tremors jolted up her arm and carried through her body in a circuit board of panic. They had Ashton. Vogel's people had Ashton, and she had no idea where they were taking him.

Her imagination jumped to the worst possibilities, and visions of her friend plagued her mind. Cold, dead eyes staring at her, void of his signature gleam of mischief and effervescent joy for life. And it was all her fault. Whatever happened to Ashton was on her.

Everything was falling apart, and it was all she could do to remain standing. If she moved, she might break. And if she broke, she wouldn't get up. It was too much. Her whole world was crumbling to ash and no matter what she did to fix things, it only got worse.

She was drowning.

Voices whispered around her, laced with a scared yet excited edge to them that dragged her back to reality. People hovered near, necks stretched to get a glimpse of what was happening. None of them approached her, keeping a wary distance until one brave soul stepped forward.

The woman had skin like aged paper, her face covered with more lines than a map of the London underground. She spoke to Maggie, and although she didn't understand the words, the sentiment was clear. *Are you okay?*

Maggie shook her head, biting down hard on her lip. She was not okay. Far from it. She didn't think she'd ever be okay again. Not if anything happened to the ones she loved.

The old woman gave her a sympathetic smile and rubbed her back, her hoarse voice soothing as she said something Maggie assumed was meant to be comforting. She caught the word 'polizei' somewhere in there and didn't need a translator.

Except the police would not help her.

In all likelihood, Interpol already knew about her. A wanted fugitive on the run. Guilty of cold blooded murder and treason. Armed and extremely dangerous.

Maggie smiled at the woman's kindness, though it

came out more like a grimace, and cradled her crimson-stained arm as she crossed the street.

More people clustered around the area as the sirens drew close, only a few streets away now. She had to get out of there.

The pain from Nina's blows settled over her, the gash in her forearm throbbing in time with her erratic heartbeat. The back of her head ached, along with most of the rest of her body, each wound fighting for attention.

A shiver ran through her, and she had to clench her teeth to stop from chittering. Her body was suffering an adrenaline dump, every bit of energy she had left reduced to nothing but bone-weary exhaustion. Her eyelids grew heavy, but she could not succumb to it.

Finally, Maggie reached the van. The door lay ajar, and she peeked around it.

Leon still lay in the back, but he rolled to the side and released a groggy groan, coming back around. Maggie captured a cry of relief before it could escape and forced it down her throat. The urge to check on him and fall into his arms was strong, but she resisted. Leon was alive, but he could have just as easily died at Nina's hands.

A wave of gratitude for Nina filled her, and Maggie almost burst out laughing. The whole mission was botched thanks to Nina's terrible timing.

Maggie allowed herself one final look at Leon before she closed the door. The police would be too busy chasing her to discover him. He'd retreat as soon as he was able, as any good agent should. Just as she was about to do.

Nina wouldn't come back to finish him off. Leon wasn't her current target, and she wouldn't risk exposure to the police. Besides, if she felt half as bad as Maggie did, then she'd take some time to recover before making any second attempts.

And if she did, Maggie wouldn't give her a chance to try a third time. Nina was only doing her job—and Maggie didn't blame her friend for making the wrong conclusion—but if she had to choose between Nina and her own life, she wouldn't hesitate to end things.

Maggie took off up the street as police cars whizzed around the corner, lights flashing and sirens wailing. She continued down the adjacent street, took a left at the next corner, and then maneuvered through a series of connecting alleyways. Her choices were random, doubling back and travelling through cordoned off areas where no vehicles could follow.

She reached the Eisner Steg footbridge and crossed the river Main.

"Maggie, Ashton, do you read me?" Leon's voice crackled in her ear.

Maggie leaned against the railing of the bridge for support.

What had she done? How could she let the people she cared about most get involved? It was stupid of her. Selfish. Dangerous people were out to get her, and she allowed

Leon and Ashton to help. All because she was scared, because she didn't want to do it alone.

Bishop told her she had to learn to work as a team, but he was wrong. She never should have dragged them into her mess. She should have sucked it up and carried on alone.

Losing them in Madrid wouldn't have been hard for her. There were opportunities to break free from them, even if they refused to let her go through it alone. She could have been long gone by now, covering her tracks so they couldn't find her. She could have kept them out of it, kept them safe.

But she didn't. She'd let them in. Relied on them when she should have been strong enough to do it on her own. It wasn't like she was unused to being alone. For years, all she had to rely on was herself. Involving others was a mistake, and now Ashton was paying the price for it.

She couldn't let Leon pay for her mistakes, too. She would get Ashton back, but she would do so alone. Once he was safe, she would leave. Go far, far away where she wouldn't hurt anyone else.

"Guys, come in." Leon's voice was panicked now, desperate.

Maggie took out her earpiece and dropped it into the river below.

Chapter 28

Maggie risked returning to the loft apartment to clean up and gather her belongings. She knew Leon wouldn't come back straight away. His loyalty made him predictable, and he would be out there looking for them, refusing to give up.

If he'd seen Nina before she knocked him out, then he'd try to find her, too. If not, he was in the dark about what happened. Either option worked well for Maggie.

Leon was out cold when Vogel's men abducted Ashton, which meant he had nothing to confirm either of their whereabouts. He was good at tracking people, but not that good. Piecing together what he'd missed would take time, and Maggie intended to be long gone before Leon figured it out.

After a quick shower to wash away the blood, Maggie gathered a needle and thread and began the slow but necessary process of patching herself up. Thankfully, the bottle to the head hadn't broken the skin, so she could focus on her forearm. Maggie hissed with each stitch, willing the painkillers she guzzled down to take effect.

Yet the pain also served a purpose. If she stayed focused on her mission, the pain could bury all her other emotions. It could keep her from crumbling or curling up in a ball of despair. Ashton needed her, and she would not fail him. Not this time.

Aliases made it even easier to shut down her emotions and focus on the task at hand, but she wouldn't use one for this mission. This time it was personal, and Maggie wanted Vogel to know the real her when they came face to face. She wanted to see the look in his eyes, to capture the moment when he realized he'd messed up and fucked with the wrong woman.

Framing her was his first mistake, but taking Ashton would be his last. She'd stop at nothing to get him back. Payback was a bitch, and hell hath no fury like a pissed off Maggie.

She balled her fist, making sure her injuries hadn't damaged any nerves. The movements sent sharp shooting pains up her arm, but it didn't matter. She focused on the pain, channeling it. Her injuries would feel like a spa day compared to what she'd do to anyone who dared lay a finger on Ashton.

Vogel's men were probably questioning Ashton right now. They'd have him tied up somewhere no one could hear him scream. They'd threaten him at first, promising to kick the shit out of him like they had back at Vogel Enterprises.

From the sounds she'd heard through the earpieces, it had taken more than a few men to take him down. Now that they had him, they'd assure him things would only get worse if he didn't talk.

Maggie grinned as she shoved on fresh clothes, lacing her steel toe boots up tight and concealing a knife at her ankle.

Ashton would talk alright. He'd hit them with a slew of colorful and inventive slurs, using every fowl and offensive word he knew in their language. Oh yes, he'd talk, but he wouldn't give them what they wanted.

Then would come the torture.

Vogel would want answers before they killed him. The who, what, where, when, and why of it all. And given the previous assassin in his employ, she knew Vogel wouldn't hesitate to take Ashton out.

Ashton was fluent enough to pass for German. He'd play the part, and take whatever they threw at him. While he wasn't cut out for the Unit, Ashton was one tough bastard.

Back in training, he lasted longer than any other student against their teacher's skilled interrogation techniques. Waterboarding, electric shocks, whatever they did to him, he took with a laugh. Bishop declared him one of the craziest recruits he'd ever met, which should have been a clue as to how difficult Ashton would be to control. Rules were meant to be broken, in Ashton's opinion. Why make rules up in the first place unless they expected people to break them.

Ashton wouldn't bend, but she knew what happened to things that didn't bend.

Maggie only hoped he could hold on until she reached him.

Grabbing Ashton's laptop, Maggie brought up everything they already had on Vogel Enterprises. As a large multinational corporation, they had property and offices all over the world, but they only had two locations in Frankfurt registered in their name.

In addition to his headquarters, Vogel had a large warehouse positioned just outside the city in an industrial estate. It was close enough to take Ashton there fast, yet out of the way enough to avoid attention. Herman struck Maggie as the kind of man who liked to oversee everything, his penthouse location a clear indication of his need for dominance. He'd want to control everything he could, including the location.

Maggie bet all she had that Ashton was inside that warehouse. Her gut told her Vogel would be there, too; he wouldn't trust his staff to carry out the job without his supervision. She hoped he didn't mind unexpected guests, because she was about to pay him a visit.

Maggie closed the laptop and gathered what she

needed. She was going to rescue Ashton, and she'd tear apart Vogel's whole bloody building to do it.

Barbed wire crowned the iron fence surrounding the warehouse.

It was a large, two story building, square and dull gray to match the rest of the bland terrain. Fields of dead grass circled the building, the nearest neighbor five hundred yards away and facing the opposite direction.

Vogel owned the most secluded warehouses in the industrial area, most of the others huddling together in rows which imitated a small town. Vogel wasn't the type to associate with the townsfolk. In his world, he was king.

A few cars were parked near the front entrance, but most of the spaces in the lot lay abandoned. Vogel had emptied the warehouse. His workers would have left without question, all too eager to head home early or too scared of Vogel to say anything.

Amid the scattering of cars was the vehicle that had carried Ashton away from Vogel Enterprises. Maggie let out a small sigh of relief. She'd guessed right. Ashton was inside.

Maggie spent the next hour staking out the area, gathering as much intel as she could. While a part of her wanted to charge in with guns blazing, her logical side held her back. She was alone, outnumbered, and didn't know the situation inside.

Breaking in effectively required strategizing.

The element of surprise was her best shot. Vogel and his crew may have guessed Ashton wasn't working alone and planned for other unwanted arrivals. They likely had heavily armed guards stationed inside. Maggie had already counted three men walking the perimeter, each carrying semi-automatics. Like Vogel's personal guards, their demeanor suggested ex-military.

For a supposed legitimate businessman, Herman had a lot of muscle, and it occurred to Maggie that she was not the first enemy he'd made.

Counting how long it took each of the guards to complete their rounds of the perimeter, Maggie had a four-minute window of opportunity. Three to be safe.

It was tight, but not out of the realm of possibility. She just needed to work fast and efficient.

The canisters would slow her down, but they were vital to her plan. Driving up to the entrance was out of the question as it would draw attention, so she set off on foot, the muscles in her wounded forearm roaring as she carried the heavy load.

Slipping in through the gate, Maggie darted in a zig-zag path up the hill, avoiding the paved road and sticking to the grass. If the security cameras caught her, she'd be done before she even started.

Taking full advantage of noted blank spots, Maggie

dodged the cameras and reached the left side of the warehouse. She checked her watch and cursed the time. The non-direct route had taken longer than she anticipated, thanks to her injury. A guard should be turning the corner any moment now.

Maggie dropped the canisters and coils of rope slung over her shoulder and pressed herself against the wall. The rough brick snagged at her hoodie as she inched along to the edge. Maggie checked her watch again and counted down the remaining twenty seconds.

Footsteps echoed from around the corner, coming her way. Her fingers brushed over the gun at her waist, but it was no use to her now. One bullet and Herman's whole squad would be on her in seconds.

Instead, she leaned her weight on her back leg and stayed on her toes, ready to pounce.

Just as the unsuspecting guard turned the corner, Maggie jumped him.

She was fast, and had her arms wrapped around his neck in a choke hold before the man even thought to reach for his weapon. He fought her, writhing in her grasp, his neck thick and arms thicker.

Maggie hopped on his back and held her prey in a vice grip, making sure to press down hard on his trachea to stop him from yelling out and alerting the others.

It didn't take long for him to lose consciousness. The exertion from all his thrashing expended his oxygen supply with an efficiency Maggie appreciated. He collapsed, and Maggie broke his fall as best she could to prevent an unceremonious thump to the ground.

She couldn't leave him there, though. The other guards would find him and be on her before she got inside. So Maggie dragged him back the way she came, acutely aware of how much time it cost her. She dropped the guard at the top of the incline and watched him roll down to the front gates. He'd probably lose his job, if he was lucky.

With the man out of the way, Maggie collected her tools and continued to the building's rear loading bay. There were crates of wooden frames and bricks piled high along one wall with forklifts parked beside them to carry the heavy cargo into the backs of delivery trucks.

Maggie rubbed at her forearm. She could have used one of the forklifts for the big lump of a guard.

Bags of cement and sand were stacked in piles on the opposite end of the bay, along with fixtures, fittings, and other miscellaneous construction equipment used for Vogel's developments.

She uncapped the first canister and let the gasoline tip free, making the most of the wood and other flammable inventory, allowing the liquid to seep in. A quick run around the bay emptied the first canister, and Maggie tipped the second out behind her as she travelled out from the bay and around the perimeter to the parking lot.

The fumes burned at Maggie's nostril and irritated her

eyes as it snaked over the ground and dry grass in thick line behind her.

When she reached the parked cars, Maggie unscrewed the caps on the sides of each vehicle and stuck in the lengths of rope, drenching them in the gasoline before shoving each one down into the fuel tanks.

She was on the last car when hands grabbed her from behind.

Chapter 29

Fingers dug into Maggie's shoulders and forced her to turn.

She grasped her gun as she moved and shoved it in the face of her attacker, finger on the trigger.

"Leon?"

"Maggie." Leon's jaw twitched the way it always did when he was angry, gritting his teeth.

Maggie dropped her gun. "What are you doing here?"

A lump protruded from the side of his head, a trickle of dry blood carving a crimson line down to his neck. "Looking for you," he growled, so close to her their noses almost touched.

"How did you–"

"I followed Vogel from his offices," Leon snapped. "He's been in there for almost two hours."

Maggie stepped away from him, his anger scalding. She'd been right about Vogel. "He has Ashton."

"I thought he had you both," Leon hissed.

Maggie avoided his gaze, unable to meet those disappointed eyes. He was angry, yes, but she could tell she'd hurt him more than anything else. It seemed like all she ever did was hurt him.

"What the hell happened?" he asked, checking around the corner for oncoming guards.

Maggie gave him the run down, keeping it short. The clock was ticking.

Nina's presence was news to Leon, but he wasn't shocked. They knew the rest of the Unit was after her. It was only a matter of time before one of them showed up. They'd been lucky to avoid them until that point.

"And what? You decided to leave without so much as a note to say you were alive?" Leon's voice was thick with hurt. "God, Maggie, I thought the worst."

"I was trying to protect you," she explained. Not that it worked. Leon had shown up anyway, and she knew there was nothing she could do or say to get him to leave. There was no way he'd let her out his sight now.

Leon's laugh was hollow. "Oh, is that what it was? Because it looks a lot like running off on your own to me."

Maggie hushed him, not wanting to talk about it. Especially not right now.

"When will you learn to trust people?" said Leon. "To trust me?"

Maggie's heart panged under his reproach. He didn't understand. If anything happened to him, it would kill her. It took all she had to keep it together knowing Ashton was somewhere beyond those walls in pain. "It's not that. I do trust you, but—"

"Save it, Maggie. I don't want to hear any of your lies." An awkward silence filled the space between them until Leon continued. "Our boy's in there?"

She nodded.

"There's too many of them to stand toe to toe. What's the plan?"

Maggie fell into work mode. It wasn't the time or place to argue, and they both knew it. Leon could yell at her once Ashton was safe. She rummaged in her pocket and shook the box of matches. "To light a fire under their arses."

Leon nodded. "Burn them out. Create a distraction."

"Any idea where they're keeping him?" asked Maggie, as a guard rounded the corner and almost bumped into them.

Leon was on him in a heartbeat. He hit the guard in the neck with the edge of his palm, stopping the man's cry before it left his mouth. The man pointed his gun, but Leon grabbed it from him with deft hands, taking it for his own and pistol-whipping the man across the face. He crumbled to the ground, and they stepped over him.

"Vogel went through the front doors," Leon said,

checking the magazine to count how many rounds he had. "My guess is he's somewhere in the north end of the building."

"Okay, so we head there." Maggie turned to the loading bay. "Ready?"

"Light it up."

Maggie struck the match along the coarse side of the box and fire sparked into being. She flicked the match and it landed at the beginning of her trail. Fire met gasoline and ignited in a rush of flame. Heat tickled her skin as the fire travelled through her deliberate course, consuming the fuel as it went. It reached the first crate of wooden panels, and they burst into flames, the intensity of the heat licking at Maggie's face.

They stepped back as the loading bay lit up like Guy Fawkes night, the bonfire consuming everything it touched. Maggie winced at the stench of the black smoke, tinged with the chemical scent of burning plastic.

The fire danced around the bay and circled back to them, whizzing past and heading around the corner to the parking lot, spurred on by the boundless supply of oxygen.

Maggie and Leon moved as one, running in the opposite direction and ducking as they passed by rows of windows.

A massive explosion sounded from the other side of the warehouse as the first of the parked cars detonated like a bomb. A second blast followed, louder this time, and was accompanied by a fire alarm that screeched like a banshee throughout the entire building.

Sometimes the best way to break into a place was to make everyone inside break out.

People were running out the front doors by the time Maggie peered around the corner to catch a look. The parking lot resembled the pits of hell, the fire now a blazing inferno that showed no signs of calming down.

One of the men, who was either as bright as a blackout or extremely optimistic, carried an office-sized extinguisher with him as he ran toward the flames.

Thick, black smoke emanated from back at the loading bay, heading skywards like a menacing phantom. Leon pointed to the row of windows they'd ducked past further down the warehouse. The windows glowered at them with emblazed eyes as the fire spread through the building's internal organs.

With the alarm ringing and most of the people preoccupied with the pandemonium unfolding, Maggie smashed an elbow into a fire exit door and let herself and Leon in.

From the looks of it, the front of the building was used as office space. Voices called through the corridors amid the chaos, the air filled with a light haze of smoke as the fire approached. One of the guards ran straight past them, too interested in saving his own skin to make sure they weren't intruders.

Maggie and Leon kicked open every door they passed, but the rooms were empty. They turned right and found themselves looking into a huge workroom, framed by a large window. Half-constructed wooden frames lay abandoned next to sheets of corrugated metal, welding masks left on unmanned benches.

Someone unseen was yelling, bellowing orders neither Maggie or Leon understood.

Without a word, they slipped through the adjoining door and into the workroom. The fire was close. Smoke filled the area in an opaque fog that clawed at the back of Maggie's throat.

She stifled a cough as Leon handed her a dirty rag from one of the benches, covering his mouth with his own and tying it to the back of his head. Maggie followed suit, the cloth keeping out some of the smoke so she could breathe better.

A figure approached through the smoke, and the woman yelled for backup when she spotted them.

"Shit." Maggie raised her gun as four more guards ran into view. With the element of surprise lost, there was no need for stealth. She fired her gun and sent a bullet through the shin of the nearest enemy. She grabbed him before he collapsed and used him as a shield as she shot the next guard twice: once in the shoulder and once in the thigh.

The others were faster than their fallen comrades.

Maggie felt the impact of three shots as they buried into the chest of her human shield. She dropped the now dead weight and dived for cover.

Leon kneeled behind a row of metal panels across the room, bullets ricocheting off them as he risked an opening. His shot missed, and the woman who discovered them leaped on top of the panels and dove toward Leon, firing mid-air.

Leon rolled on the ground, fragments of the concrete floor bursting around him as he narrowly dodged the bullet. He turned and fired, landing a kill shot between the woman's eyes, and she collapsed on top of him.

Maggie sprung up from her spot behind a bench and used her remaining rounds against the final two guards, but she missed as they retreated into the smoke.

Behind her, Leon groaned as he shoved off the dead guard. Maggie helped him to his feet.

Tossing her empty gun, Maggie picked up a metal pipe from one of the benches. The weight was nice and heavy in her grip.

She motioned for Leon to stay at one end of the room while she crept along the other, following the guards into the smoke. Coming in from both ends would split their attention, giving her and Leon the advantage.

Creeping forward, Maggie pricked her ears for signs of movement. The smoke grew thicker by the second, the air toxic and alarmingly hot.

A creak sounded somewhere in front of her, and Maggie strode forward ready to attack.

She stopped when she saw the two guards had multiplied to four, each of them pointing guns at her and Leon as Herman Vogel watched from behind.

So much for an advantage.

Chapter 30

Maggie counted six paces between her and the surrounding guards, which was too far away to get a good swing at them with her pipe, but not far enough to avoid a headshot from one of their guns.

Leon aimed his gun at Vogel, using the only leverage they had against the guards outnumbering them. Alongside the initial two, were the man and woman they'd spotted on Vogel's personal detail. Close up, Maggie noted their toned physiques and hard faces. She knew killers when she saw them.

"Hello, Herman," said Maggie. "Nice to finally meet you."

Herman Vogel sneered behind his wall of armed muscle. "I can't say the same, Ms. Black. You were supposed to be dead by now."

"Sorry to disappoint you."

"No matter," said Vogel. Crow's feet appeared at his eyes. "We can fix that."

Vogel snapped his fingers and left them, vanishing in the smoke. The woman went with him, leaving her partner behind with the other two. Eyes trained on Maggie, the man in question puckered his lips and sent her a kiss.

"That one's mine," said Maggie, pointing with her metal pipe.

Leon nodded, and they positioned themselves back to back as their opponents circled closer like a pack of wolves.

"Now boys, why don't you put your guns down and fight like real men?" Maggie asked, inching nearer.

Before they could answer, Maggie lunged forward and swung her pipe, connecting with the nearest guard's nose with a sickening crunch. The man screamed and held his face with his hands as if he feared it might fall off, his reaction leading her to assume she had broken more than just his nose.

A shot rang through the room, and Maggie spun to check on Leon. He was locked in a brawl with the guard nearest him, fighting over a gun, his own discarded on the floor.

Maggie started towards him to help, but the smooching guard stepped between them.

"No weapons," said the sleaze with a heavy accent, tucking his gun behind his back.

Maggie arched an eyebrow. She tossed the pipe, and it clanged on the ground as she raised her fists.

The ex-military man's eyes lit with the stare of the dishonorably discharged.

He made the first move, as Maggie predicted, feigning with a jab at first before aiming a kick to her solar plexus. She dodged the attack and clipped him in the ear with a right hook.

His smile grew wider, seeming shocked at her speed. He straightened and rolled his shoulders before leaning into a mock karate stance and motioning with his hand for her to come get him.

Maggie didn't react to his taunts. She knew she'd get the last laugh.

Leon and his opponent were trading blows now, but she couldn't focus on them. Smoocher may be underestimating her, but she knew he was no joke. One wrong move and he could end her.

The guard jabbed toward her face, and Maggie threw her arm up to block it. The impact made her bones rattle at the sheer power behind the blow.

Sweat beaded on her forehead as her lungs struggled against the rising smoke.

The guard struck again before she could recover, the back of his hand meeting her face and sending her to the floor. The cooper tang of blood filled her mouth, and she spat it out, seeing red.

Maggie stumbled to her feet as the man bellowed a laugh. He kicked her in the stomach and sent her reeling back, gasping for air. Her chest tightened as she struggled to breathe, the oxygen gobbled up by the approaching fire.

A second kick to her head didn't register until she was flat on the floor, ears ringing in alarm.

His shadow approached as he knelt and leaned over her. "I'll take that kiss now."

"You'll have to settle for a Glasgow kiss." Maggie grabbed his collar and yanked him towards her, meeting him halfway with a head-butt, just like Ashton had taught her years back.

His head whipped back, and he collapsed over her in a daze. Maggie flipped on top of him and pummeled his face until her knuckles were stained with a dripping red.

Leon handed her a gun when she got up, his opponent much like her own, and they continued their search.

A spurt of coughing came from beyond the smoke, and Maggie sped up as she realized who it was. "Ashton!"

Ashton spluttered as he fought for air, the heat almost unbearable now. Maggie turned a corner and laid eyes on her friend. Vogel had him strung up on the hook of a crane, his wrists bound with rope and left to bear the weight of his bruised and battered body as it hung limp in the air.

"Help me get him down," called Maggie.

Leon jumped into the cart of the portable crane and pulled down a lever. The crane lowered and Maggie wrapped her arms around Ashton, freeing him from the hook and untying the rope cutting into his wrists.

Ashton tried to stand, but he couldn't hold himself up. Maggie lowered him to the floor. "Ashton? Can you hear me?"

"Mags?" he asked, blinking. One of his eyes was too swollen to open.

"I'm here," she said, scanning him for anything worse than a beating. "You're safe."

"I never told them a thing," he murmured, his bare chest slick with sweat and scattered with cuts and bruises. They'd really done a number on him.

"Of course you didn't," Maggie said, unsure if her stinging eyes were from tears or sweat dripping down her face.

"He needs a doctor," she said when Leon returned. Her meaning was clear: *Leon* was to take him to the hospital. She still had work to do.

"I'm not leaving you here."

"His injuries can't wait."

Leon looked down at his old friend. Ashton was in bad shape, and he knew it. "Fine, I'll go," he said, "but come with us. We'll get Vogel another way."

"No." Maggie glanced at Ashton's bloody face. "This ends now." A rage bubbled inside her at the sight of her dear friend, bruised and broken at Vogel's hand. She had a score to settle.

Leon's shoulders dropped, and he sighed in resignation. He leaned down and took Ashton from her, hoisting him up in his strong arms.

"Go, before this place comes down," Maggie warned as the building whined in pain. It wouldn't hold much longer.

Leon stepped towards her, Ashton still in his arms, and kissed her. Maggie allowed herself a moment of reprieve, kissing him back with an almost desperate need. Leon broke free and touched his forehead with her own. "Kick his arse."

"I will," she said, back in full rage mode, knuckles cracking as she balled her fists.

"We'll be at the hospital in Nordend-West," said Leon. "Come as soon as you finish here."

Maggie turned to go, but Leon pulled her back.

"Promise me, Maggie."

"I promise.," Maggie lied. "Now go."

Leon left, disappeared through the smoke like a ghost in the night.

Alone, Maggie took stock, stretching her limbs to test for injury. Her body was sore from the blows she'd taken, but nothing felt broken. She rolled up the sleeve of her hoodie to find her forearm bleeding; the stitches had burst during the fight.

It was less than ideal, but she'd been in worse shape before. Part of being a good fighter was the ability to take a good hit as well as deal them out. All she had to do was make it through one last showdown. Then she could take that vacation everyone kept telling her she needed.

Collecting Leon's gun from the floor, Maggie went in search of Vogel.

It was time to end this, once and for all.

Chapter 31

Maggie rushed through the smoke, following the path Vogel took with his remaining personal bodyguard. The fire had breached the workroom now, and Maggie stepped over the men who'd tried to kill her. From the trail of blood smeared on the floor, one of them had dragged themselves out.

The smoke was just as thick outside the workroom. Behind her, a crash echoed through the exit as part of the roof caved in and collapsed. The window overlooking the workroom looked like a framed painting of a furnace, the flames wild and consuming all they touched, leaving behind only broad strokes of enraged red, blood orange, and deathly black.

Swearing came from straight ahead, and Maggie hurried onward. The fire had slipped past the workroom, traveling down the row of offices that ran along the left-hand side and creeping toward the front of the building.

Above, the squared ceiling tiles welcomed the fire like an old lover. Maggie darted through the corridor, dodging debris as it toppled in burning piles on the carpet.

She made it to the entrance, following the panicked voice. Vogel stood, waving animated hands at the front doors. The ceiling had fallen through and blocked the way out, trapping them in the building to meet the wrath of the smothering flames.

Maggie struggled amid the clawing smoke, her lungs working overtime. She couldn't stay there much longer. The fire was too wild and unpredictable.

"We need to talk," called Maggie, gun at the ready. She glanced left down the fire exit Leon likely used as his escape. Thankfully, the fire hadn't spread down that hallway. Yet.

She wasn't the only one who noticed the path. Vogel's bodyguard looked between Maggie and her only way out.

"You don't have to die here," Maggie said. "I only want him."

The woman spat on the ground. "I'm going to make you squeal like a little pig. Just as I did with your fr—"

She never finished her sentence. Instead, the woman crumpled to the ground, grasping the hole Maggie had shot into her chest. Vogel's eyes bulged as the last of his hired muscle fell.

Maggie stepped towards him, and he pulled out a gun

of his own, aiming it at her with tremoring hands. "Don't come any closer," he ordered, unable to go anywhere other than into the pile of burning debris blocking the entrance.

"You've got some explaining to do."

Vogel spat. "Hündin."

"Watch it," snapped Maggie. "I promise, my bite is far worse than my bark."

Vogel did the smart thing and shut his mouth, his eyes filled with venom.

"Why did you do it?" Maggie asked. "Why did you set me up?"

"You were in the way."

"Of what?"

Vogel tutted at her, arrogant despite the fear that quaked through him. "Haven't you figured it out?"

The building whined above them, but Maggie stood her ground. "I suggest you tell me, and quick, because we're not leaving until you do."

"You have no idea who you're dealing with." Something about Vogel's tone surprised Maggie, like he wasn't referring to himself.

Maggie frowned, and Vogel laughed at her.

"Ah, you thought I was the only player in this game."

"The Handler?"

"Silly girl. No, he was working for me. I needed a job done, and he carried out the contract. Though he was nice enough to tell me you paid him a visit. It gave me time to prepare for your arrival."

Maggie's grip tightened around her weapon. "That was stupid of him."

"Making an enemy of the Handler wasn't the smartest move you've made. Even I wouldn't want to be on his bad side. He's a nasty piece of work."

"As am I."

"Yes," rasped Vogel, coughing as smoke filled his lungs. "He told me what you did to his favorite asset."

"An asset you paid to distract me from protecting the mayor. Did you have him kill James Worthington, too?"

Maggie pictured the man's dead face, his vacant eyes looking up at her. Thought about his young children and the devastated wife he left behind.

"Like you, he got in the way. I needed you both removed."

Vogel said it like he simply had them escorted from a building. While the German stared at her now with distain, the reasoning behind his actions weren't motivated by vengeance. It wasn't personal.

"We got in the way of *what*, exactly?" she asked, her mind fogged from the mounting smoke. "What's behind all this? Who else is involved?"

"So many questions, yet you seem to have few answers."

Maggie fired her gun and sent a bullet whipping past Vogel's ear. "If you want out of here, you better explain. And fast."

The building was volatile now, the structure ready to

collapse and let the fire demolish it. They could both see it. Vogel yanked at his tie and unbuttoned the top of his shirt, sweat dripping down his face. His arrogance seemed to dissipate under the intense heat, the need to make it out alive becoming more important than keeping up a bravado. He wilted and lowered his gun.

"It's all business," he said. "Nothing personal."

Maggie almost laughed. "Forgive me, but I take being framed for murder very personally."

Vogel shook his head, and Maggie could have sworn she caught the slightest hint of sympathy in his eyes. "You never should have involved yourself with that reporter."

"Reporter?" Maggie's mind flashed back to a yacht and the snap of a neck. "Adam Richmond?"

But Vogel never got to answer.

Just as he opened his mouth, a rumble sounded from above. A split-second later, the ceiling crashed down in a pile of blistering ember and ash, burying him in blazing rubble.

He never even had time to scream.

The mound crackled and hissed as it grew into a pyre, sparking as it devoured Herman Vogel. Maggie escaped the building before it caved in on her, too, trying to process Vogel's final words.

Her situation ran deeper than she thought, and one thing was abundantly clear.

It wasn't over.

Chapter 32

Maggie wandered back to the city center in a daze and weaved through the streets to her destination. The Bürgerhospital was situated in the Nordend-West area like Leon had said, its yellow walls and arched windows giving the false impression of a happy, welcoming place.

She loitered out front, dreading what she might find inside.

Onion domes adorned the roof above her, reminding Maggie of Saint Basil's Cathedral in Moscow. Reminding her of the Handler.

Viktor Fedorov had warned Vogel about her. Even if Nina hadn't shown up, Maggie's plan to break into Herman's penthouse would have failed. He was expecting her.

Using Fedorov's family as leverage was a fast and

effective way to find Vogel, but it also pushed him over the edge. She should have seen it in him, heard it in his threats. By warning Vogel, Fedorov could get the personal revenge he craved and the damage control his business needed.

Not that it worked.

Fedorov would regret his decision one day—Maggie would make sure of that—but right then, she was too busy regretting her own decisions to worry about him any further.

Maggie entered through the sliding front doors and winced at the familiar hospital scent. It didn't matter where you went, hospitals all had the same sterile sting of antiseptic that failed to mask the presence of sickness and death.

She passed the front desk and glanced into the little shop beyond, lined with helpless visitors who could do little more than buy flowers and magazines for their bedridden loved ones. A pile of newspapers sat on the counter, leading her thoughts to Vogel's last words.

The reporter.

It didn't add up. How did Adam Richmond tie into the assassination of the mayor? And why did Vogel and his as-yet unknown partner choose to frame Maggie for the murder?

Maggie replayed everything she knew about her last successful assignment before her world fell to pieces. Richmond had been selling classified information to the highest bidder in the black market. At least, he was going to before Maggie stopped him.

Did Richmond's information include Vogel? Did he have information about the businessman that Vogel didn't want his rivals to know about? If so, it made sense why Vogel would frame her. If he thought she was privy to the information, he couldn't let her walk free. But she didn't know anything. Adam Richmond hadn't stored his secrets on his laptop.

And even if all that were true, where did the Mayor of London come in? Was he involved with Adam Richmond? Was he planning to buy the information about Vogel? Maggie shook her head. James Worthington had seemed like the rare politician who cared more for his constituents than his own pockets. Then again, most people weren't what they seemed. James wouldn't have been the first bent politician in history.

Maggie had cleaned up for more than one elected official since becoming an agent, their fuck ups resulting in very real dangers to public relations and national security. Not to mention threatening the already strained relationships with other countries.

Yes, politicians were far from angels. Could James have fallen with them? Taken advantage of his position of power?

It was possible.

Maggie's gut told her James had been a good man, one of the few who strived to do good for the people he represented and wanted to make a real difference in the world. He was the exception to the rule.

Did that exception put him in the line of fire? Vogel said he needed to get rid of them both, that she and James had gotten in the way. But in the way of what?

There was a piece to this puzzle she didn't have, something that linked it all together. And now her only lead was dead.

Maggie reached the accident and emergency wing and asked the front desk about a British man. Leon wouldn't have used Ashton's real name, but she doubted many other Brits would have run through the doors seeking medical attention in the last couple of hours.

After a few stilted exchanges, in which Maggie again made the mental note to learn some German, she was directed to a ward on the floor above.

Doctors and nurses strode past her, overworked and understaffed like most hospitals. A row of them queued at a vending machine which dispensed coffee into little polystyrene cups, the stream of dark liquid looking more like dirty dish water than anything else.

The ward was large, and Maggie popped her head into a bunch of rooms, six beds a piece in most. She stopped before the fourth room and peeked around the window looking in.

Maggie suppressed a cry and covered her mouth.

Ashton lay in the bed against the far wall, beneath a large arched window that someone had opened to allow fresh summer air into the stuffy ward. Even from where she stood, Maggie could see the stark contrast between his pale, fevered skin and the ghastly purple of his puffed eye.

A dark part of her was glad Vogel and his guards were dead. The part of her she went to great effort to ignore, yet couldn't deny. They deserved far worse than their fates for what they did to Ashton.

Brushing the thoughts aside, Maggie watched the two men she cared for most in the world, taking them in one last time. Leon—not without his own, lesser wounds—sat by Ashton's bedside. His hand covered Ashton's with a gentleness no one would expect from a big hard man like him.

Leon's lips moved. Ashton laughed, before falling into a coughing fit. He sat up on his bed, face wincing with pain as he reached for his ribs under the sheets.

When he stopped coughing, Leon lowered Ashton back down on the bed and made sure his pillow was positioned just right. Ashton patted Leon on the shoulder and closed his unwounded eye.

Maggie caught a tear before it fell. Despite everything, one good thing had come from this nightmare. It made her feel a little less guilty about her decision, knowing Leon and Ashton had reconciled. That their friendship had finally been repaired.

It was too bad her last memories of them had to be tarnished, both battered and bruised. Though their fates could have been worse. So much worse. Which was exactly why she had to do it.

There was no other way out. Not without risking more people. Causing more damage.

It was safer for all of them.

Leon would think she lied to him about coming to the hospital, but she'd followed through on that promise at least, even if he would never know.

Maggie wished and wanted for so many things—to see her friends healed and happy and well. To tell Leon all the secrets in her heart. But she was out of time. Nina would have contacted the Unit by now, detailing her run in and ultimate failure to take Maggie out.

In her report, Nina would have mentioned Leon's involvement, his betrayal of orders by helping Maggie, and his direct defiance of the Unit. As far as the Unit was concerned, Leon would be just as much a traitor as Maggie.

Ashton, too, if Nina had learned enough about Maggie's little team before she went in for the kill. While already on the Unit's shitlist, Ashton was never a major concern for them. His exploits involved conning and robbing criminals. If anything, his self-serving actions helped the Unit, depleting the finances and resources of known offenders, causing rifts between allies and pitting them against each other. Not to mention keeping them preoccupied and off the streets while it all happened.

That would all change now. The Unit had always

considered Ashton a liability, but he had never given them cause to permanently remove him. Until now. Now he was a threat, and it was all because of Maggie.

But she wouldn't let them suffer for her mistakes. Not anymore.

Vogel was gone, along with any information he had about the mayor's assassination and her role in it all. With no more leads, she had nowhere to turn. No more tricks to try or tactics to implement. She was done digging her own grave. And she sure as hell wasn't going to keep digging graves for her friends.

The Unit wanted Maggie. And maybe, just maybe, she could trick her colleagues into giving chase and leaving her friends behind, untouched. She'd lead the Unit halfway across the world before Leon and Ashton even realized she was gone. While handing herself over to certain death wasn't an option, she couldn't continue fighting a losing game.

Going underground, vanishing from everyone's radar, was one thing she knew she could do. She could leave her old life and walk into the distance, never to be seen again. Become someone new. Someone from far away and live a quiet, normal life. Someone whose past would never come back to haunt her because she didn't have one.

Maggie could do it. It was her specialty, after all.

Of course, it would mean being constantly on the move for a while, changing appearance just as much as she changed her location, never staying in one place for too long, or too little. It would take a while before they gave up searching for her. Maybe they never would.

But eventually, she could settle down as a new person. She could be anyone.

Anyone but her true self.

It was a small price to pay to ensure the safety of those she loved. She just had to make sure they wouldn't be condemned for helping her. It wouldn't be easy, but there was one person who could make it happen. A man she trusted just as much as Leon and Ashton. The only other person who believed in her innocence.

Time to call in one last favor.

Maggie tore her eyes from her friends and turned to leave, but a nurse was standing next to her. She hadn't even noticed the woman, her keen senses dulled as she'd said her silent goodbyes.

"Sorry, I don't understand," Maggie said when the nurse spoke to her in German, a short little woman who was quickly approaching retirement.

"You're hurt," said the nurse in perfect English.

Maggie caught sight of her reflection in the window. Her pulled back hair was ratty and covered in dirt, her face much the same thanks to smudges of soot from the fire. The bleeding had stopped from her forearm on the way to the hospital, but it throbbed with a pulsing pain, constant and strong like her heartbeat.

She looked like she had been dragged through hell.

Smelled like it too, thanks to the stench of smoke that clung to her like a cheap perfume.

"I'm fine." Maggie shrugged it off and pointing a thumb into the ward. "I'm here to check on a friend."

"Oh, him. Nice boy." The nurse smiled before her wizened face grew harsh. "I hope they catch the ones who mugged him."

"Will he be okay?" Maggie asked.

"He'll be fine. Broken ribs, dislocated shoulder. Cuts and bruises. All will heal with time and rest." The nurse gave a pointed look to Maggie's arm, the blood stains visible despite the black material. "You'll need to have that seen to."

"I can't," said Maggie. "I have to go."

"Come with me," ordered the nurse, taking her in by the hand in a grip firmer than her frail arms suggested.

"Really, I don't have time."

"I'll be quick," she said. "You're not the first person to come here afraid of registering your name. But that doesn't mean you don't deserve help."

The nurse led Maggie into an empty room and closed the door, ushering her to take a seat on the table.

"I'm Jana, by the way," she said, helping Maggie peel off her hoody before examining the damage.

"Maggie," she replied, unsure why she decided to go with the truth. Then again, it wasn't like it mattered. She'd be long gone soon enough.

Jana nodded like she didn't believe her and got to

work. She cleaned the wound with a swab dipped in stinging alcohol and began stitching. Her hands were skilled and efficient, and she finished much faster than Maggie had in her own attempt.

"All done." Nurse Jana returned her tools to a drawer. She rummaged in a second one and handed Maggie two bottles that rattled when she took them. "Take three of these antibiotics each day for the next week to avoid infection. The other ones are for the pain."

"Thank you, Jana," said Maggie.

"You're very welcome."

"Is there a phone I could use?" Maggie asked as she slipped her hoodie back on.

"Down the hall, first left."

The urge to hug the old woman came over her, and before Maggie knew it, she had her arms around her. "Thank you, Jana. Take good care of my friend for me."

Jana patted Maggie's back. "Of course. And you take care of yourself."

Maggie gave a little smile. "I always do."

M aggie leaned against the wall as the phone rang with the international dial tone. Bishop answered on the third ring.

"Hello?"

"It's me."

The sound of a door closing came from the other end, then Bishop's lowered voice. "Maggie. Where are you? Are you okay?"

"I'm fine," she said, avoiding the first question.

"No, you're not."

"I'm not," she agreed, twirling the cord tight around a finger, "but that's not why I'm calling. I tried to fix things, but I've only made them worse."

"What are you doing in Frankfurt?"

"Nina's checked in then?" Maggie knew she would. It was standard procedure.

"She briefed the Director and I a few hours ago."

"Are more people coming for me?"

"You have a two-hour window before you can expect to run into anyone."

It was all she needed. In two hours, she'd be long gone.

"Leon and Ashton were only trying to help me," she said, getting to the point. "You have to believe that."

"I do."

"Promise me they won't suffer for it."

"You know I'll do what I can," he replied, but it wasn't enough.

"Promise me, Bishop. I know I have no right asking, but please do this for me. Say whatever you must, just make it happen. Tell the Director I coerced them into it. Lied or blackmailed them. Just make sure they'll be safe."

Bishop was silent a for a moment before answering her. "You have my word."

"For them both? Not just Leon?"

"Yes."

Maggie leaned her head back against the wall and let out a deep sigh of relief. "Thank you." They'd be safe. Bishop wouldn't let her down. Not with something like that. Not when he'd given her his word.

"Let me help you, too," he said.

"You know what will happen if I turn myself in." With the kill order in place, the evidence stacked against her, and no proof to clear her name, her hands were tied. As were Bishop's. He couldn't be seen trying to help her. As far as everyone else was concerned, she was a known traitor and terrorist. Any hint of lenience from Bishop could rouse suspicion.

"You don't have to come here," continued Bishop. "Tell me where you are and I'll come get you. To hell with the Unit."

Maggie's eyes grew wet. "I can't tell you how much that means to me, but I can't get you involved. Ashton's in a bad way. Leon could have died too. It's too dangerous."

It was over. She'd tried and failed and didn't want to try again. Not when she had no way of discovering anything more than what Vogel had told her. Not when the rest of the Unit was on her tail. Not when it endangered those around her.

It was time for Plan B, and that meant counting her losses and disappearing.

"We can work this out." Bishop's voice was desperate now, panicked. "Let me help you."

"You know, I've never really thanked you for everything you've done for me."

"Maggie."

"I mean it. You saved me. You offered me a second chance when no one else would. Gave me a life I didn't dare dream I could have. I'd be in prison now if you hadn't come for me. Or dead."

Maggie never knew her father. Her mother never spoke about him, from what little she could remember. Her mother died when Maggie was six, taking anything she knew about her father with her.

In many ways, Bishop was the closest thing she had to a parent. Someone who guided her, protected her, and wasn't afraid to call her out on her shit when needed. He saw something in her no one else did. Took her in when she was at her most desperate.

"Confirm your location for rendezvous," Bishop snapped. "That's an order."

"I can't." Tears snaked down Maggie's cheeks.

"Listen here, you may be on the run, but you are still my agent and you will do as I say."

"I have to go now," she whispered.

"Maggie, please don't hang up."

"Goodbye, Bishop."

Chapter 33

LONDON, GREAT BRITAIN
1 JUNE

It was bittersweet for Maggie, stepping onto British soil for the last time. A whole day had come and gone since she'd left Leon and Ashton in Frankfurt. With agents on her tail, she left the city and made her way to Belgium where she caught an early evening flight with her Ekaterina alias, under the guise of a business trip.

The Unit would focus their search outside of England. As far as they were concerned, Maggie wasn't stupid enough to risk a return home, never mind brazen enough to hop on a direct flight to one of the country's most heavily surveilled airports.

Normally, Maggie reveled in thwarting people's expectations, but her heart held nothing but sadness as she made it through security and border control unscathed. She was back in London in time for the ten o'clock evening news.

Asking the taxi driver to stop a few streets away from her destination, Maggie walked the rest of the way. She'd travelled light, having left most of her things back in Frankfurt, but she'd held on to her new identities.

The Thames was quite beautiful on summer nights, the lights from the buildings sparkling over the surface, coated in warm pinks and purples that brushed over the sky like watercolors.

Maggie would miss it.

She'd miss a lot of things about living in London, her home ever since she ran away from her last of many foster families. Life on the streets had been more appealing, and safer in some ways, than the constantly changing foster homes.

Yes, the tube was a nightmare during rush-hour. The streets were filled with tourists year-round, walking infuriatingly slow and stopping every five seconds to take pictures or to simply gawk at the famous sights. And don't even get her started on the parking tickets the city council dished out like sugar-free sweets at the dentist.

But London had its good points, too.

From fish and chips served out of food trucks in Canary Wharf, posh afternoon tea at Harrods, or some good old pie and mash in the East End, you were never short on choice for a good meal.

The British Museum and the Tate Modern always had new and exciting exhibits, a perfect way to spend your day off, wandering through a maze of history and art.

Whether she was drowning her personal sorrows or celebrating a successful mission, The Golden Lion always welcomed her with her usual whisky over ice when she walked through the door.

Then there were the walks through Hyde Park in the autumn months when the leaves turned shades of fire and danced along the pavement with the growing wind.

Maggie always meant to catch more West End shows, but she never got around to it, figuring she had all the time in the world to see them.

She would need to say goodbye to all of it. Yet another farewell she wasn't ready for.

It would be a while before she could really call a place home again, and she hadn't decided where to head first. Until then, she had one last stop to make.

Maggie was hardly shocked to discover a detail at the entrance to her apartment building, which included plain-clothes Unit members, trying their best to mask as civilians. The young woman going for a jog. The middle-aged man walking a too well-trained dog.

She also wasn't shocked to see them stationed on her floor, as she risked a peek up to see them pacing the hallway through the large windows designed to capture the views of the river.

They were simple enough to slip past. Maggie used the back door of the building, which led out to the bins, and took the stairs, going up an extra flight.

From there, she picked the lock on the door to the apartment directly above hers, knocking first to make sure no one was home. Thankfully, her kind and helpful neighbor, Dr. Gupta, still worked nights at Kingston Hospital.

Once inside, she ventured onto the balcony and proceeded to climb over it. Maggie dangled in the air, her nearest foothold not for another five feet below her. She counted down from three, and before she thought better of it, let go of the railing.

Her body met nothing but air, and Maggie reached out as she fell, gripping on to the side of her own balcony before swinging her leg over it and fumbling to safety. She lay there for a moment, catching her breath.

Maggie never locked her balcony, assuming no one would be daft enough to pull a stunt like the one she just did. Leon would chide her for the breach of security, but she figured if anyone made the mistake breaking into her flat, they were in more danger than she was.

Everything was much the same as she left it, though she knew the entire apartment would have been searched from top to bottom for evidence or clues about where she disappeared to.

Slipping off her shoes, Maggie tip toed to the front

door and peered through the peep hole to find someone standing on the other side keeping watch. Like she would really waltz out of the elevator and expect no one to be there waiting for her. It was almost insulting.

A part of her was tempted to leave a note to let them know she'd been there, right under their oblivious noses.

Amateurs.

She wasn't there for much, and her exit route didn't exactly allow for much baggage.

First, she changed out of Ekaterina's clothes and into her own: worn in jeans, boots, and simple t-shirt and jacket. She almost felt like herself again.

Next, she removed a back panel from her fitted wardrobe and was happy to discover the excavation crew failed to dig up her secret stash. Tucking her Glock into her jeans and pocketing a few extra magazines, Maggie brought out a little box she hadn't opened in a while.

The locket was the only thing she had left of her mother. A plain, oval-shaped pendant with a filigree design that hung on a silver chain and held a little picture of them both, smiling at the camera.

Maggie couldn't remember when or where it was taken, being a toddler at the time. Still, it brought back memories of her mum, memories she clung to in her darkest hours and always feared she'd fabricated in her mind to make up for time that was stolen from them.

Her mum was around Maggie's age when it happened, the beat-up car she drove crashing and catching fire with her trapped inside. Maggie had her blue eyes and pinched nose, the blond hair most likely inherited from her father. In her youth, she thought her mum looked happy in the picture, given her wide smile. Now, she wasn't so sure, the look behind her eyes hinting at someone who bore a burden.

Maggie closed the locket with a snap and put it around her neck. It was the one thing she couldn't leave behind. The one thing from her past that would follow her into an unknown future.

Back in the living room, Maggie heard the familiar noise of scratching. Willow the cat waited for her by the balcony with an expectant stare. Maggie might be risking her life being back home, but as far as Willow was concerned, she still had to feed her.

Maggie slid open the glass door and the cat slinked in on elegant paws, weaving between Maggie's legs and purring. Shushing her, Maggie scratched behind the cat's ears and prepared a final supper of canned tuna for the little stray.

Willow would be okay without her. The cat was nothing if not resourceful. Her kitten days were far behind her, and life in the streets wasn't easy. Maggie watched her eat, saying yet another farewell to a part of her life.

A flash of red blinked from her answer machine. Out of habit, she picked up the phone and listened to the only message left in her absence.

"Hello, it's Laura from First Class Travel. Just calling

again to let you know about some of our hottest summer deals. From an all-inclusive escape to the Maldives to a romantic weekend getaway to Venice, we've got you covered for the perfect holiday. Call me back when you can. Bye for now."

Maggie deleted the message, hoping Laura had better luck with her other calls.

She was going on a permanent vacation.

Besides, she had already had a romantic weekend in Venice. Deadly too, but still romantic. It felt like forever ago now. A past life. So much had happened in the ten months since. So many decisions that had led her to this point.

Something Leon said during their mission in the drowning city came to her then, a memory from when they were seemed to be no closer to the truth. He'd said the best thing to do when lost, was to go back to the beginning. In the end, he'd been right, the answer to their problems hidden in plain sight from the start.

Maggie tapped a finger on the counter. The beginning.
Adam Richmond.

Crossing the room, Maggie scooped up her laptop where it lay abandoned on the couch since she first scoured the reporter's files. The Unit would have searched it, too, of course, but they had returned it right where she left it to hide their presence. Bringing the files back up, Maggie went over everything she'd previously read.

Vogel said she never should have gotten involved with

the reporter, so there must be something she'd missed. Something linking all the different pieces together. It may not have been clear when she originally saw it, unaware of the larger picture at the time.

Adam had been working on a story to expose the shady dealings of a company named Brightside Property and Construction Limited. The company purchased government-owned council houses and increased the rent exponentially, which forced most residents to move. The company wanted to demolish the houses and build commercial property in its place, but to do that, they needed the residents gone. All of them. Richmond had gathered reports from the last remaining residents that detailed a variety of intimidation tactics, presumably bankrolled by Brightside.

With a little more digging, Adam had found other alleged instances of the same methods being used in several areas of London. Based on the police files gathered about the death of an elderly man named Eric Solomon, it appeared the reporter believed Brightside Property and Construction resorted to murder to ensure no one contested their plans for new developments.

Maggie bolted upright as visions of a warehouse circled in her mind. Of wooden frames, corrugated metal roofing, and piles of bricks.

Jumping online, she searched for Brightside Property and Construction and brought up their website. Maggie scanned every page, reading everything there. She found it at the bottom of the 'About Us' page. The missing link.

Brightside Property and Construction Limited is a subsidiary of Vogel Enterprises, GmbH.

Maggie's mind raced to put all the pieces together. Brightside was a British branch of Herman's multinational corporation. It was Vogel's business.

Vogel must have learned Richmond was planning to expose him, to bring the murder of Eric Solomon to light and take down Brightside. It would have ruined Vogel's dealing in the UK, irrevocably tarnishing his worldwide brand, and most likely landing him in prison.

Vogel must have thanked his lucky stars when he learned Adam Richmond was assassinated on a yacht in Cannes, thanks to his little side business of selling secrets. The reporter really had a knack for unearthing things others wanted to remain hidden.

It would have come as a great relief to Vogel, until he learned someone had stolen Richmond's laptop—*and* the damning files. And that someone was Maggie.

So Vogel's last words were true. She never should have gotten involved with the reporter. Had she not, she wouldn't be in the position she was now. If she had looked at the hard drive back on the yacht, she would have realized the classified secrets weren't on his personal computer. In the rush of the moment, she would have thought nothing of the research he was doing on some company in London. That was for his day job. It had nothing to do with his dealings in the black market.

Taking the files and removing the laptop had been her downfall.

It all made sense, the connections she couldn't see now clear as day.

But two vital questions niggled at her. How did Herman Vogel know Maggie had been the one to kill Richmond and take his files? And where did James Worthington fit into it all?

Back to the beginning.

Maggie met the mayor at the Baltic Hotel the night of the conference. The night he died.

Vogel said he needed both her and James out of the picture. That it was nothing personal. Just business.

The mayor's death had been planned. She'd known that from the beginning since the Handler's asset had travelled from Spain and booked a hotel room. A booking he would have made far in advance given the packed conference.

Maggie wasn't supposed to be there. She'd only received the job earlier that day. Which meant the plan to kill James came first, long before she was in the picture. Before she even learned about the information Adam Richmond had on Vogel.

Yet before the Handler's asset died in the Midnight Lounge, he told Maggie he was hired to distract her. To lead her away from the mayor, allowing someone to slash his throat in the meantime.

Had his orders changed? Did her last-minute presence at the conference force them to come up with an alternative plan?

Maggie sat back in her chair and marveled at the brilliance of it.

It was the very definition of killing two birds with one stone. Vogel and his elusive partner needed both Maggie and James Worthington gone. By carrying through with their original plan to kill the mayor, with a small adjustment to pin the murder on Maggie, they managed to eliminate them both.

Vogel said she was supposed to be dead when she surprised him at his warehouse. He must have planned for the police or her colleagues to do the rest of his dirty work for him, as punishment for her supposed crimes.

It was simple, yet undeniably effective. Maggie wasn't dead, but it wasn't through lack of trying on the Unit's part. The Director had given the kill order, just like Vogel had wanted.

But who killed the mayor? Who knew Maggie would be there? Who knew she had obtained files incriminating Vogel?

Back to the beginning.

The Baltic Hotel had CCTV. Bishop sent her a clip of the footage, supposedly showing her slashing the mayor's throat. The footage had been grainy, but it was more than enough to frame her. From the same black dress she wore that night to the blond hair, the slasher had done their homework.

Maggie closed all the reporter's files and did some digging of her own.

Inked International, the stationery supply company behind which the Unit carried out their business, had their own simple website that garnered a couple of hits per month from those not in-the-know. The rest of the visitors were part of the secret intelligence agency and each had a unique login to access an intranet used for secure communication.

Maggie's logins still worked, which wasn't surprising. By logging on, the Unit would be able to gain the IP address of the computer she was using and use the online fingerprint to discover her location. Right now, the Unit techs would be furiously at work, trying to track her down. Speed was of the essence.

With the computer whizzes too busy trying to find her, she used the distraction to do some hacking of her own, and worked her way to the stored footage the Unit had gathered from the Baltic Hotel. While she had only seen a snippet of the footage, the Unit had acquired all the CCTV files for that night and the entire week.

Maggie scoured through the files for the right ones and finally found the cameras that recorded in and around the conference room. Skipping through the hours leading up to the conference, she narrowed in until she caught sight of her and the mayor heading down the stairs and going to the back stage of the podium in preparation for James's speech.

Moving to a new file, Maggie switched cameras and watched as she and the mayor stepped into the back room, closely followed by James's security. Maggie prepared herself for what she was about to see, the footage replaying like a memory. The Handler's asset arrived and tried to attack the mayor, taking out his two men in the process.

Maggie gave chase and left the mayor alone, a mistake which cost the man his life. He stayed backstage like she told him, checking his men for any sign of life.

A few minutes later the footage played out the mayor's death, the imposter slashing his throat and leaving him to bleed out.

Maggie searched for the camera that would have captured the killer's exit route and played the file, ready to discover their identity once and for all.

Only it never came. One moment, the footage played, and the next it stopped, the screen fizzling out into a snowstorm of static. Maggie fast forwarded the file, but it was no use. The file was corrupted.

Maggie noted the time hop when the footage returned to normal. A full three minutes were obliterated. The killer's exit had been deleted. Someone had wiped the footage clean to cover their tracks.

The urge to throw the laptop across the room boiled inside her.

Someone had tampered with the evidence, and that someone had to be Vogel's accomplice.

Maggie dug her nails into her palms, fists clenching until her knuckles turned bone white. It couldn't end that way. Not when she was so close to the whole truth. There had to be another way.

Another camera.

The footage of the departure may be gone, but that was only one of the many cameras inside the hotel.

Time was ticking, and the techs would soon learn of her whereabouts. A detail was already there, which meant she had even less time get herself far away. Once the Unit contacted them, all they had to do was open her front door.

Maggie brought up four different camera feeds, each of them located in and around the conference room, and played them all at once. Leaning close to the screen, Maggie kept a sharp eye out for anything that seemed out of place in the time leading up to the mayor's assassination.

Agonizing minutes passed, each second like a countdown to her capture. The detail could charge through the door any moment. But she couldn't go. Not yet. There had to be *something*.

The conference room exploded in a mass of panic as gunshots fired from backstage. Guests ran for the doors, rushing into the foyer to reach the front doors and get far away from danger.

The feed on the top right caught her attention as the guests spilled out from the hotel. Maggie watched a figure until they fell off screen and then moved to the lower right camera, tracking the movements of her new suspect.

Then she saw it. The evidence she so desperately craved.

Maggie's heart plummeted as she watched the familiar face stare back at her.

Vogel's accomplice.

She picked up the phone. It only rang twice. "We need to meet."

Chapter 34

Wind gusted over the Thames and swept Maggie's hair behind her as she stared at the ominous dome in the city skyline, lit with a sinister glow amid the midnight darkness.

The path to the meeting point unfurled before her, lights glowing underfoot as she crossed the Millennium Bridge. A chill enveloped the city. Overhead, a cluster of black clouds approached from the west in complete disregard of the impending summer.

It was the British way.

From the elegant steel suspension bridge, Maggie continued up Peter's Hill and crossed at Queen Victoria Street. The switch from modern office buildings and the City of London school to the historic landmark before her was like stepping into another world.

London was alive and ever-changing, with new buildings like the Shard rising to display a bold vision of the future. But the city's history ran deep, its roots spreading through the streets that had endured plagues, saw leaders rise and fall, and survived vicious wars.

Bronze statues of heroic firefighters battling flames during the blitz of World War II pointed her in the right direction, and she continued to the south side access to the building.

The main entrance to St Paul's Cathedral was locked, the place of worship and popular tourist attraction closed until the early morning prayer service at seven-thirty.

Maggie closed the large door behind her and went inside.

He was waiting for her on the cathedral floor.

She crossed the black and white checkered floor, moving down the long central aisle with rows of seats set up on either side. Her footsteps echoed in the empty, cavernous room, shadows reaching out like ghouls in the dim light.

"Maggie," he said when she reached him, and she couldn't help but fall into his arms.

The musk of his aftershave tickled her nose, and he still wore a suit despite the late hour. Though for someone like him, work never really finished for the day. It was a full-time gig, with agents across the world in different time zones, and unexpected emergencies—like the one now—that required his immediate attention.

"I've been so worried about you." Bishop's voice was thick and rumbled in his chest.

Meeting at the Unit headquarters felt too risky. While she trusted Bishop, Maggie knew the building was full of agents who would shoot her the second they laid eyes on her, full of secret cameras and microphones, constantly recording. It was only natural for secret agencies to spy on their spies.

"Thank you for meeting with me," she said.

"Of course."

"Strange rendezvous point."

Their voices carried all the way up the famous central dome, scenes of the life of Saint Paul depicted around the oculus in an intricate architectural design, painted in gold like the eight arches that surrounded it.

Cathedrals freaked Maggie out. Never one for religion of any sort, the medieval-inspired Baroque design felt imposing and a little too cultish for her liking.

"I know the night manager," Bishop said in explanation.

Maggie broke their embrace and straightened her back. She had information to report. "I have news, and you're not going to like it."

"I assumed as much. Any good news to soften the blow?"

"I can prove I'm not the one who killed James Worthington," she replied, though she knew the truth would still punch him in the gut.

"How?"

Maggie brought out her phone and handed it to him, hitting play on the collated CCTV footage she had uploaded to it.

Images of the Baltic Hotel appeared on the screen, and Maggie watched the surveillance for the fifth time. She still couldn't quite believe it, yet there it was, playing out on the screen. Again.

The foyer overflowed with a congregation of panicked guests, each struggling towards the door as staff failed to calm them. Amid the mass of people, a figure helped a man towards the door, shoving people out of the way to make room.

Maggie recalled being in the foyer, searching for the assassin before she followed him upstairs.

The man and his protector made it to the exit, but only one of them left. Instead of following the rest of the guests into the street, the culprit headed back the way they came, weaving through the crowd with purpose.

Switching cameras, Maggie's pieced-together file of clips jumped to the side of the large foyer where the person in question entered the bathroom as people continued to run by, the rest of the hotel's guests—those not attending the conference—entering the fray of terrified people.

To the untrained eye, it appeared that the brunette in the green gown never came back out.

But she did.

Now in a black dress and a blond wig, the woman exited the restroom and headed towards the backstage area of the podium, checking over her shoulder before going in to assassinate the Mayor of London.

Her colleague's face looked right up at the CCTV camera, her guilt undeniable.

"It was Nina," Maggie said, yet still the words sounded wrong on her lips.

Bishop switched off the phone and slid it into his pocket before meeting Maggie's eyes. "I know."

Chapter 35

hen?" Maggie asked. "How did you find out she killed James?"

"Isn't it obvious?" came a voice from the shadows.

Heels clicked against the floor, and Nina stepped into the light from the south aisle. She walked up behind Bishop, running a hand over his chest, and kissed him, her eyes never leaving Maggie as she did.

A wave of nausea crashed inside Maggie as her mind spun. Nina and Bishop. They were both involved. The betrayal wouldn't compute.

Maggie knew Vogel had an accomplice, but she never thought Bishop was capable of something like that. Nina was a surprise, but deep down it didn't come a as complete shock. There had always been something a little off with her. Unhinged. She killed too easily, showed no signs of remorse or hesitation. Even back in training. Nina took to wet work like a duck to water.

But Bishop?

"You bastard," Maggie said through gritted teeth.

Bishop locked eyes with her when Nina released him, but he quickly looked away.

"You bloody bastard." Maggie made for Bishop, but Nina spun on her, looking down the barrel of her gun.

"I wouldn't," she warned, and Maggie froze.

"And you had the cheek to call *me* a traitor." Maggie's rage simmered, thinking of Nina's performance in Frankfurt.

Nina shrugged. "You're not the only one skilled at acting." Her jaw showed signs of Maggie's handiwork, the bruising a blotched purple and yellowed stain on her otherwise beautiful face.

"You'll need stage makeup to cover that," Maggie jibed.

Nina ran a hand along her jaw, her foundation doing little to mask the damage. "You don't look much better yourself, love."

"Nice move with the dress, by the way," Maggie said, stalling for time. Nina had changed into the exact same ensemble as the one Maggie wore to the conference. When Nina killed James, she looked just like Maggie on all the hotel's cameras.

"The devil's in the details." Nina smiled, clearly

pleased with herself. "You always wear that dress to fancy events. It hides your gun and holster well."

She'd been predictable. A slight on her part, though Maggie never for the life of her assumed she'd need to worry about her fellow Unit members setting her up. She'd trusted them.

Speaking of trust... Maggie turned to Bishop, her whole body shaking with rage. "How could you?"

Bishop stared at the floor and shook his head. "It wasn't supposed to go like this, Maggie. I never wanted you involved."

"You've got a funny way of showing it. You framed me for murder."

"I thought it was genius myself," came another voice, this time behind her. "Bishop's always been quick on his feet."

Maggie spun to find yet another familiar face. "You, too?"

George Moulton, the Foreign Secretary, stood with three armed men by his side. "Just business, I'm afraid."

"Herman Vogel said the same thing." Maggie paused and scowled at the man who'd been sloppy drunk when they'd first met. "Right before he died."

Moulton shrugged. "He may have been my business part-ner, but I never liked the man. Call me old fashioned, but I don't trust Germans. One might even say you did me a favor. Now I can run Brightside myself and carry on with my plans."

"Your shopping malls and private apartment buildings?" Maggie sneered. Everything about Moulton disgusted her, from his shoddy tan to his nonchalance and complete lack of empathy.

"I'm making London a better place to live," Moulton insisted. "Cleaning out the riffraff."

"By raising people's rent and forcing them out of their homes," Maggie yelled, her voice booming through the cathedral.

"If they can't afford the new rates, then they have no business living there. It's all perfectly legal."

Maggie itched to smack Moulton's smug face, but she was outnumbered six to one. "Murdering Eric Solomon wasn't legal."

"That wasn't me. Vogel solved that little problem."

"And you agreed to it?"

"Of course. You can't argue with the man's efficiency. Once the stubborn git was dead, we had no hold ups with our development. We started work a few weeks after the old boy's funeral." Moulton chuckled, like he was telling a joke to his pompous politician friends by the bar inside Westminster.

"You're a monster."

"What I am, is rich. Exceptionally so, once we're finished with the new location. Bishop, too, for his contracting services. Like I said, dear, it's just business."

"Is that what I was?" she asked Bishop. "Just business?"

"No," he replied, barely audible despite the acoustics.

"Then what? Spit it out, Bishop. You owe me that much."

Bishop rubbed his forehead, face grim. "All you were supposed to do was eliminate Adam Richmond."

Maggie's heart drummed in her ears as all the anger and fear and betrayal fought inside her, threatening to send her over the edge. She needed to calm her emotions before she did something stupid.

"Typical Maggie Black." Nina grinned, clearly enjoying herself. "Always sticking your nose into things that don't concern you."

"Talk to me again, and I will end you," Maggie promised.

"Try it," Nina said as she lunged for her, Maggie moving to meet her in the middle.

One of the Foreign Secretary's men sent a shot into the cathedral floor between them and both Maggie and Nina jumped back.

"Now girls," said Moulton, with giddy excitement, "don't go hurting those pretty faces of yours."

Maggie panted, struggling to keep her cool. Shady politicians like Moulton were common as muck, even if he was significantly more corrupt than his peers. But Bishop and Nina? These were people she'd worked with. She'd fought alongside Nina on missions. Gone through training with her. They were supposed to be friends and allies, not enemies.

Bishop hurt the most. He had saved her all those years ago. Took her in and gave her a new life. Now he was trying to end it.

"Were you even interested in the secrets Adam Richmond was selling? Or was it all about the files on Vogel and that piece of shit," Maggie asked Bishop, nodding her head towards Moulton.

"Oh, he was never selling secrets," answered Moulton. "He was working on an exposé to out my operation with Vogel."

Bile rose in Maggie's throat. "He was innocent?"

"I don't know about innocent," Moulton said, "but he wasn't a secret seller."

Maggie closed her eyes as the weight of his words bore down on her. Adam Richmond wasn't selling classified secrets in the black market. He wasn't about to betray his country by giving them to the highest bidder. He never had them in the first place. It was all a lie.

Bishop had turned her into a contract killer. Hired her out to criminals to cover up their illegal dealings, just like the Handler did with his assets. Bishop had used her.

"You sent me on a mission to kill an innocent man. A man who was trying to do the right thing and let the world know what they were doing?" Maggie's stomach churned. She had snapped Adam's neck. Severed his spinal cord with one vicious twist. He was innocent, and she had killed him.

"You were never meant to know." Bishop pleaded with

her, like she could ever possibly understand. "All you had to do was kill him and then you were out of it."

Like it was that simple. Like what he tricked her into doing was okay, if only she hadn't been over diligent and accessed what was on Adam Richmond's computer.

"But I read the files," she said.

"It was never part of the plan. You knew too much."

Maggie marveled at the level of his betrayal. It cut into her like a blade, the laceration bleeding and raw. The more he said, the more salt he added to the open wound. He made her a pawn in his game. A game she never knew he was playing until it was too late. Adam was dead by her hands, and she could never fix that.

"So what? You thought you'd just off me, too?"

He'd been so calm when she reported her findings from Adam's laptop, acting like all of it was news to him. Bishop was one of the best, a Unit legend, and she could see why. He played her like a mark, and she had fallen for it. Killing Adam, and then toddling off to look after the mayor for the evening, all because he asked her to. Not once did she question him.

"I tried to get you to come in after it happened," he said.

"To take the fall?" Maggie looked at Bishop with new eyes, finally seeing the real him. Bags hung heavy under bloodshot eyes, both of which weren't there the last time she met with him. His usual clean shaven face was dusted with unmanned stubble, the shirt he wore untucked and crinkled like he'd slept in it. The risk of his criminal life being exposed was doing quite a number on him.

"If you handed yourself in quietly and without fuss, they would have let you live."

"To rot in a cell," added Nina, winning her a glare from Bishop.

"But I ran away and forced the Director's hand. She had no choice but to issue the kill order." Maggie let the pieces fall into place. A chain of events orchestrated by those surrounding her.

"Which is still in place, in case you've forgotten," said Nina. "I might even get a raise for killing you."

Maggie ignored her and focused on her boss. "Why did James Worthington have to die?"

"Unlike his predecessor, he wouldn't cooperate." Again, Moulton answered the question she directed at Bishop, like he couldn't help but gloat about their nefarious plans.

"Worthington's constituents caused a lot of fuss about having to move from their homes." Bishop's voice was robotic, completely void of emotion. "He wouldn't agree to the planning permission for the developments on Brightside's latest location."

"He simply had to go," added Moulton, like the mayor had been a contestant on some Saturday night talent show.

James had only been mayor for a few months. The previous mayor, Edgar Johnston, had died from a heart attack at the beginning of the new year. Edgar must have sold the houses to Moulton but died before he could pass the planning permission.

"I get it," said Maggie. "Kill James and bribe someone else." James had been doing the right thing, just like Adam. Now they were both dead.

"Precisely." Moulton checked his watch. "Should we get this over with? I have an early morning meeting with the PM."

Nina aimed her gun at Maggie.

"Don't you have the balls to do it?" Maggie asked Bishop. "You got me into this mess. You might as well finish what you started."

Bishop balled his hand into a fist, but he made no move to interject or help her. He was in too deep, and removing Maggie from the picture was the only way to ensure he got away with it. When it came down to it, he would save his own skin over hers.

"You should have kept running," Nina said, her finger inching toward the trigger.

"And you should have done your job and checked the vicinity."

Nina dropped her aim as a spark of fear shone through. "What do you mean?"

Ignoring Nina again, Maggie spoke to Bishop. "You weren't the first person I called."

Right on cue, Leon and Ashton stepped out from behind one of the surrounding arches.

"Did you get all of that?" Ashton asked, eye still

swollen closed and his right arm tied into a sling due to a dislocated shoulder. His free hand held a gun to even the odds a little.

Leon rewound the recording on his phone and played back the conversation. "Every word," he said, hitting send. "I'm sure the Director will be very interested in what you all had to say."

Maggie smiled at Bishop as the blood drained from his face. "You always said I should learn to work as part of a team."

Chapter 36

Maggie was on them before they even registered what was happening.

She kicked high and disarmed Nina to the pleasurable cracking of fingers. The gun slid out of sight across the tiled floor as the others began to move.

"Shoot them," Moulton ordered, and his men took aim.

Right then, Ashton brought something from his pocket and smashed in on the ground. There was a flash, then a *bang*, as bursts of darkness exploded around them all as the smoke bomb did its job.

Shouts of anger and blind shots fired amid the confusion, but they were next to useless in the gloom.

"Stand down," called Nina, who had been in the firing line with Maggie before the smoke hit.

The gunshots stopped, and Maggie headed in the direction of Ashton and Leon.

A grunt came from her right, and Maggie narrowed her eyes just enough to catch Bishop hightailing away from the chaos.

A hand touched her shoulder, but she knew the owner.

"Go get him," Leon said, leaning close so she could make him out. "We've got things under control here."

Maggie nodded and left them to it. Her boys could handle themselves.

Leaving the sounds of battle and the irate cries of George Moulton behind, Maggie charged through the smoke and went after Bishop. He ran out of the main cathedral floor and headed for the front entrance, Maggie hurrying to catch up.

"Shit," Bishop hissed as he reached the door only to discover it locked, clearly forgetting he had told Maggie to take the south entrance for that very reason.

Maggie was gaining on him, and he spotted her as she closed the gap, blocking the way to the exit. He'd have to get through her first.

Bishop swore, and darted off to the side through a doorway.

Maggie picked up her pace and followed. The doorway led to a set of stairs, and Bishop was bounding up them, taking two at time.

"Bishop, stop." Maggie took out her gun and aimed. A bullet in the leg was all she needed to bring him down, but she didn't have a clear shot.

Bracing herself, Maggie began the ascent.

One set of stairs led to another, the second set tight and closed off. Bishop was out of her line of sight, but his footsteps sounded above her, and she soldiered on.

Up they went, the steps never-ending in a dizzying spiral. Maggie's legs burned and the beginnings of a cramp chomped into her side.

Finally, the steps ended and gave way to a series of thin, narrow corridors. They were dark and damp with the smell of abandonment. Maggie moved slowly, carefully as her eyes adjusted to the darkness.

Her legs shook with exertion and the adrenaline pumping through her veins was the only thing keeping her going. "It's over. Stop running!" She still couldn't see him, but she heard him. He wasn't far now, his labored breathing loud in the empty halls.

The corridors twisted and turned, only wide enough to fit one person. The walls were rough and unloved. The crumbling bricks were exposed and adorned with nothing but dirt and cobwebs, making it clear this part of the cathedral was not open to the public.

From the sight of it, Maggie doubted anyone had been through there in years.

A rusted creak rang through the barren walls, and a gust of wind careened inside, sending dust and grit into her eyes. She continued until she reached an open metal door, the lights from the dome above giving her a clear view as she stepped out into the night.

Maggie found herself on one of the cathedral's lesser roofs. She hesitated near the edge and gawked.

It was a long way down.

The wind was treacherous so high up. It whipped at her face and howled to the moon where it hung full in the starless sky. The clock tower was across the way and displayed the time. It was minutes until two o'clock.

A click came from behind her.

"Don't move," ordered Bishop.

But Maggie didn't take orders from him anymore. She turned around in a split second and matched him with her own gun.

They stared each other down, neither dropping their weapon.

"There's nowhere to run," Maggie said.

A row of saints and apostles lined the side of the roof behind Bishop, their backs turned in disapproval like they knew what he had done.

"I never wanted it to end like this. You have to believe me."

"I do," Maggie said, overwhelmed with disappointment towards the man she had looked up to for so long.

Bishop leaned forward and rested his free hand on his knee, short of breath from the steep climb. He looked older than she had ever seen him. Worn.

"Why?" she asked, fighting back tears. Her gun rattling in her grip. "I don't understand."

Bishop swiped at his eyes, his gun lowering until it pointed at Maggie's hip. "I was gambling. A lot. I don't know why, but I couldn't stop. Didn't want to stop. When June found out I'd lost the house, she left me. Took the girls with her. She'd had enough. Said that the job was one thing. The late nights, the not coming home, the distraction when I *was* home. Missing parents' nights and dance shows with the girls. Not spending time with any of them. The gambling, the house, that was the last straw."

Bishop sat down on the thick ledge of the roof, his shoulders slumped like every last bit of his strength had crumbled away. "After the divorce, things just spiraled. I was nearing bankruptcy."

"You hid it well." Maggie thought back to when June had left him three years ago. She had no clue he was struggling. Like everyone else, she assumed it was the job that caused them to separate. Bishop hadn't been the first, and he wouldn't be the last. Divorce was one of the many risks that came with working in the Unit.

"Spies make the best liars," he said. "I managed to cover it up enough so the Director never found out."

"You should have told her. Or me. We could've helped you."

Bishop bowed his head. "I was ashamed. I'm ashamed of everything I've done."

"Then why did you do it?"

"I'd lost everything. June started custody proceedings.

Said I was an unfit father. Too busy with work, and pissing away everything we had when not at the office. I had no home for the kids to stay in. I couldn't afford to pay a decent lawyer. She was going to take them away from me. I couldn't allow it to happen. I needed money, so I started taking contracts."

Maggie had been inching towards him, but she stopped dead. "There were more?"

Bishop looked up at her and his eyes glistened. "Yes."

"How many?"

"A lot." His voice broke.

Maggie didn't want to know the to answer to her next question, but she had to ask. "Did you send me on any of them? Besides the last one?"

Bishop let out a retched sob in reply, freely crying now.

"Oh god, Bishop."

"I know."

Despite everything, Maggie found it hard not to feel sorry for him. The affection she had for him was still there, even if the respect was obliterated.

She gave herself a shake and hardened her shell. Her feelings weren't facts, and the fact was that Bishop had ordered her to kill innocent people for his financial gain. Had helped set her up and put her life—and the lives of those she cared about—in jeopardy. He was just as bad as any of the real criminals she had taken out. Worse.

He could sit there and feel sorry for himself all he

wanted, but she would not show him pity. She would not show remorse.

"You said you were supposed to get the girls next week when I briefed you on Adam Richmond," Maggie said, keeping her voice firm. "If you got joint custody, then why have you continued with the contracts?"

"I'm in too deep. I involved myself with some bad people. They'd have my head if I refused them now."

"And they know you can't ask the Unit or anyone else for help."

"Not without exposing myself."

"And Nina?" Maggie asked, moving closer towards him with each question. "You both hid that well, too."

"Since June left, I've been so lonely. I just needed someone to be close with. Some company. It's nothing serious," he said, though Maggie suspected Nina would view it as much more than that.

"And you got her involved in your little side business?"

"She found out and offered to help. I was hardly in a position to refuse."

Maggie couldn't tell if Bishop believed what he was saying, or if he was trying to convince himself of it. He chose to allow Nina to get involved. He chose to keep the contracts going and send other members of the Unit to carry out the dirty work.

Maggie stood over him now, still holding her gun. "What you've done goes against everything the Unit stands for. What you are supposed to stand for. What I stand for."

"I'm sorry." He sniffled, furiously wiping away his tears, like he was angry at them for existing, for showing how much he hurt.

"It's too late for that. All you can do now is confess to your crimes and accept the punishment given to you."

They both knew what that meant.

Bishop raised his head to her and something changed in his eyes.

A clang reverberated around them, as the clock struck the hour and the bells rang. The roof vibrated under their feet and sent a trill though Maggie's entire body.

Without warning, Bishop leaned backwards on the ledge and sent himself off the roof.

"No!"

Maggie dived.

Her torso leaned completely over the edge of the roof, and she caught Bishop by the arm. He swung out in the open air, Maggie his only lifeline. She wrapped her legs around one of the stone statues and pulled with all her strength.

Bishop barely moved, his weight too much as her shoulder writhed in pain at the joint.

The soft fabric of his suit made it hard for her to maintain her grip, and she felt Bishop slip through her fingers.

"I'm sorry, Maggie."

Maggie clenched the muscles in her thighs as her legs

slid free from the statue. If she held on any longer, they would both topple over.

The hard ground waited for them below. It was only a matter of time.

Their eyes met, and they both understood.

"I'm sorry, too," Maggie said, and she released her grip.

Chapter 37

Maggie made her way back down from the roof with a heavy heart.

She was hollow. Everything she had—her mind, her body, all of it—felt zapped, her energy completely gone.

For the past two weeks, she'd barely slept, always on the move and looking over her shoulder. Never knowing when they would find her, or if Death would come to pay her a visit. She couldn't afford to stop. To really process everything that had happened, or allow it to sink in.

It was sinking in now.

The memory of Bishop falling to his death would haunt her already troubled dreams for the rest of her life.

His body lay on the road in a bloody mess, waiting to be scraped off the pavement. She'd never be able to scrape the sight of it from her mind.

Tears wouldn't come, though. She'd done enough crying. She didn't have the energy for it. All she wanted to do was curl up into a ball and sleep for eternity.

Her clothes were sticky from exertion, and her teeth chattered as the sweat dried in, either from the cold wind on the roof or the shock of what she witnessed.

A part of her should have felt glad. She'd cleared her name and found the ones responsible for setting her up. She accomplished what she'd set out to do, somehow managing to stay alive in the process. She was safe now.

But Maggie couldn't bring herself to rejoice over a mission accomplished. It didn't feel like a win.

She traipsed down the final flight of stairs, in no hurry to return to the cathedral floor. Leon and Ashton could handle themselves, and from the flashing sirens she'd seen approach the building, they had already called it in.

Voices echoed through the cathedral, and though she couldn't make out what they were saying, her friend's Scottish brogue chimed through with an air of ease to it.

Maggie walked down a hallway, strobes of blue and red shining through the stained-glass windows from the police cars outside, covering her path in an angelic aura.

Outside, they would be cordoning off the area, redirecting traffic away from where Bishop had landed. A group of officers marched past her as they entered from the main entrance, led by a disheveled looking clergyman still in his slippers. Maggie made to follow them, when something sounded from behind.

Nina limped towards the door in an attempt at a quick exit.

"Stay where you are," said Maggie, reaching for her gun.

Nina stopped with her back to her.

"Don't even think about it," said Maggie, catching the slightest shifting of weight as Nina moved to the balls of her feet to make a run for it. "Turn around and put your hands on you head."

Nina complied, sneering as she did. If looks could kill, Maggie would have been assassinated right there. A trickle of blood slipped from the corner of Nina's lip, along with a fresh welt across her sharp cheekbone.

Maggie trained her weapon on Nina, thinking of everything the woman had done to her. Maggie could have killed her back in Frankfurt. Nina would have done it to her if their roles had been reversed. Maggie shook her head, thinking about it now. Nina found them when she did because the Handler had warned Vogel to expect a visit from Maggie. One call to Bishop, or perhaps George Moulton, had sent Nina to Germany, ready to take Maggie out. All Vogel had to do was sit tight and wait for Maggie to make the first move.

"Do it, then." Nina raised her chin in defiance. With her arms stretched to place her hands on her head, Nina's shirt rode up and revealed her belly.

Maggie gasped when she saw it. She placed an automatic hand over her own stomach, flat where Nina's showed the beginning signs of life.

Nina was pregnant.

Maggie simply blinked for a moment, her gun a barrier between them. "Is it Bishop's?" she finally asked.

"Yes." For the first time, Maggie saw real fear in Nina. Saw the maternal panic for her unborn child.

Maggie's finger hovered over the trigger.

Nina wasn't far along. Twelve, maybe sixteen weeks, tops. Maggie hadn't noticed in Frankfurt, or at the conference. She'd worn a jacket when she attacked her, and a green dress which would have easily hidden the signs. While Maggie had been concealing a weapon, Nina had been concealing a baby. Bishop's baby.

She knew what turning Nina over meant. Pregnant or not, the Unit would kill Nina for the very same reasons they had wanted Maggie dead. She was too much of a threat to keep alive.

There would be no prison cell for her, no plea deal or bargains made. Exile wasn't part of the worker benefits. The risk of exposure was too great for the Unit. Nina knew too much. She was a liability. Should Maggie turn her in, all that awaited her and her unborn baby was death.

Maggie warred over her options, but she had already decided. Her gun stayed right where it was, aimed between Nina's eyes. She clutched her mother's locket.

"I need you to listen to me very carefully. When you walk out of that door, it's for good. You'll disappear. You'll leave behind the life you have. All of it. You won't contact your family or anyone else. As far as they're concerned, you're dead."

Nina nodded.

"I don't want to ever see or hear from you again," Maggie continued, slow and deadly clear. "You'll stay far away from me and the ones I love, and if I ever see you again, I won't hesitate to blow your bloody brains out. Do I make myself clear?"

"Yes," whispered Nina.

"Then get the fuck out of my sight before I change my mind."

Nina left without another word and never once looked back.

Maggie watched her as she slipped out of the cathedral and vanished into the night. It pained Maggie to see her go after everything she had done. To allow her to live when people like Adam Richmond and James Worthington were dead. But she couldn't let an unborn child die due to the actions of its mother. That wasn't Maggie's choice to make.

It was the right thing to do. She only hoped she didn't live to regret it.

The cathedral floor was filled with enough people to hold mass when Maggie returned.

Leon and Ashton were standing over George Moulton and his men, each of them covered with signs of a good and well-deserved arse-kicking. They were sitting on the floor with their hands secured in zip-ties like slightly bashed packages ready to be shipped off and delivered to the nearest jail.

"You have no idea who you're dealing with," said Moulton, stopping mid-sentence to spit out a mouthful of blood.

Maggie was pleased to note at least one of his front teeth was missing.

"I am a member of parliament. I have connections. I won't go down for this, just you wait and see." Moulton never saw Leon's foot coming, but that didn't stop it from catching him in the jaw. The man was out before his head hit the floor.

"Sorry." Leon flashed a sheepish grin as everyone stopped what they were doing and looked at him. "He was doing my nut in."

Maggie regarded the politician and nudged him with her boot. "I like him better this way."

Everyone went back to what they were doing, seeming very busy for people who arrived after all the hard work was done. A few Unit members were there too, but they kept their distance.

"We lost Nina," said Ashton, chipper even in his beat-up state.

"I don't think we'll need to worry about seeing her again." Maggie pressed a palm over Ashton's forehead. "You have a fever."

Ashton wiggled his eyebrows. "Is that your way of telling me I'm hot?"

"You should be in hospital," said Maggie, suppressing a laugh.

Ashton dug in his jeans pocket and shook a brown bottle of pills. "Who needs hospital when you've got these. I can barely feel my face."

Maggie looked at Leon for back-up, but he only shrugged.

"It wouldn't be fair to leave him behind and miss out on all the fun," he said, wrapping an arm over Ashton's shoulder and messing up his hair.

Usually, Ashton would have bit the hand off anyone who dared touch his pristine hair. Instead he smiled and allowed it to happen, his cheeks blushing. It was like nothing had ever happened between them, falling easily into their old, carefree friendship.

"Bishop's dead." Maggie's words sounded absurd even to her own ears. None of it felt real.

Both boys sobered.

"We know." Leon cleared his throat and tried to hide how much it was affecting him. "I can't believe he was behind it all."

"I don't think we ever really knew him at all," said Maggie. Not the real him. They only knew the man Bishop presented to the world. Maggie knew a thing or two about aliases.

They grew quiet, each lost in their thoughts. Maggie would have to tell them the full story. Tell them about the other contracts and how deep Bishop's betrayal went. The whole Unit would need to be briefed. They were all involved, even if they weren't aware. There was no telling how much damage each of them had unknowingly caused, or what long lasting impact Bishop had caused.

Maggie glanced at Leon. There were many conversations that needed to be had.

But, there was a time and a place, and all of it could wait. Right now, all Maggie cared about was that they made it through alive. It was finally over.

"Thank you," Maggie said, breaking the silence. She pulled them both in for a hug, squeezing them tight and ignoring the aches and pains that decorated her whole body. "I couldn't have done it without you both."

"You would have managed," said Leon, his hand on the small of her back. "We just helped speed the process up a little."

"I'm just glad I had you both on my side."

Ashton leaned into her. "Always."

"It's nice to see you accepting help," added Leon. "For the most part."

"Sorry again about running off," said Maggie as she released them.

Leon laughed. "You saved the day, so I think we can let you off on this one."

Maggie took each of their hands. She'd never be able to express how thankful she was for them.

Bishop had been wrong about so many things, but he was right about letting people in. Though it didn't come naturally, the habit of doing everything on her own a stubborn one, she would try and get better at it. There were some things you just couldn't do alone.

"Well," said Leon, checking his watch. "I think the boys in blue have got it from here. Fancy a drink?"

Maggie nodded. "I'd say we've earned it. Though I don't think The Golden Lion is opened this late."

"Not to worry," said Ashton. "I've got plenty of drink back at my place."

"Surprising absolutely no one," jibed Leon with smile.

Maggie linked arms with them both, and they headed for the door. "Come on you two, let's get out of here."

Chapter 38

Maggie sat back in her seat, having just finished recounting the entire series of events that took place, from the mission in Cannes to the death of Brice Bishop.

It was late afternoon, and Maggie had only been awake for a couple of hours. She'd slept like the dead, her mind and body needing to recharge after what had to be the most taxing couple of weeks of her life.

Director General Grace Helmsley clasped her hands on the table. She wore her trademark power suit which was tailored with precision. The shoulders were dominant, the lapels cut in blade-sharp angles just like her bob of gray hair. Her eyes held a wisdom behind them from her sixty years of life, and they never missed a thing.

"I commend you for actions and outing Brice Bishop for what he was."

"Only doing my duty, ma'am," said Maggie.

They were in one of the Unit's conference rooms, Helmsley's official office inside the SIS building at Vauxhall Cross. Given that the Unit didn't officially exist, the Director's presence inside headquarters was a rare sight. But the situation called for it.

"Though you should have reported to me the instant you suspected foul play within the Unit," the Director chided.

Maggie only knew of Nina's involvement before heading to meet Bishop in St. Paul's. If she hadn't met with Leon and Ashton beforehand, then things could have turned out quite differently, their original purpose for being there to make sure Bishop hadn't been followed by any members of the Unit still hunting her.

"You had a kill order out on me," Maggie pointed out.

"In accordance with the evidence."

"I don't blame you," said Maggie. Nina had flawlessly executed the set up.

"Good," said the Director, "because if you expected an apology, you would be disappointed."

Maggie smiled. She'd always liked the director. "What will happen to George Moulton?"

The Director's lips thinned at the mention of his name. "He'll rot in prison. I'll personally make sure of that."

"Good."

Maggie wasn't sure how they planned on breaking the news about what really happened to James Worthington. Reports had already made the online news sites about an incident in St. Paul's, yet it seemed the Director had it under control.

"We're still on the case with Nina," she said. "It's only a matter of time before we find her."

Maggie had been forthright when briefing the Director, but she left out the part about letting Nina go. She wouldn't understand.

The Director closed the file opened on her tablet with a tap of her finger. "I have a proposition for you?"

"Oh?"

"I want to offer you Bishop's old role. Help me rebuild the Unit to serve its original purpose."

Shocked, Maggie couldn't form a coherent thought. If not for the intensity in the Director's gaze, she would have assumed her boss was making a joke. But the Director wasn't known for her humor, and she awaited a response.

Maggie sipped her glass of water and stalled for time. "I appreciate the offer, really I do."

"But?"

"But it's not for me."

"You're sure?"

"I'm sure."

She'd felt the niggling worry that something in her life needed to change, and the past fortnight had only cemented the urgency of that need. She'd become so wrapped up in her work, had sacrificed so much, that she felt like she'd lost the real Maggie somewhere along the way. The realization lost didn't sit well with her. Taking on Bishop's role and the monumental responsibilities it entailed would only further the issue.

The Director recovered quickly, though she'd clearly expected a different answer. "I'd be lying if I said I wasn't disappointed. Very well, I shall find another for the position."

"If I might make a suggestion, Special Agent Leon Frost would be the ideal candidate."

"How so?"

"He's proven himself in the field, so people respect him. His leadership abilities are second to none, and he's skilled at bringing people together to work as a team. Most importantly, he truly believes in the work we do here."

"And you don't?" the Director asked, not missing a beat.

Maggie bit her lip. "I'm not sure anymore."

"Take some time. You've been through a lot. Return when you're ready to get back to work."

The Director made to leave, pushing her chair out from under the table.

"And if I don't want to return?" Maggie's heart raced in her chest.

The Director sat back down. "Are you saying you want out?"

In all honesty, Maggie didn't know what she wanted. She needed to take stock of her life, needed to reevaluate what was important to her. What her aspirations were outside of any job. Continuing her life as an agent wouldn't allow for any of that. Not when she'd be sent off to go undercover somewhere, living as one alias after another. She needed to discover who she, Maggie, was after years of service.

"Yes," she finally said, before she changed her mind.

The Director watched Maggie like she could see into her soul. Whatever she saw there made her release a sigh of resignation. "You're a talented agent, Ms. Black. One of the best to walk through those doors. If you wish to leave and give up a career you've spent years building, then I won't stop you."

"Just like that?" Maggie asked.

"I can't have an agent doubting their reasons for being here. I can't have any weak links in the chain, not after this whole mishap." Tapping at her tablet, the Director brought up a new file and slid it across the table to her. "Sign here," she said, passing Maggie a stylus.

Maggie read over the resignation document and signed on the dotted line. "Anything else?"

"No, we're done here." The Director gathered her tablet and got up.

"Thank you," said Maggie, offering her hand.

The Director gave her a single shake and released her firm grip. "You can hand in your gun and security pass at the front desk. I'll have someone collect your other weapons tonight. I trust I don't have to remind you about the Official Secrets Act?"

"No."

"Very well. Goodbye, Ms. Black."

And with that, the Director left, taking Maggie's old life with her.

"How'd it go?" Leon asked when she returned to the downstairs lobby. He waited with Ashton, who was chatting to the cute guy behind the front desk before he cut the conversation short and joined them.

Maggie took a deep breath, jittery from the rush of her decision. "Better than expected. I'm out."

"Out?" repeated Leon with a frown.

"I'm no longer an agent."

"Congratulations!" Ashton crushed her in a hug. "You're free," he said, making her chuckle.

"Maggie, are you sure about this?" asked Leon. "You don't have to make any rash decisions."

"I'm sure. I've thought a lot about it, and I can't do this anymore. It's time for something new." Maggie didn't expect Leon to understand her decision. He believed in the Unit with every inch of his soul, even after the revelation of Bishop. If anything, it only solidified his loyalty to the cause. The Director would be lucky to have him by her side.

Finally, Leon nodded. "If it's what you want, then you have my full support."

"I appreciate it." Maggie went to the front desk and handed over her pass and Glock. She looked around the lobby one last time, thinking of the countless times she'd gone in and out those doors. Year after year, mission after mission.

There was nothing for her there anymore.

"So, what are you going to do now you don't work for the Man?" asked Ashton.

"I don't know," said Maggie. "I'm sure I'll think of something. After a long holiday in the sun, that is."

If anyone had earned a vacation, Maggie had. She played with the idea of returning to Spain, only this time she could be a tourist. Soak up the culture, eat all the tapas and drink as much sangria as she wanted. Even catch up on the pile of unread books by her bedside she hadn't found time to read.

She could do whatever she wanted. Go wherever she pleased.

Outside, the sun was out, bright with potential in the

cloudless sky. Perhaps they were in for a good summer after all.

Maggie left the Unit headquarters with her friends by her side and stepped out into her new life as a free agent.

WANT TO LEARN MORE ABOUT MAGGIE?

The Maggie Black Case Files is a prequel series of self-contained missions which Maggie completed prior to the events of the main Maggie Black Series.

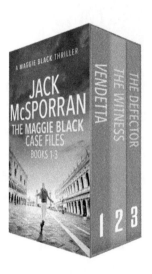

If you want to find out what really happened in Venice, and join Maggie in some of her most explosive missions during her time at the Unit, check out the Maggie Black Case Files today!

Thank you so much for reading Kill Order. I hope you enjoyed it!

I have so much more coming your way. Never miss a release by joining my free VIP club. You'll receive all the latest updates on my upcoming books as well as gain access to exclusive content and giveaways!

To sign up, visit

https://jackmcsporran.com/vendettasignup.

Thank you for reading KILL ORDER! If you enjoyed the book, I would greatly appreciate it if you could consider adding a review on your online bookstore of choice.

Reviews make a huge difference to the success or failure of a book, especially for newer writers like myself. The more reviews a book has, the more people are likely to take a shot on picking it up. The review need only be a line or two, and it really would make the world of difference for me if you could spare the three minutes it takes to leave one.

With all my thanks,

Jack McSporran

Acknowledgments

No book reaches publication without help. I want to give a special shout out to some of the members of my own Unit:

Big thanks to Steve Searby (aka Doris), Jan Makellky, Shannon Robinson, Kim Lennon, Beth Kavin, Sylvia Foster, Alix Lopez, Nigel Gambles, Ted Camer, Teresa Stump, John McShane, Seadly Swayne, Brenda Garcia, Shannen Clements, Steve Fitzgibbon, Jaimi V, David Johnston, Lois Ann Welsh, Bucksmom, John Kennington, Susan Rasdale, Christine Matinale, Jennifer Herkert, Jim Hunter, Barry Jackson, Diane Barriere, and everyone else involved. You lot are the best!

Gloucester Library
P.O. Box 2380
Gloucester, VA 23061

CPSIA information can be obtained
at www.ICGtesting.com
Printed in the USA
LVHW02s1715260218
567900LV00003B/648/P